Operation Capitol Hill

Copyright © 2006 Ronald P. Wolff
All rights reserved.
ISBN: 1-4196-3796-7

Library of Congress Control Number: 2006904519

Registered WGAw #964382

To order additional copies, please contact us.
BookSurge, LLC
www.booksurge.com
1-866-308-6235
orders@booksurge.com

Operation Capitol Hill

Ronald P. Wolff

2006

Operation Capitol Hill

ACKNOWLEDGEMENTS

This novel has benefited immensely from the comments and critiques of many people who generously shared their time and expertise. Cindy Fabricius-Segal encouraged me to begin the project and offered both moral support and helpful suggestions as the novel evolved. Members of the Writers' Group at Borders in Montclair, California, provided valuable assistance. Two professional editors, Mike Foley and Patricia Hernandez, commented on the initial draft—barely 20,000 words—and made important suggestions regarding plot and characterization. Following a major revision, Patricia also did a thorough line edit, engaging me in an enjoyable and productive creative dialogue. Joyce Frevert contributed useful insights and proved that she is the best proof-reader in the world, bar none.

I am especially grateful to the members of my immediate family—my mom, brothers HJ and Marty, and sisters-in-law Linda and Nancy—for their interest, support, and creative suggestions.

Writing fiction is by far the most difficult creative task I have ever attempted. I welcome comments from readers who find themselves intrigued by this book, and I eagerly anticipate, from a lively exchange of ideas, enhancing both my craft and my understanding of complex social issues.

Ronald P. Wolff
Claremont, California
OpCapitolHill@aol.com

"Why has government been instituted at all? Because the passions of men will not conform to the dictates of reason and justice without constraint."
        Alexander Hamilton
        The Federalist #15

"The necessity of reciprocal checks in the exercise of political power, by dividing and distributing it into different depositories, and constituting each the guardian of the public weal against invasions by the others, has been evinced by experiments ancient and modern, some of them in our country and under our own eyes. To preserve them must be as necessary as to institute them…..[L]et there be no change by usurpation;…it is the customary weapon by which free governments are destroyed."
        George Washington
        Farewell Address, September 19, 1796

CHAPTER ONE

Friday, November 9, 2040
I came to the White House expecting simply to engage in an evening of polite conversation with our capital's socially and politically elite, then take the train back to Trickle Down Community #327 and get a good night's sleep snuggled up to my beautiful wife. I left less than two hours later, obsessed with an astonishing dilemma: did an introverted man like myself, whose last elective office was sixth grade hall monitor, have the courage and the capacity to preserve, protect, and defend the Constitution of the United States against two of the most powerful politicians in the country?

***

As a journalist who had covered politics in Washington, D.C. for more than a decade and a life-long friend of the President, I was well known to the Secret Service. Nevertheless, with the country's terror alert system perpetually on red, precautions were to be expected.

"ID please."

I handed my federal identification card to the uniformed guard at the gate, who scrutinized it under ultra-violet light, then scanned it. His printer sprang to life, producing my picture as well as a description: Roland Raines, five foot ten, brown hair, 175 pounds, clean-shaven. He looked at me, evidently satisfied. "All right, Mr. Raines, put your palm here on the sensor." After a few seconds, a green light came on. "Nice to see you again, Mr. Raines," the guard offered, his tone brightening considerably.

"Proceed down the walkway to the North Portico, and you will be escorted to the East Room." Then he turned his attention to a man I thought I recognized as the Ambassador from Guatemala.

A Marine opened the door crisply without looking at me, and I stepped carefully over the threshold. I did everything carefully in the White House, despite having been there more times than I bothered to count. It had an aura. Hundreds of people used it every day, but nothing was ever out of place. You could search in vain for a scratch in the paint or a speck of dust. Even the air had a distinctive smell.

A young lady with an impeccable smile approached me. "Would you follow me, sir?"

We passed enormous oil paintings and antique upholstered chairs casually, as if they had been found at a two-for-one sale at VOXMart. But I knew better; they all had a story to tell. I lingered. It hit me suddenly—they were all in exactly the same location every time, hung on the wall or placed on the luxurious carpet with the care and precision of an artisan's eye, symbolizing stability in a grand governmental experiment that had survived two civil wars and an international community frequently subject to the whims of dictators and terrorists.

"Is everything all right, sir?"

"Oh, I'm sorry. Yes. As many times as I've been here, it's always impressive." I caught up with her, and we proceeded down the hallway more rapidly. When we reached the entrance, she turned and smiled. "Have a good time." Then she returned the way we had come, presumably to escort additional guests. I stepped into the great hall.

To be honest, the East Room was not my favorite place in the White House. Other than a single full-length portrait of a smiling, splendidly-attired George Washington, staring into a rectangular room larger than most people's homes, it was stark—devoid of the historical paintings and period furniture so common throughout the rest of the mansion. Simple but tasteful off-white wallpaper with golden vertical stripes stretched from the baseboard to the twenty-six foot high ceiling. It was in this room that Abraham Lincoln had lain in state, and Jackie Kennedy and her two young children had paid their last respects to the country's fallen President more than seventy-five years ago.

Tonight the mood was festive. Three elegant cut-glass chandeliers cast a cheery light on perhaps two hundred people engaged in energetic conversation, most of them helping themselves to the bountiful hors d'oeuvres being passed around by tuxedo-clad waiters. The occasion: the 58th birthday of President Jadon P. Hamilton. In fact, it was a double celebration. The President had just been re-elected two days earlier, carrying all but twelve of the fifty-one states, achieving the highest total of votes in the electoral college since 2028. Waiters uncorked bottle after bottle of champagne as the evening advanced, continuing long after sobriety had become a feeble memory. I had voted for the opposition but helped myself to a glass anyway.

"Happy Birthday, Mr. President," the Chief of the Council of Economic Advisors shouted, unaware that Hamilton was out of earshot half way across the room.

"Happy re-election, Mr. President," the Chief Political Advisor bellowed, clinking glasses flamboyantly with his counterpart.

"Happy Emvironmentally Protected, Mr. Resident," slurred the Chief Executive Officer of Mineral Reclamation through Strip Mining Corporation, still light-headed from being designated earlier in the day as head of the Environmental Protection Agency.

I retreated to a corner of the room, hoping that my eardrums had not yet been unalterably shattered, trying to decide how long to stay. I hadn't yet said hello to Vice President Andrew Tyler, chomping on his omnipresent unlit cigar. "Shorty," as he permitted his friends to call him in private, standing five foot seven in thick socks, was gesturing emphatically, apparently having some sort of disagreement with the Ambassador from India. He had jettisoned his tuxedo coat, revealing a slightly rumpled white shirt with one stud missing and extra-wide flag-colored suspenders that succeeded in keeping his too-short pants from dropping below his ample waistline. He excused himself from the conversation to follow a waiter carrying a succulent collection of pastries, allowing his blazing white socks to peek out over his shoes with every step.

Jadon knew I despised Tyler, who had been chosen for his role as running mate largely for his ability to draw votes in key southern states. He had gradually worked his way up the political ladder, acquiring a reputation for thinking seldom and speaking often. Beginning as a school board member in Jackson, Mississippi, Tyler had promoted a policy of "zero tolerance" toward anyone not saying the Pledge of Allegiance in a loud enough voice. As a city council member, he had once slugged a city manager in public for lambasting his lack of impulse control. Nevertheless, the voters had elected "Tantrum Tyler" as their Governor—three times. From there, he'd gone on to the United States Senate, where as Majority Whip he had ruthlessly punished members of his own party for votes not conforming to the prevailing philosophy. Jadon would want me to be polite to the man, but the task stretched my social skills far beyond their capacity. I decided it was better not to say anything to him at all.

Twenty feet or so beyond Vice President Tyler, First Lady Vanessa Hamilton chatted amiably with the Ambassador from

Canada, an attractive woman in her fifties wearing a low-cut formal black gown and a gorgeous string of pearls that glowed in the reflected light of the chandeliers. They probably weren't discussing politics. Vanessa didn't much care for it, and I knew the Ambassador abhorred most of the policies of Jadon's administration. Attending social functions was her way of smoothing over deep-seated disagreements and maintaining a sufficiently cordial relationship between the countries to avoid being put on the highly classified but frequently leaked "targeted for invasion" list.

Pete Chesterfield moved into view, dressed in a shiny black tuxedo with royal purple lapels, adorned on both sides with American flag pins. He approached the First Lady and the Ambassador, who welcomed him with handshakes and smiles. Champagne glasses clinked as they glanced in Jadon's direction. I assumed they were toasting the President's election victory, because the Ambassador had her fingers crossed behind her back. Childish, I thought; but acceptable ways of disagreeing with the administration had become severely limited.

Chesterfield had been selected as Attorney General for the first term and had already held a press conference to announce that he was certain the President would ask him to continue in that capacity. A native of Chicago, with a law degree from the University of Illinois, he had learned politics at the hands of the masters in his home state, sometimes interviewing them in jail so as not to miss an educational opportunity. Elected twice as Lieutenant Governor, he lost a squeaker for the top job in 2036 and was thereby relegated to the political junkyard, where those more successful with the voters often found their high level appointees. He had been content to stay out of the headlines during the first term, but I suspected that he exercised considerable influence from the sidelines. Known for his conservative views on just about every topic that entered the realm of public policy, Chesterfield had built his reputation writing essays supportive of the series of Constitutional amendments that had successfully repealed or modified the liberties guaranteed by the original Bill of Rights.

A waiter carrying a large tray of hors d'oeuvres stepped up to the group, blocking my view, and my gaze wandered. Behind me, a single champagne bottle sat on a huge silver tray, resting on a table. Korbel Brut, Russian River Valley, Western California, 2036. I was pleased to see a product from one of the insurgent states being consumed at the White House. I could understand the President banning imports from France after that country supported the North in Civil War II, but the practice of boycotting goods from states that had tried to protect the original First Amendment had lasted too long, in my opinion. Reconstruction was one thing; lingering recrimination was another.

Suddenly, the President materialized at my side, clearly a bit tipsy. Normally flawless in appearance, the result of his career as a network television news anchor, he looked tired. A few strands of gray hair fell randomly over his forehead, and his black bow tie sat slightly askew against his pressed white shirt. "Well, Roly, are you having a good time?" he roared. The President was the only person in the world permitted to call me "Roly"—short for "Roly-Poly"—a leftover from my high school days when I had admittedly been just a bit plump. I preferred Roland.

"Yes, wonderful party, Hammy," I said. "Congratulations." He hated it when I called him "Hammy." But he wouldn't remember in the morning.

"Well, have some more bubbly! Glad you could be here!" The President gave me a hug, wrapping his long arms around my back, miraculously managing not to spill his drink in the process. Then he was gone, along with the entourage of ten or so obsequious hangers-on who almost tripped on his every step.

I lifted the wine bottle from the tray, intending only to pour a socially appropriate half glass to last the rest of the evening, but it was empty. A Secret Service agent who had observed my interchange with the President approached. "I can get you a waiter, Roly," she said, emphasizing the last word through a skimpy smile and pronouncing it the same way the President had.

"That's all right, Madison. I'm fine." I gave her a warm smile. "And don't ever call me Roly." We had met when she first joined the Service nine years ago, and I had liked her immediately. She was solid physically, presumably the result of many hours spent in training, buffered by a soft feminine perimeter. The product of a law enforcement family, her dad had been a special agent with the FBI before his retirement, and her mother was a criminal defense attorney. Apparently there had been some spirited dinner table conversations. Not wanting to take sides, she had learned at a young age to appreciate all points of view and weigh evidence carefully. A husband with a drinking problem had abandoned her after fathering two children, but she seemed stronger without him than with him. There was something about Madison that said "I'm a real human being" thrusting its way through the required professional veneer. You don't meet many people like that—people you know in your gut have a common decency immune from emotional and intellectual corruption. We had gotten to know each other well enough for our kids to attend each others' birthday parties. I thought her promotion two years ago to Chief of the White House Security Detail was long overdue.

Madison laughed, then quickly resumed a more subdued demeanor. "Actually, I was hoping you'd be here. I'd like a few minutes of your time." She paused and surveyed the room with a subtle, practiced sweep. "It's important."

"All right, sure." I didn't have a clue.

She leaned toward me. "Come with me. Make it look like I'm giving you a tour." She turned ninety degrees to the right and headed toward a door leading to the Cross Hall. "The Blue Room is used primarily to entertain foreign dignitaries," she said loudly.

I played along. "Is that a fact? I didn't know there were too many foreign dignitaries who still wanted to visit."

Although the Hall was deserted, Madison evidently felt obligated to keep up the charade a little longer. "There are 132 rooms in the White House, including 35 bathrooms. These chandeliers," she said, pointing to the ceiling, "were made in London in 1775."

"They're gorgeous," I answered. I had seen them so many times I had stopped noticing. "I sure wouldn't want to pay the light bill."

We walked another ten feet. "Oh, here's the desk President Jeb Bush used to sign the legislation revoking the Freedom of Information Act. It's made primarily out of Florida pine. Do you see the alligator motif in the carved legs?"

"Yes, it's quite unmistakable." Madison was being exceptionally cautious. I searched her face for a clue, but she offered none.

"Have you ever been to the Map Room, Mr. Raines?"

"No, I haven't."

About halfway down the corridor, she led me down a small staircase. At the bottom, we made a hard left, and after walking another twenty feet or so down a corridor devoid of lavish furnishings, Madison abruptly opened an unmarked door. She flicked a switch, revealing a small, stark room with a bank of computers.

I was intensely curious now. As soon as she shut the door behind us, I whispered, "Madison, what the hell is this all about?"

"Wait." The entire side wall was covered with filing cabinets about as tall as I was, each containing drawers about three inches high. She opened a drawer marked "October, 2040," removed a flat memory chip that had been color coded, inserted it into one of the computers, and entered a password. "Sit down. Watch."

After a few seconds, a low quality video appeared on the computer screen. Vice President Andrew Tyler and Attorney General Pete Chesterfield were sitting in an office I did not recognize, talking in hushed though audible tones. The camera looked on from the side. "We got this election tied up tight, like a pig ready to roast over an open fire," Tyler said, doing his best to give the word "fire" two lazy syllables.

Chesterfield didn't comment on the Southern drawl. "Yes, sure looks that way. Operation Capitol Hill is going to be a huge success."

"Absolutely." The Vice President's grainy head bobbed up and down. "Who's writing the speech?"

A wicked smile spread across the Attorney General's face. "I am, Shorty. We can't trust the speechwriting staff not to leak something this big." Chesterfield leaned forward and pointed to the breast pocket of his suit. "I'm almost done."

"But won't they be writing their own speech?"

"Of course. And we'll let them. Here's the way it plays. The President doesn't see either speech in advance. You know he prides himself on reading fluently with no rehearsal. We tell him it's a great speech, very straightforward, and no rehearsal is necessary. We keep him so busy the week before the inaugural, he won't even have time to think about previewing it. We fly in million dollar donors from around the country and schedule him for non-stop entertainment. On the big day, at the last minute, we simply switch our speech for the one his staff wrote."

Tyler's eyes grew big, like a kid witnessing his first public flogging. "You're a genius."

Chesterfield ignored the compliment. "Hamilton comes out in favor of eliminating Congress as no longer necessary to the preservation of our democracy and a deterrent to efficient government. The people will eat it up. They are pretty well conditioned now to believe whatever they hear on the news. This one will be easy to spin. In a year or less, we'll have three-fourths of the state legislatures behind us, and voila! No more obstructionist, unpatriotic speeches from would-be statesmen."

I looked at Madison, hoping she would be stifling laughter—eager to discover that the video was an ingenious hoax or a very bad practical joke. Her stern face directed me back to the screen.

"And I won't have to stay in town for those awful meetings of the Senate. Rather be out huntin' possum." Tyler seemed genuinely relieved, exhaling deeply. Then he frowned. "You don't think the President will object when he finds out what he said?"

"I don't think he will. He's not the sharpest knife in the drawer." I noticed a distinct smirk from Chesterfield. "But he won't know until it's too late. Once he says it, he'll stand behind it. Hamilton would rather see his own mother humiliated than lose face himself."

Tyler produced one of his rare thoughtful expressions. "Can you imagine the outcry if anyone found out he didn't give the right speech?"

"Nobody will find out," Chesterfield insisted. "We'll offer lifetime compensation to the real speechwriters on condition that they never reveal what happened. If they don't agree, we'll incarcerate them as enemies of the state and plant a story. Abducted by the French military. In training to become the first men on Mars. Whatever."

I looked at Madison again. "Nobody could be this brazen—could they?"

"Watch."

"Good plan," Tyler continued. "And in four more years, they'll be callin' me 'Mr. President.' " I swear, his chest stuck out another two inches.

"And I'll be your Vice President," Chesterfield added confidently. "I'll help you write your speeches too if you like."

Tyler didn't seem to grasp the implication. "Are you that good?"

"I don't suppose it's the Gettysburg Address. Well, judge for yourself." Chesterfield pulled two typewritten pages from his breast pocket. "Now, picture Hamilton saying this in front of ten thousand people at the Capitol and millions more watching live on the OmniScreens." He cleared his throat. "My fellow Americans, thank you for trusting me with a second term as your President. I will serve you proudly and effectively.

"Our country has witnessed a great deal of turmoil in its long history. Having recently celebrated the two hundred and fiftieth anniversary of the adoption of the original constitution, it is valuable—indeed, it is necessary—that we examine our complex and often difficult history. There are lessons to be learned.

"We were led into battle in the Revolutionary War by George Washington, a brave and noble man. Washington risked his life to defeat the evil British Redcoats. He knew the difference between freedom and tyranny. He would approve of the course of action we must take from this day forward."

"People love George Washington," Tyler interjected. "That'll get'em."

"Wait. It gets better," Chesterfield continued. "Abraham Lincoln was another brave and noble man. He freed the slaves and crushed the first civil insurrection. Lincoln understood that unusual times dictate the use of unusual measures. He would also approve of the course of action we must take from this day forward.

"Arnie Sassenbruger was a brave man. He terminated Iran, Syria, North Korea, and China because they didn't understand what freedom was all about. We are a peace-loving nation. But when evil rises up against us, we must destroy it. Sassenbruger understood that when people try to take our freedom away from us, we must kick their ass. He would approve of the course of action we must take from this day forward."

"I love it. That's the way *real* Americans talk."

"Shorty, are you going to let me get through this?"

"Sorry."

"Here comes the important part." Chesterfield traded his disapproval for a scholarly tone. "Today we are confronting a harsh reality. Evil—always insidious and clever—has invaded even the institutions of our great American democracy. I speak, my fellow Americans, of our Congress, that great deliberative body that has served us well, until recently. Today Congress is harboring dissidents and evildoers, people who refuse to acknowledge the new era. These traitors promote dissension where there should be unanimity; they promote discord where there should be harmony. Something must be done to derail them before they wreck our great nation. Therefore, during the first year of my new term as President, I will convene a new constitutional convention for the purpose of transferring the legislative function of government to the executive branch. The result will be a smoother, more efficient, and more effective administration of the policies the vast majority of Americans want and demand. I ask that you support me in this effort.

"My fellow Americans, never in the history of the world has a nation been blessed like America, with hard-working, straight-thinking, God-fearing people. Together, we will overcome the evil that lurks, even eight long years after Civil War II, in a few dark corners of our country. We will root it out and punish the perpetrators. As our great President George W. Bush said, 'They can run but they can't hide.' Only then will we know the true meaning of the legacy of freedom left to us by Washington, Lincoln, and Sassenbruger, and together we will all say 'God Bless America.' "

Tyler whistled. "Wow. You're fucking eloquent."

"Well, thank you. I enjoyed writing it." Chesterfield refolded the pages and tucked them away carefully. "I think it will do the trick."

Tyler stood up, walked off-camera for less than a minute, and returned with a bottle of wine and two glasses. Looking at the label, he announced "California, 2037. A good vintage from a great state." He poured.

"I have a feeling 2041 will be even better," Chesterfield replied. "Here's to Operation Capitol Hill."

"I'll drink to that."

Madison pressed a key, and the image froze with the two glasses touching. "There's more, but you get the idea. You and the President are good friends. I thought you'd want to know."

As a journalist, I'm not usually at a loss for words. I sat there simply stupefied, trying to comprehend the scenario I had just witnessed but coming up empty. "Are you sure this isn't some kind of rehearsal for one of those roasts where all the politicians give speeches making fun of themselves?"

"No, Roland, I'm afraid it's quite real." I had never seen a more somber look on her face.

"Where did this happen, anyway?"

"The Vice President's office, in his official residence at the Naval Observatory. He knows all the meeting rooms and offices in the White House are bugged, but he doesn't know we got his office as well."

"How can he *not* know that?"

"He had all the bugs taken out before he went to Antarctica to visit our troops. While he was gone, we reinstalled a system that uses wireless nano-devices—they're almost molecular in size. I don't understand the technology, but I guess they're practically undetectable." Madison stooped down and examined me more closely. "Are you all right? You look pale." I felt like someone had punched me in the gut. Thoughts formed, but I couldn't get the words out. I held up my hand, in a stop sign gesture, and Madison let me catch my breath. "Can I get you some water?"

"No, thanks. Say, is there a back door or something? I need to get out of here."

"I'll get in a lot of trouble if anyone finds out I showed you this."

"Of course. Don't worry." Then as an afterthought, "Why *did* you show me?"

"I...um...well, as a Secret Service agent, I'm not supposed to express personal political views. But this strikes me as wrong. I don't want to see the President duped. Like I said, you're his friend. I hope there's something you can do." As I look back on it now, I see it wasn't the continued dismantling of the Constitution that offended her. The plan violated her sense of fair play.

I wanted to reassure her, but I wasn't feeling sure about

anything at the moment. "I don't know. I'll need time to sort this out. It certainly would be a big story." First and foremost, I was a journalist. The idea that I should probably do something about this, rather than just write about it, didn't hit me until later.

"If there's anything I can do to help...?"

"For starters, you can get me a cab."

"Yes, of course. That's a perfect excuse, if anyone wants to know where we've been or what happened. You got sick from drinking too much champagne, and I helped you get home. Okay?"

I wanted to hug her.

Inside the cab, the astonishing plot to abolish Congress began to settle in. Did they really think they could pull this off? Was it possible to get three-fourths of the state legislatures to simply undo the most important element incorporated into the Constitution—the balance of powers? Considering they had voted, some of them under duress, to abolish the Bill of Rights, anything was conceivable.

What kind of country would we have if they succeeded? It wasn't just that the administration could accomplish its political goals; it was doing that already. The little opposition that remained would be silenced forever. There would be no protected forum for the expression of any views other than those sanctioned by people in power. And what power! Without Congress, there could be no impeachment. Without Congress, the administration could declare war under any and all circumstances and appropriate whatever resources it decided were justified. Without the Senate, there would be no "advice and consent" on cabinet-level appointees or judges. The more I thought about it, the more I realized the genius behind the notion. These guys were not just abolishing Congress; their plan would emasculate the independent judiciary as well, resulting in nothing less than a legal dictatorship!

Was I prepared to do anything about it? Is that the proper role of a journalist? Did I even have the ability to prevent it from happening if I chose to get involved?

I caught the 11:42 out of George W. Bush Memorial Station, and as the mile markers flashed by, the questions started turning into answers. By the time I slipped into bed, I knew what I had to do.

CHAPTER TWO

Saturday, November 10

Like a woman whose common face and too-wide hips had appeared attractive in the subdued light of a bar at closing time, my plan had lost its appeal by morning. I couldn't help but laugh at my naiveté and my silly illusions of audacity. What had I been thinking? How could one glass of champagne have killed off my capacity to reason—and a small glass at that? Yes, the plot to abolish Congress was a problem of monumental proportions, one that demanded action. But from whom? I was a journalist. I had never even contemplated running for public office. My job was to report the news. What right did I have to intervene in the affairs of state?

I opened one eye to look at the clock by the side of the bed, then realized I didn't have to work. *Good.* I needed more time to sort things out.

A journalist! Of course! I could just write a column about Operation Capitol Hill and explain why it would be even more damaging to the country than the elimination of the Bill of Rights. I'd expose the sons of bitches before they could implement their heinous act.

I realized just as quickly that it would never work.

"Roland, could I talk to you a minute?"
"Sure, what's up boss?"
"Well, it's this article you wrote about the plot to abolish Congress. Where exactly did you get this piece of shit?"
"It's true, a Secret Service agent at the White House tipped me off."

> *"Yeah, and the Pope tipped me off when the next earthquake was gonna hit."*

Even if the editor did approve it, the publisher would never print it. He'd call the White House Press Secretary, who would deny everything in good conscience and threaten reprisal, and I'd get reassigned to the NASCAR beat for the rest of my career. No thank you, I'll just live with a guilty conscience, taking my knowledge to my grave.

I turned over. Alycia had gotten out of bed already, probably doing the daily food shopping. I felt badly that another responsibility had been added to her already crowded schedule, but there was no alternative now that we had decided to use the refrigerator only for special occasions. On the bright side, using less of the revoltingly expensive electricity, we had a little more money for essentials. We had even started splurging on chicken for dinner twice a month.

I noticed a piece of paper on her pillow.

> *Honey, I hope you had a good time last night. You didn't sleep well, is everything okay? I'll be back around nine. Kiss Devon for me, will you? I love you.*

I threw the covers off, knowing I'd be greeted by a blast of cold air. So far the fall had been unseasonably chilly. Jeans, shirt, and shoes, quick! Still shivering, I hurried to the basement, where a couple of shovels of coal into the fireplace churned up sparks of hope and warmth. *Thank heaven for cheap plentiful coal, even if it does pollute the air. Who the hell can afford natural gas at $120 a cubic foot?*

Back upstairs in the hall, on my way to Devon's bedroom, I passed my favorite group of family photos: Mom and Dad at their wedding, looking unbelievably young and trim in formal wear; a similar pose with Alycia's parents, although they were older—a second marriage for both of them; Alycia at thirteen, petite but already attractive at her middle school graduation, with high cheek bones and dark brown hair; and a darling Devon, just starting to sit up at six months.

Devon was waiting for me, eyes blazing with curiosity about what the day would bring. Perhaps even more than other children, he greeted every morning with excitement and anticipation. I sat down on the edge of his twin bed, easily big enough for the body of a twelve-year old who would never grow to normal size. "Hi, sweetheart." I kissed him twice. "The second one is from Mommy." He tried to laugh but choked on the accumulated saliva he had trouble swallowing. "Okay, up you go." I lifted him to a sitting position, which helped clear his airway. "Are you hungry?"

He moved his head up and down.

"Mommy will be back home soon with the milk. Then we'll have some cereal together, all right? Do you want to go outside today? We can go to the park."

A thousand candles would not have made the room any brighter. How incredibly lucky we were that this boy had an inexhaustible spirit. A diseased liver and a malfunctioning hypothalamus had no chance against his eternal smile. We'd had friendly debates, Alycia and I, about Devon. At the age of two, he'd made a habit of giving unsolicited hugs to every kid in the neighborhood. "Psychologist," she would say. "Social worker, maybe." But he was good with his hands, too, and put wooden blocks together in imaginative patterns that astounded me. "Engineer," I countered. "Surgeon, maybe."

Then, when he was five, VOX Pharmaceuticals, one of the many corporations controlled by the trillion-dollar-a-year VOX conglomerate, came out with a pill that caught the country's imagination. Stalled in the approval process until the retired CEO of the manufacturer took the helm of the Food and Drug Administration, the little orange chewable was promoted heavily as the next wonder drug, in the same league as penicillin and Viagra. The product was promoted unceasingly on OmniScreens, billboards, and bus benches, courtesy of the National Institutes of Health. Trusting the claims that eVOXtabs improved resistance to all manner of diseases, caring parents across the country administered the drug to a hundred million children, until it was discovered that it caused auto-immune reactions in three percent of the kids who took it. Complications caused such extensive brain damage that Devon lost his mobility and most of his verbal capacity. The doctors said he would function at the intellectual level of a five-year-old for the rest of his life, and his physical growth would be sporadic at best.

We sued for medical damages and lost. VOX claimed that its scientific studies had generated no evidence of auto-immune reactions. The FDA backed it up. The jury never did hear all the evidence, sealed until 2250 under the terms of the Transparency in Government Act of 2011. We sold our house in Georgetown and moved to TDC #327, using the capital gain to purchase an annuity that would enable us to provide for Devon for the rest of his life. With government programs to help people with disabilities no longer being funded, Alycia quit her job as a music teacher to become a full time caregiver.

"I'm going to read a few minutes, okay? Then Mommy will be back, and we'll have breakfast."

Devon nodded.

I retreated to the computer desk in my tiny home office and signed onto the on-line version of VOX News. Responding to a White House press release, Winslow Bell, Minority Leader of the Senate, was quoted briefly as saying he did not regard Switzerland as an imminent threat to the security of the United States. Five high level administration officials were provided with ample time to denounce the Senator as a traitor for daring to question the President while the country was in grave danger. The Vice President and the Attorney General were especially vitriolic in their condemnation of Bell's criticism. My stomach turned, and I signed off hastily. It was all too obvious—groundwork for the plot was already being laid.

What would stop them from doing this? How many people even knew about it? What kind of responsibility did I have, an American citizen who had reluctantly become the recipient of the most important piece of news since the abolition of freedom of speech in 2036?

Was I reluctant or just overwhelmed? I normally didn't carry this kind of burden. I could point to no part of my formal education as a journalist that prepared me to deal with matters of this kind. The only reason Madison had approached me in the first place was that I covered the White House, and I was a friend of the President. Jadon and I did go to high school together, and I got to know him fairly well. Maybe I *was* part of some grand plan.

***

I had been a sports reporter for the student newspaper at Santiago High School in Corona, California. Jadon was second string quarterback on the football team as a junior, standing five foot seven and weighing all of 140 pounds. The starting quarterback was a talented athlete recruited to UCLA at the end of the season, so Jadon didn't play much. I don't think he got more than a paragraph from me the entire year.

Late in the season, wondering if watching from the sidelines got him down, I asked Jadon why he had tried out for football, rather than track, or swimming, or debate.

"Du-bate!?" he responded sarcastically. "Du-bate!?" I guess he figured that reply was sufficient. And, after thinking about it, I realized it was.

The truth is, football attracted girls, and Jadon wanted to be where the girls were. The feeling was mutual, too. While short of stature, he nevertheless had a cute face and a mop of curly brown hair that apparently made him irresistible.

During the summer before his senior year, Jadon became a man. I remember bumping into him one day by chance in late July. I was going in to see my counselor for a conference on college selection, and he was on break from summer school algebra. He had shot up to five foot ten and gained at least thirty pounds. He still needed pads to be seen on the field next to the hulking linemen, but he had a talent for executing plans and a nickname for all the cheerleaders, which increased his popularity for reasons I don't claim to understand. The coaches decided to give him a try as first string quarterback, knowing they would have to send in every play from the sidelines.

I interviewed Jadon after the third game of the season—we were 3 and 0, by the way. I wrote a complimentary article about him. Honing his political skills, probably without knowing it, he sent me a note. "Thanks, Roly," it said. Even then Jadon was a man of few words and simple ideas.

A few weeks later Jadon was waiting for me at my locker before school.

"Hey, Roly," he said with a practiced smile.
"Hi, Jadon. Thanks for the note."
"You're welcome. Good article. Got a favor to ask."
"Yeah?"

"Yeah. Can we talk a minute? In private?"

I glanced at my watch. I had fifteen minutes until class started. *What in the hell would Jadon Hamilton need to talk to me about in private?* "Sure, I guess."

He guided me onto the football field, obviously a place he felt very much at home, and sat on the bench, motioning for me to follow suit. The stands, occupied during games by hundreds of screaming classmates and parents, sat abandoned. The sprinklers spread their life-giving circles of water in a vain attempt to preserve a semblance of greenery despite the daily bludgeoning the grass took from twenty-five pairs of cleated shoes. I have to admit it felt creepy.

"You gotta promise never to tell anyone about this."

"Don't worry about it, man. Reporters know how to keep secrets."

Jadon pulled a piece of paper from his back pocket, unfolded it, and handed it to me. "See, I got a love note from Jennifer."

I read it, feeling very much the voyeur. I knew they were dating, but what did that have to do with me? "Lovely," I said, handing the note back to him. "Nicely written."

"That's the point. I can't write."

"You don't need to write. Just tell her you liked her note and you love her too."

"No, I need to answer it." He leaned closer to me, as if he were about to share the highly classified code that would authorize detonation of a nuclear weapon. "Other guys are hot for her too. I need an edge on the competition."

I started to get the gist of where he was headed, and he confirmed my suspicion immediately.

"You're a writer. You know how to say things so people believe you. Do me a favor, man, help me out."

I had to give the guy credit. He wasn't smart, but he was resourceful. "Do you really think that's a good idea?"

"Would I have asked you if I didn't think it was a good idea?"

Okay, maybe he did have just a smidgen of the debater in him. "But isn't that really dishonest, passing off someone else's words as your own?"

"You're helping me, that's all. If I don't like something, I'll change it."

"But won't she figure it out?"

"No. I'll copy it into my own handwriting. Just don't use any big words."

I looked at my watch again. I hated being late for class. "Look, Jadon, I've got to go. Give me some time to think about this, okay? I'd love to do you a favor, but..."

"Think if you want to, Roly. But think fast, 'cause I need a love poem by tomorrow morning."

Needless to say, he was waiting at my locker when I arrived the next day. "Here," I said, handing him a piece of paper. "It's not very good." The truth is, I had scratched it out in about ten minutes, wondering why I was doing it at all.

He grabbed it out of my hand and skimmed it in about five seconds. "No, it *is* good. Thanks, Roly." He started walking off, then called back over his shoulder, "Nice work, Cowboy." To my knowledge, I had never been within fifteen hundred miles of a live cow. Jadon used the word as a term of affection, a hold-over from the early twenty-first century.

Shortly after lunch I saw them kissing by her locker. My little love note, bearing no resemblance to a Shakespearean sonnet, had apparently done the trick. Despite my misgivings, I have to admit I wore a smile around school the rest of the day. Jadon Hamilton, star quarterback, owed me, cub reporter, a favor!

A few weeks after that, Jadon met me again at my locker.

"Tomorrow's Jennifer's birthday," he said.

"And that involves me because…?"

"You figure it out, Einstein. I'll meet you here tomorrow morning, eight a.m. sharp."

I wrote Jadon Hamilton's love notes to his girlfriend the rest of the year. The irony didn't escape my notice. I hadn't yet summoned the courage to ask a girl out myself, though a few of them attracted my attention, and here I was writing love notes for a jock who was barely more than an acquaintance. I began to put some effort into them, living vicariously through Jadon. I would look across the room at the diminutive blonde I adored but couldn't talk to for fear my legs would crumple beneath me, pouring out my feelings in the most eloquent poetry a seventeen-year-old brain could fashion, then substitute the relevant details to make it sound like Jadon had written it for his true love.

Sometimes he would read my stuff and just shake his head in amazement. "How do you know I feel that way?" he asked me once.

"Don't ask," I said, and he never raised the issue again.

Unfortunately, this state of affairs mirrored the rest of my life as well. I was not predisposed to action; I was a scared child living in a teenage body. The psychologist my parents had taken me to said I was just overly shy and would grow out of it. My parents encouraged me, unsuccessfully, to try out for parts in the school play, or even to join the chess club. My older brother taunted me, dared me, to get involved with sports, to no avail. My little sister bounced all over the community, belonging to so many different groups that my parents finally had to restrict her activities until she did at least an hour of homework every week. My siblings were my opposites; I just wasn't a joiner.

Journalism provided the perfect outlet for me. It enabled me to be in places where interesting things happened without feeling any responsibility to get involved. Subject to the intellectual immaturity so common in young people, I extrapolated the role of reporter far beyond anything justified by common sense. When my best friend ran for class president, he asked me to campaign for him. I wouldn't even help make signs, claiming that the journalist's role is to report the news, not to help make it. "Journalists don't join the parade," I told him, paraphrasing a lesson from our faculty advisor. "Our job is to report on the parade." Writing became the only public part of my life. I finished my assignments for the student newspaper, played video games when I got home, and satisfied myself with fantasies of dating the girls who starred in my wet dreams.

Jadon surprised me one day when I handed him one of my creations. "Are you seeing anyone?"

I was surprised that he didn't know, but in retrospect, he probably had difficulty comprehending anyone being afraid to ask a girl for a date. "Umm...no," I stammered. "Not right now."

"Well, I'm going to do *you* a favor, Cowboy. Cindy Tovary thinks you're cute." He punched me in the upper arm playfully, man to man.

As luck would have it, Cindy had appeared in my nighttime productions more than once. "Is that so? I don't even know Cindy Tovary."

"The blonde cheerleader in your history class, numbskull."

"I know who she is. I mean, I don't *know* her."

"That's about to change. Give her a call. Here's the number." He slugged me again.

I ran into the boy's bathroom to contemplate this unexpected event. After an anguishing and obsessive search for courage lasting three days, I dialed Cindy's number. To my complete amazement, she was pleasant. She was more than pleasant, she was charming, excited that I called. Did she want to go to the movies on Friday night? Yes, she most certainly did!

Thus began a months-long romance, the only one I ever had before I met Alycia. Its success gave substance to the fragile bond Jadon and I shared. We became friends. I eagerly shared the details of the memorable evenings Cindy and I spent together, knowing he enjoyed that sort of information, hoping that if she dumped me he would bring me another phone number. I actually started caring whether his football team won or lost. The day before we graduated, I wrote in his yearbook "Good luck, lover boy. Glad I could help." In mine, he wrote, "Been great knowing you, Cowboy. If I can ever do you a favor, anytime, anyplace, just name it." He signed it "Your favorite athulete, Jadon P. Hamilton."

***

I was staring at the computer screen when Alycia came up behind me and put her arms around my shoulders. "What are you thinking about, honey?"

"Nothing. Well, Jadon, in high school."

"You were pretty lost in it. Is everything okay?"

"Sure, sweetheart. Did you get the milk? Devon and I want to have cereal."

"It's on the table."

I went to the kitchen and filled two bowls with Cheerios and milk. Alycia wheeled Devon in from the bedroom, and I fed him small bites so he wouldn't choke. He loved the way the little circles bobbed up and down in the milk when I pushed them with the spoon, and I enjoyed seeing him giggle. After breakfast I brushed Devon's teeth and bundled him up for a trip to the park. It had warmed up to about 55, but he had little resistance to disease; it was better for him to be too warm than too cold. I grabbed a light jacket for myself. "We'll be back in a couple of hours," I told Alycia.

"Take your time, I've got plenty to do."

I intended to take my time. I had a lot to think about. We went out the back door, where my neighbor Matthew had been kind enough to build a wheelchair ramp out of boards from a fence rotting on the abandoned lot across the street. Moving to the front along a dirt path, I asked Devon the standard question: "Do you think we'll see any birds today?"

He nodded an enthusiastic yes, communicating hope rather than expectation. Birds had become rare in the TDC, poisoned by left-over toxic waste or starved from the lack of bugs and insects that had also fallen victim to the chemicals the EPA claimed did not exist. Nevertheless, we spotted an occasional sparrow, and Devon always reacted with unfettered delight.

The sidewalks had been abandoned to large cracks and crabgrass, so I chose to push the wheelchair in the street. It was still fairly level and just as safe, since the chances of encountering a motor vehicle were about as great as those of seeing a bird. A few persistent autumn leaves dotted the otherwise desolate branches of the red bud trees that survived in the front yards of every fifth or sixth house, adding a painting-like quality to the bare wooden facades of the standard 900 square foot bungalows. Thin columns of black smoke rose from most of the chimneys. Under foot, the leaves that had abandoned their perch cracked in our path, signaling a dry winter.

We headed north about a mile along Buchanan Avenue, then turned right onto Main Street. Four more blocks put us squarely in the business district, passing first the small market where Alycia had purchased the milk. Momentarily without customers, Mr. Dash was relaxing in a wooden rocking chair, the customary and comforting squeaks emanating from hundred-year-old joints. I'm not sure why I noticed the weather-faded sign hanging crookedly in the window above his right shoulder: "No Beef Today"; it had been there for three years. Nobody in the TDC could afford it anyway. When global warming moved the last domestic herds of cattle to Alaska, the transportation costs alone became prohibitive. I picked up Devon's hand and waved it toward Mr. Dash, securing a friendly wave in return.

A few doors down, on the other side of the street, I spotted Matthew, fourth in line to get into Doc Wheeler's office. I had noticed an increased intensity in his chronic cough lately. I hoped he didn't have bronchitis, knowing he would not be able to afford antibiotics. His wife had been a good friend to Alycia when we moved to the TDC. I cried at her funeral, not so much for her, or for him, but for my wife, who had lost a pillar of emotional support. Devon and I waved and got a broad smile back, followed by a coughing spell that hadn't yet subsided when we reached the end of the block.

We crossed First Avenue, and I quickened my pace as we passed the pillory fastened into the cement in front of the courthouse. The grotesque medieval device had only been used once, when a newcomer to the TDC had attempted to shoplift a loaf of bread from Mr. Dash. Ordinarily, the hungry man would have received a lecture in ethics from the mayor, and the residents would have taken up a collection to buy him and his family a few days worth of food while he searched for odd jobs. Unfortunately, he chose to commit his crime while the circuit judge was in town to complete a foreclosure. With trial by jury available only to those with money or political connections, and the room in the courthouse formerly used for jury deliberations now filled with odds and ends confiscated from local residents in lieu of fines they couldn't afford, the thief had been sentenced to spend four hours with his head and wrists trapped in steel. Humiliated beyond human endurance by his inability to feed his family, and too new to the community to realize that his plight had engendered sympathy, not scorn, he exercised one of the few rights still granted to him by the new United States Constitution: he purchased a cheap handgun the next day and blew his brains to pieces.

A small post office occupied the northeast corner of Main Street and Greenleaf Lane. The postmaster, Ed Martin, was emptying the mailbox in front. "Big haul today?" I asked him.

"The usual," he muttered, meaning "not much." With most people communicating electronically and no businesses of any size located in the TDC, volume had dropped off dramatically in the last twenty years. The administrators of the Postal Service had tried to close the building down eight years ago, and they would have succeeded had the residents not organized a strong political protest. I had never seen them so agitated. It wasn't just saving Ed's job that was at stake; having a post office was a symbol of respect in a city nearly devoid of any other indication that the nation even knew it existed. Although nobody articulated it quite so explicitly, losing that institution would have killed the spirit of the community.

"Maybe there will be more tomorrow," I suggested.

"I doubt it."

Ed and I played poker together occasionally, venturing into politics between hands. He was a true liberal, a man who saw the country going downhill fast and didn't mind letting you know he was plenty upset about it. He believed in the American way he had been raised with—telling the truth, taking care of the sick and the elderly, delivering the mail on time through rain, snow, and sleet. Ed resisted the occasional government snoop who came into town looking for a quick and dirty way to pry into the affairs of one resident or another. I didn't know anyone better suited to the job of postmaster.

We turned left onto Greenleaf Lane. Still using the street as my thoroughfare, I pushed Devon another two miles, finally lifting his wheelchair over the curb into the single park that served the 45,000 residents of TDC #327. Occupying a full city block, the "Oasis," as some people called it, was lined around its perimeter with trees and flowers. Somehow there was always money for landscaping, a symbolic shield of greenery set against the depressingly brown exterior that surrounded it. Six or seven groups of people were scattered around, playing football on the makeshift gridirons or just sitting and talking on the dilapidated picnic benches. I nodded hello to the people who noticed us and headed over to the playground. A young mother was pushing her toddler in the swing, and I moved the wheelchair back and forth in synchronization with its motion. Ten minutes later, Devon nodded off.

Knowing Devon usually slept about half an hour, I wandered to the edge of the playground, keeping an eye on him. Meticulously mowed grass and carefully weeded begonia beds lined the monument sign dedicating the park to Arthur Laffer, the twentieth century economist whose famous "Laffer Curve" predicted that decreases in tax rates would increase government revenues. An entire school of thought had developed around this theory, supporting among other things the idea that leaving wealth in private hands would trickle down to all segments of the population, benefiting the rich and the poor alike. Walking to the park would have been sufficient evidence that the idea simply didn't correspond to reality, but the people who still subscribed to the theory had never seen *this* community.

A sparrow landed on the monument, and I watched it gulp a worm down hungrily. Then it excreted, leaving a large white spot on the red marble. Devon, facing me about twenty feet away, was still asleep. He would be devastated if he found out he had missed such an unusual event. I moved toward him, quickly yet quietly, trying not to scare off the sparrow, but the bird flew off just as Devon opened his eyes.

"You just missed a small hungry sparrow," I said. "I'm sorry."

He looked at me, disappointed, perhaps just a bit distrusting. Sometimes it was difficult to know exactly what his eyes tried to reveal. "Look, I'll show you." I wheeled him over to the monument and pointed to the evidence. His eyes lit up. "Are you ready to go back?" Devon nodded. I pushed him out of Laffer Park, through downtown once again, past the blighted bungalows, arriving at home just in time for lunch.

CHAPTER THREE

Tuesday, November 13
I followed my usual routine the next few days as much as possible. I wrote for the paper, had breakfast with Devon and took him to the park, and loved every minute I was able to spend with Alycia. But Operation Capitol Hill haunted me. I hadn't said anything about it to anyone yet; the entire episode still seemed surreal. It even occurred to me briefly that Madison might be playing a practical joke on me. Yet the facts contradicted that notion; it would have been totally out of character for her.

Assuming it was true, I had a gigantic dilemma on my hands. What, if anything, was I going to do? My journalistic instinct, and my natural proclivity for inaction, told me to stay out of it. My predicament might be totally hypothetical. As much as I might feel a responsibility to the country, presidential security would probably make it impossible for me to foil Operation Capitol Hill anyway. If this were true, I could tell Alycia what I knew, explain that there was nothing I could do about it, and return to a relatively normal life. Without divulging my source, I would tell my editor that I had heard rumors about a new Constitutional amendment—not just talk, but an actual plan. Then I would observe the unfolding events with a heavy heart but a clear conscience.

To the contrary, my concern for the country, and secondarily for my friend Jadon Hamilton, told me I had to get involved. But did the plan I had developed after the meeting with Madison in the White House have any chance of succeeding?

Finally, what should I tell Alycia about the whole affair? Trusting her was not the issue. The question was whether I would be putting her in jeopardy, and Devon as well, giving her information about an activity that would engender hostility from people at the highest levels of government. That would make her an accessory, potentially subjecting her to prison, or worse.

There was only one person I could trust to clear up my confusion: Madison. Yes, she was a Secret Service agent. But she had deliberately informed me of the plot. She had even asked me if she could help, although at the time neither of us had any notion of where the revelation about Operation Capitol Hill would lead.

All right, then, how would I go about arranging a meeting with her in a safe location? There had to be absolutely no chance that our conversation would be compromised. The newspaper office was only a few miles from the White House, but taking her to lunch was out of the question—way too public. Calling her on the phone was equally absurd. It was too likely that our lines would be tapped. There was only one way: I would have to gain access again to the White House and talk with her in the computer room, where she apparently felt secure.

The solution arrived in the next day's mail—an invitation to attend the annual ceremony where the President spares the life of the Thanksgiving turkey. Ordinarily, this was an event I skipped, a feel-good public relations affair with no hard news value. I sent in my RSVP immediately. For all I knew, Madison would be off that day, but it was my only chance.

***

I arrived in Washington the day before Thanksgiving on the 9:12 a.m. train, purposely giving myself extra time in case of unexpected delays. With the ceremony not scheduled until one o'clock in the afternoon, I had a few hours on my hands. I figured I'd get a cup of coffee at the station, browse around the Capitol—home of the Congress Tyler and Chesterfield were determined to obliterate—then walk down Pennsylvania Avenue to the White House. I handed the attendant at the walk-up café a twenty-dollar bill for a black coffee and a mini-muffin, using the change to buy the morning paper. **Switzerland May Be Stockpiling Nerve Gas**, the headline screamed, quoting the Secretary of Defense. *"Enemies of the United States descend from Alps and now hold near-majority in Swiss government; pose imminent threat."* Won't be long before they ban imported watches and cheese, I predicted silently. I tossed Section One in the wire mesh trash enclosure near the rickety table. Maybe the local news would be more entertaining.

It wasn't. **Bell Goes Shopping, Doesn't Return**, caught my eye, a short article below the fold. *"Barbara Bell, wife of Senate Minority Leader Winslow Bell, has now been listed officially as a missing person following her disappearance during a shopping trip twenty-four hours ago. Senator Bell indicates he knows of no reason she would leave town or change her plans without notifying him. Local police have no clues and have requested assistance from the FBI. Attorney General Pete Chesterfield, speculating that terrorists may be responsible, has assumed full charge of the investigation personally. Senator Bell, secluded in his Washington D.C. home, would not comment for this article."*

I didn't want to contemplate the worst, but what alternative did I have? The idea that two of the highest officials in the United States government would engage in kidnapping to silence the opposition was gaining credibility at a frightening pace. And not just kidnapping—possibly blackmail as well, and certainly conspiracy to obstruct justice. If this were true, my plan was more risky than I'd originally thought, but all the more urgent.

I dumped section two in the trash and jumped up the stairs two at a time to street level. I still had more than two hours.

I had fallen in love with Washington, D.C. the first time I'd seen it. Architecturally speaking there were few buildings of note, except for the national monuments, but I appreciated the sense of history that permeated the city and the natural beauty of the expansive public spaces, graced by thousands of trees and well-kept flower gardens. With gasoline at $43 a gallon, most of the private automobiles had disappeared from the wide streets, resulting in an almost serene ambience.

I decided to visit one of my favorite landmarks, the Lincoln Memorial, work my way east along the Mall toward the Capitol, then go back to the White House. I never tired of seeing the nineteen foot high statue of our sixteenth president, seemingly relaxed in his white Georgian marble armchair, looking down on all that his statesmanship had preserved for almost two hundred years. Would he be so serene if he could somehow have known that the Union had split again, spilling the blood of seven million Americans in Civil War II? How would he feel if he could somehow observe from his magnificent outlook that the Capitol—constituting one of the main elements of his view—was in jeopardy of being dismantled, literally and figuratively?

From the base of the Memorial's broad steps, I walked north of the reflecting pool toward the Vietnam Veterans Memorial. Certainly the most somber of the historical structures ever dedicated in Washington, D.C., the black granite etched with the names of more than 55,000 casualties brought back memories to visitors more than half a century after the war had ended. As I stared at its elegant, inspired shape, a woman about forty years old appeared and searched for a name. When she found it, she took a piece of paper out of her purse, placed it against the granite, and rubbed it with a pencil. My journalistic curiosity got the better of me, and I moved toward her. "Hello," I said quietly.

She looked at me with watery eyes. "He was my grandfather. I never knew him. Neither did my mother. He was killed six months before she was born." She turned away, clearly not expecting a reply.

I moved toward the reflecting pool. On the other side stood the Korean War Veterans Memorial. I recalled that it had originally been called a "conflict" or a "police action"; however, the soldiers were just as dead. This memorial was potent emotionally not only because of the events it represented but because of its technical artistry. I decided to come back and pay my respects another day.

I walked toward the eastern end of the reflecting pool nearly half a mile away, where the National World War II Memorial honored 16 million Americans who served in the military, including 400,000 who died. Plans were already being made to use the site for the 100th anniversary of Pearl Harbor Day. I had nothing against celebrations of historical events, but sometimes I wondered why we didn't put more energy into providing necessities for people who were still alive.

Reluctantly but inevitably, I stopped next at the series of war memorials commonly referred to as the "Crescent of Death." Situated between the Washington Monument on the south and Constitution Avenue on the north, four separate structures honored the members of the armed services who had lost their lives in Iraq, Iran, Syria, and China. Each one was impeccably designed and constructed from finely polished gray marble. The "forty-years war"—a term not yet fully accepted, since no one knew how much longer it would take to achieve peace—represented, in my opinion, one of the great tragedies of mankind's modern era.

I lingered at the Syrian War Memorial, which paid tribute to 12,484 brave Americans who lost their lives between 2027 and 2032. Devon's older brother was one of them. Charles D. Raines—"Chad" to his friends—had been drafted at the age of 18. One year later, he'd given his life to his country, blown to pieces by a suicide bomber about the same age. Every year, on the anniversary of his death, we made a special point of explaining to Devon how brave and wonderful an older brother he used to have; we knew he didn't understand, but doing it made us feel like we were honoring Chad's memory.

Throughout the forty-years war, and in all previous wars as well I supposed, friends and relatives of the deceased asked whether their loved ones had died in vain. I think they asked the wrong question. What I wanted to know was, did they *live* in vain? Had they experienced joy and happiness during their days on earth? Had they been provided with opportunities to grow as people and contribute meaningfully to society? Perhaps most important of all, had they been given enough time to experience love?

Love: a simple word, a complex phenomenon. It seemed to me that people are capable of three types of love. Although some might quibble with the definition, certainly there is sexual love. Secondly, there is emotional love, possibly the strongest of bonds between two living people. Third, there is intellectual love, still an emotional bond, but between a person and a concept. Soldiers fight and die for many reasons, among them a loyalty bordering on love for their leaders and the members of their units. But they also fight for country—for principle. Patrick Henry and the other patriots of the Revolutionary War valued liberty above life itself. The soldiers of World Wars I and II went to Europe to make the world safe for democracy, and hundreds of thousands died in the process. Did I value freedom any less than they did? Was there some reason I should be exempt from making sacrifices for my country just because I was too old to get in the way of flying bullets?

This Mall I was walking on was conceived as a symbol of America's democratic values, including a government accessible to its people. How accessible is dictatorship? Would I be able to live with myself if I failed to exercise every conceivable method of preventing the government of the United States from collapsing into the tyranny that would inevitably follow if Operation Capitol Hill were successful?

Passing the Washington Monument, lifting its white pinnacle more than 550 feet into the air, I began to notice the Capitol, almost a full mile away. The huge cast-iron dome, basking in a strong sun, seized and held my eyes. It never failed to send a chill down my back. What would happen to this architectural wonder if Operation Capitol Hill succeeded? Would Chesterfield and Tyler let it stand as a historical monument? No, they would be too paranoid, concerned that the past might come back to haunt them. They would dismantle it and ship the pieces incognito to a graveyard inside some mountain in Utah.

With every step I took toward the Capitol, my resolve grew stronger. No, I didn't think I was going to stand by and let Article I of the Constitution expire at the hands of power-hungry tyrants.

Tourists hadn't been allowed to wander through the Capitol unaccompanied since September of 2001—the day everyone still referred to as "nine-eleven." My press pass got me past the gate with a stern warning to stay in the public areas. Venturing into the meeting rooms or the legislative chambers would result in my immediate arrest. Fine with me, all I wanted to do was kill some time.

It had been three years since my last visit.

Twenty yards from the Rotunda, I discovered that the State of the Month for November was South Dakota. A mini-museum had been set up depicting, in various displays arranged in a circular fashion, the topography, the climate, the history, the economy, and the people. In the center, a small replica of Mount Rushmore had been constructed, complete with the faces of the five U.S. Presidents whose faces were carved into the mountain: Washington, Jefferson, Lincoln, Theodore Roosevelt, and George W. Bush. I had heard a rumor that Bush had bought his way into this esteemed company with the leftover proceeds of his campaign fund, which had generated over $300 million for his second re-election effort. The guide would neither confirm nor deny.

One floor down, an attractive lady about twenty-five years old invited me into a small electric-powered vehicle about the size of a golf cart. With straight black hair reaching just to the top of her shoulders, wearing medium-high heels that brought her up to around five foot seven, she was dressed to impress. "Watch your step, please. Welcome to the Hall of Rights."

"Thank you. I'm getting a personal tour?"

"Why not? If you weren't important, you wouldn't have been allowed to tour the Capitol by yourself." She extended a hand. "I'm Karen."

"Hello, Karen." I liked her handshake, feminine yet firm.

"Have you visited the Hall of Rights before?"

"It's been a few years."

"Things haven't changed much. It's been five years since the Bill of Rights was perfected."

Perfected! The word bounced mercilessly into every corner of my brain. How dare she make such an outrageous claim? But I held my tongue.

Karen turned the key and wheeled the cart toward the entrance to the exhibit. The familiar diorama of the framers of the Constitution came into view on the right hand side. Life-sized and life-like, but silent, Jefferson, Franklin, Hamilton, and a few lesser known men made debating-like gestures as a document on a desk nearby glowed, as if it were the Ten Commandments illuminated by a light from Heaven.

"The original Constitution didn't include a Bill of Rights," Karen explained, sounding like an elementary school teacher. "It was an add-on, promised to the people as a political device to encourage them to replace the Articles of Confederation. Alexander Hamilton actually argued against the need for a Bill of Rights, calling the lack of such a document a 'pretended defect.'"

Fortunately, I had taken American History in college. "Yes, Federalist Paper #85. But he merely argued that the Bill of Rights didn't need to be voted on simultaneously. He went on to say that, with three-fourths of the states in concurrence, individual amendments could be subsequently enacted." It was difficult to see in the subdued light, but I thought she lost a little color in her face.

"I can see you're something of a skeptic, Mr. Raines. I hope this tour will renew your appreciation for the process we have been engaged in the last few years to improve the underlying documents that govern our great nation."

"I'm a journalist, Karen, and we're skeptical by nature. What brings you here, by the way?"

"I taught school back in my home town. Cheney Elementary, in Atlanta, sixth grade. It got boring after two years."

"And is this bringing you more adventure?" I imagined her parents, probably large political donors, calling the office of their local congressman to see if there were any federal jobs available for their deprived, bored-to-tears daughter, being disappointed when the tour guide position was the best he had to offer.

She hesitated a second, then did a pitiful job of covering up. Her face flushed. "Yes, well, Washington is where the action is."

I didn't have time to pursue the natural line of questioning, which involved an attempt to discover the type of action she was looking for. An illuminated map came up on our left, showing which states had supported the repeal of the eighth amendment in 2014. Beneath the map, barely legible because a bold red strikeout line had been drawn through the entire sentence, were the original words: **Excessive bail shall not be required, nor excessive fines imposed, nor cruel and unusual punishment inflicted.**

"The eighth amendment was vague," Karen explained, "and it prohibited the government from protecting our way of life against revolutionaries, both foreign and domestic." She sounded rehearsed. But the language didn't strike me as the kind a sixth-grade teacher would use. I guessed she had graduated from tour guide school with honors.

"It was purposely vague." I could have reminded her that the language of the eighth amendment was adopted directly from the British Bill of Rights written one hundred years prior to its incorporation into the Constitution, but I sensed it wouldn't have done any good. Her next statement confirmed my hypothesis.

"The return to public whipping, use of the pillory, and other forms of humiliation have reduced crime in this country by twenty percent."

"If these punishments are so effective, why do people still commit illegal acts at all?"

"Jealousy, perversion, and lack of self-discipline," she answered confidently.

"You mean, like having the desire to eat?"

"Oh, Mr. Raines, you are dramatically oversimplifying to justify a position that is indefensible. Surely you don't believe that stealing is justified under any circumstances."

I wasn't sure that I derived any significant benefit from engaging Karen in debate, but the battle had been joined. "I don't believe that five percent of the people holding ninety-five percent of the wealth is justified under any circumstances. I agree, it is not desirable to steal. But the effect of the tax code as it has evolved over the last forty years has been to concentrate money and power in the hands of the few, leaving the many to live in squalor and poverty. Of course some of them are going to steal. They think it's unfair to work ten hour days and earn barely enough to feed their families."

"And when they do steal, we will continue to cut their hands off."

She's probably never been hungry a day in her life. How would she understand the power of an empty stomach?

The next part of the exhibit came up on the right. "Fifth, sixth, and seventh amendments repealed, in 2020," Karen stated in a matter-of-fact voice. She turned to me, and I noticed defiance in her eyes. "I suppose you believe everyone should have the right to a public trial by a jury of his peers?"

"What would the exception be?"

"Think about it, Mr. Raines. In any criminal trial, there are two kinds of errors that can be made. We can release someone who is guilty, or we can convict someone who is innocent. In both cases, we will be wrong. But the first is far riskier than the second. In the first case, a criminal goes free, and society pays the price when the culprit continues to destroy our way of life.

In the second, the person is punished without cause, but society is protected. This is a dangerous world, Mr. Raines. We allow evil people to commit acts of violence without retribution at our own peril. It is far more effective and expedient to have these important decisions made by judges rather than by juries."

How quickly ignorance turns three hundred years of jurisprudence on its head.

The next exhibit came into view, the one most tourists considered the highlight of the tour. An eight-foot high statue of Charlton Heston, rifle in hand, towered above us. "2026," Karen said. "Rewording of the second amendment."

"The right of the people to keep and bear arms of any kind and in all circumstances shall not be infringed," I quoted.

"Exactly. The reference to a well regulated militia may have been appropriate historically, but it kept interfering with the real meaning of the amendment."

"But the words 'of any kind and in all circumstances' effectively removed from the legislatures and the courts any ability to mandate safety locks or reduce the proliferation of military-style assault weapons," I countered.

"Safety locks are unnecessary if people are properly educated in the use of their weapons."

I looked at her closely and concluded that she actually believed what she was saying. People are products of their environment. Growing up in the South, her dad had probably talked about the beginning of hunting season months in advance, using language that would make a little girl think it was almost as important as the Second Coming. In school, part of the science curriculum would probably have been studying the beneficial impact of hunting on animal population. Nevertheless, I couldn't resist offering my rebuttal. "I saw a study the other day. Since this amendment was passed, the rate of accidental shootings in this country has doubled, and 23,850 children have died of gunshot wounds just in the last five years."

She was unmoved. I got the feeling her reaction would have been identical had I said that two million children had been killed. "We can't let a few unfortunate incidents distract us from one of the most fundamental rights upon which this country was founded." Lapsing into reverential silence as we passed the statue, she added, "It's just too bad Mr. Heston didn't live to see this amendment adopted."

A few unfortunate incidents! I marveled at the power of the human mind to ignore facts that contradicted preconceived conclusions and deeply held beliefs.

"Are you ready for the tunnel?" Karen continued evenly, apparently schooled in the art of ignoring conflict when it served her purpose.

The tunnel, I knew, was the last and most dramatic part of the exhibit. "No, wait. What about the Ninth and Tenth Amendments?"

"Those changes are difficult to portray visually. Most people don't really care about them anyway."

I thought I had seen something in the exhibit about them during my last visit, but maybe that was wishful thinking. "Wouldn't it be important to have at least a little display about the removal of the concept of popular sovereignty from the Constitution?" I asked acerbically.

"I suppose you think so," she replied, mimicking my sarcasm.

"Yes, I do. I think every American ought to be able to recite the language of the 32nd Amendment: **No State shall grant any rights to any citizen that are not expressly stated in this Constitution.**"

"I know what it says, Mr. Raines."

"I'm sure you do. But do you know what it means?"

"I think you're going to tell me."

"I'll give you my interpretation, for whatever you think it's worth." I presumed she would rather swallow glass. "This amendment was the most powerful change to the Constitution ever made. It reversed the concept of power being reserved to the people and established the federal government as the ultimate authority."

"It's dangerous to give the people too much authority, especially in time of war. It invites chaos. As for the states, it makes no sense for them to provide rights to people that the Constitution no longer grants. It's inconsistent."

I supposed Alexander Hamilton to be turning over in his grave. *The people surrender nothing*, he had argued in The Federalist # 84, urging a favorable vote on the proposed Constitution. *WE, THE PEOPLE retain everything.* "Karen, would it be fair to say then that you believe there is no situation in which the people have the right to rebel against the government?"

"The government *is* the people. The people elect the president. They vote for the person who best represents their point of view. Once the majority speaks, the minority has to go along. You know as well as I do that unanimity is impossible. What happens, Mr. Raines, if we allow people to rebel every time they disagree with an action of the duly elected government?"

She had pushed one of my buttons, and I saw no reason to stifle my reaction as long as I didn't exhibit the intense anger that was building inside. "You are trivializing and distorting an important concept. Nobody is suggesting that the government should have no power to enforce legitimate legislation. But when government usurps for itself total control, power unchecked, used for its own advantage *against* the people, shouldn't the people have a remedy?"

"They can elect a new government."

"And if the government rigs the elections? Or changes the laws to prolong terms of office, making elections so infrequent that they might as well not be held at all? Have you read no history, Karen? These things happen!"

"You have a vivid imagination. May we just finish the tour, please?" Karen headed the cart directly into a tunnel. "The darkness is symbolic of the next chapter of American history," she explained. "Let's not talk through this part. And hold on."

Our vehicle came to an abrupt halt. I knew what was about to happen, but I could still feel my heart pounding. My eyes strained to pick up light that simply wasn't there. The sharp rat-a-tat-tat of rifle fire sounded in the distance, then quickly approached. The sound of bombs whizzing through the air pelted the silence, followed by explosions of light. Finally, accompanied by a violent rocking of the vehicle and a deafening roar, the blinding flash of a simulated nuclear explosion lit up the side of the tunnel. As the mushroom cloud grew in size, over a period of several minutes, it also diminished in intensity. When the ambient lights faded in, Karen started the cart.

"2035," Karen said. "Simplification of the First Amendment. Fifteen states secede from the union in protest, causing Civil War II."

I wasn't sure I had heard correctly. Had the propaganda machine finally thrown caution to the wind? Four hundred years of philosophical development had been poured into the First Amendment. It had been phrased carefully by people who appreciated the nuances of language, and countless Americans had gone to their graves defending it. "Did you say 'simplification'?"

"Yes. It was long, convoluted, and unnecessary. Freedom of speech, in particular, had become destructive of our country's way of life. People were criticizing the federal government for its foreign policy, its environmental protection procedures, and even alleging that the administration was lying about the rationale for the trade embargo of Europe. Likewise, freedom of the press. Peaceful assemblies were getting out of hand. Enough is enough."

"I still don't think it was necessary to nuke Cleveland."

"That was just a warning. Boston would have been next, had the insurgents not capitulated. That little bomb saved a lot of lives, surely you will agree with that."

"My brother lived in Cleveland."

She paused for less than a second. "Oh. I'm sorry. But we had to save the Union, you know." I surmised she would have killed her own mother to save the Union. "Anyway, we were magnanimous in victory, accepting Western California as the fifty-first state in the union despite its participation in the rebellion."

We moved slowly past the text of the revised First Amendment, glowing in saturated holographic colors on the right side of the vehicle: "Congress shall make no law prohibiting the free exercise of religion."

"Simple, short, and eloquent," Karen said.

"Gutted and gutless," I replied. The veneer of public politeness I had been trying to maintain had finally been shattered.

She stopped the cart. "Must we have this kind of discussion on each and every improvement that has been made in the Bill of Rights? Do you not approve of anything that has been accomplished in the last thirty years?"

I decided to test her knowledge of social psychology. "Karen, are you aware of the experiments of Solomon Asch in the mid-twentieth century?"

She shrugged her shoulders and looked besieged by the question. "I can't say that I am. How would that be relevant?"

"Bear with me a minute. Asch demonstrated that many people can be influenced by a group to ignore what their own senses tell them. In one experiment, he asked people simply to say which of three lines was the same length as a comparison line. In the absence of group influence, they answered correctly. When a group of Asch's confederates purposely gave the wrong answer in the presence of the subject, the subject frequently gave the wrong answer as well."

"People like to be part of a crowd. So what?" She started forward again, apparently believing she had countered successfully.

I continued, despite the smug look on her face. "If you're deciding which blouse to wear, it doesn't make much difference. If you're deciding whether to go to war or not, it makes a big difference. The point is, any kind of social pressure to conform will decrease the variety and intensity of views expressed. And when people keep their opinions to themselves, voluntarily or otherwise, other people who might be influenced by their arguments are deprived of hearing potentially useful information."

"And you feel comfortable in generalizing some silly experiment with college freshmen to the behavior of citizens in the greatest country in the history of the world?"

"Absolutely. In fact, it was suggested by Arthur Schlesinger, Jr. that even a single dissenter might have prevented President Kennedy from going ahead with the disastrous Bay of Pigs invasion of Cuba. The absence of any dissent can cause what is known as 'incestuous amplification,' in which a group of people reinforce each others' prejudices and biases, resulting in stronger convictions, even though those convictions might be incorrect."

"Aren't we getting pretty far afield from the Bill of Rights?"

"Not at all. The point I'm making is that dissent helps groups of people come to informed, wise decisions. The framers of the Constitution understood this and purposely chose a system of government with built-in checks and balances, both within the government and outside the government, in the form of the right to popular dissent." Karen looked at me vacantly, so I added one final thought, knowing our tour was coming to an end. "In 1943, the Supreme Court said, 'If there is any fixed star in our constitutional constellation, it is that no official, high or petty, can prescribe what shall be orthodox in politics, nationalism, religion, or other matters of opinion, or force citizens to confess by word or act their faith therein. If there are any circumstances which permit an exception, they do not now occur to us.' "

For this she had no rebuttal, except the well-worn phrase that many of her would-be boyfriends had probably heard on second dates: "I'm getting a headache."

We rode in silence another minute or so, as the vehicle came gradually to a stop in a facsimile train station decorated with outlandish shapes and gaudy colors. "Thank you for exploring the Hall of Rights," Karen intoned, trying her best to sound professional. "We disembark here, at the Station of the Future, standing firm in the knowledge that our country is on the right course, standing optimistically as the administration of Jadon P. Hamilton leads us into the future."

"Thank you, Karen," I said as I got out of the vehicle. And I meant it. The tour had reinforced for me the importance of an idea Thomas Jefferson had expressed in one of his letters: "A bill of rights is what the people are entitled to against every government on earth." Unfortunately, Jeffersonian democracy was no longer in vogue.

Back on street level, I walked to the White House, taking advantage of a balmy day and the unusual luxury of an hour to spare. I also knew my boss would appreciate my not turning in a cab fare on my expense account.

Pennsylvania Avenue was desolate, almost eerie. What had once been a major thoroughfare, clogged with traffic, had become a wide alley separating the office buildings on either side. What an incredible story this street would tell if it could somehow verbalize the thoughts and feelings of all the famous people who had traveled its length. What was going through James Madison's mind as his horse-drawn carriage carried him to the White House, becoming the fourth man to occupy the office he had written about so eloquently in the Federalist Papers? What did Woodrow Wilson really think about the Senate that blocked the nation's membership in the League of Nations, his noble but unsuccessful attempt to form a world government that would prevent all future wars? How had world leaders regarded John Kennedy when they'd marched down this street seventy-seven years ago, following his simple horse-drawn, flag-draped casket?

Security at the White House was routine, and within fifteen minutes of my arrival I was standing on the South Lawn, along with about four hundred other guests, waiting for the grand entrance of the President and the turkey. Standing nearly two hundred feet from the mansion, I scoured the multi-storied patios for Madison. I circulated within the crowd, trying to get as close to the front as possible. No luck.

At precisely 12:55 p.m., a live turkey was brought out in a large cage, followed shortly by the President. Madison was at his side. Would she see me? How could I get her attention without arousing the suspicion of every other agent? She gave no sign that she even knew I was there. The President completed the routine faultlessly, and the crowd started filing out. I had no choice but to head toward the exit along with everyone else.

"Mr. Raines?" A uniformed security guard monitoring the exit motioned me aside.

"Yes?"

"I've been asked to issue you a special invitation, sir. Would you like a personal tour of the White House?"

Madison! Bless her heart.

"I can't think of anything I'd like better."

"Please follow me."

Madison met us at the east door. "I'll take it from here, Doug. Thank you." Striding at a rapid clip, she turned to me a few seconds later and added, "We don't have much time. All the other agents are with the President in the West Wing. I'm on break. Play tourist and just look around until we get to the basement."

I happily obliged. Madison walked directly toward the room we had used during my previous visit. When we arrived and the door had shut behind us, she gestured for me to sit down.

"I gathered you wanted to see me. You've never attended this monumentally important event before." Even without her smile I would have known she was joking by the intonation in her voice.

"You're good, Madison. Exactly what I was hoping for." With people like Madison protecting him, Jadon was in no danger—physically. "Has anyone discovered that we've been meeting?"

"No. The cameras in the hall are monitored only when the President is in the vicinity."

"Is anything new?"

With Madison, what you saw was what you got. Unlike some politicians who grabbed your hand with both of theirs and shook vigorously at the same time they were plotting your demise, she told only the truth, embellished simply by alert eyes and an earnest face. "Events are unfolding just as you would expect. As far as I can tell, there's nothing standing in their way. And they've activated a small but powerful security network to detect any potential obstacles. I have people looking into it for me. Don't worry, they're not aware that you know anything about it." She shifted gears seamlessly. "You were pretty overwhelmed the last time I saw you. What's happening on your end?"

"I want to run something by you. It's pretty far out."

"I'm not going to permit an assassination."

"You know I would never do that. First of all, I know you couldn't and wouldn't collaborate. You'd do everything you could to stop it, and I respect that. Secondly, Jadon is my friend. Not to mention that Tyler would then become President, making it even easier for them to implement their plan. I have a better idea."

She brightened. "And that would be?"

"The President has just been re-elected. He'll have the entire world at his fingertips on Inauguration Day, a fact clearly not lost on the opposition. Despite the back-stabbing and behind the scenes maneuvers of his enemies, he's still the person people look to for guidance as far as the proper direction for this country. I'll write another substitute speech for him! We'll beat them at their own game!"

She didn't seem to comprehend the idea at first. "The President will give a speech—written by you?"

"Yes. I've studied quite a lot of history. I know what he

should say. I think I do, anyway. At the very least, it won't advocate the abolition of Congress!"

She looked around the room as if she were seeing it for the first time. "I really don't know, Roland. I've never heard of such a thing."

"It's not as bizarre as it sounds. Presidents always have speechwriters. Jadon has speechwriters. Only this time, he has two he doesn't know about. One wants him to abolish Congress. The other wants him to restore the fundamental principles on which this country was founded."

"What would you say? I mean, I know you're a journalist—and a good one—but isn't that substantially different from writing an inaugural address?"

"I suppose it is. But what options do we have? It appears we have to make a choice for the President that he will presumably never know about. We can let him read the speech written by the Attorney General, or we can arrange to have him read mine. We can lose Article I of the Constitution, or we can stand up for what we think is right."

"A persuasive argument, I admit."

"I thought so." I risked a smile, which was well received. "The question is, can we pull it off?"

"I think so, but I'll have to check on the technical details. My job is physical protection." She sighed deeply.

"There must be a way. Otherwise, how will Tyler and Chesterfield substitute their speech for the one Jadon's regular staff is writing?"

"Good point. I'll find out, okay?"

"I'll work on the speech."

"Roland, listen, don't get your heart set on this. I admire your plan. But it's not going to be easy. These guys are cunning and vindictive. They'll crucify anyone who tries to get in their way."

"That reminds me. I noticed in the paper this morning that Senator Bell's wife is missing. Is there a connection?"

Madison's shoulders slumped in anguishing slow motion. "I was afraid you were going to ask about that. Okay, I think you have a right to know." She stood up and withdrew a microchip from one of the cabinets. "Watch this."

Once again, Tyler and Chesterfield were talking in the Vice President's office.

"Where is she?" Tyler asked.

"Gitmo." From the expression on his face, Chesterfield could just as easily have said "Ohio." The coldness in his voice reminded me of a video I had seen once, the story of a psychotic serial killer who had no more conscience than a vulture. Tyler looked confused. "Guantanamo Bay. It's the most secure facility we have for enemies of the state. We rigged part of it to look like a third world dungeon. She thinks she's in South America."

"How's the Senator taking it?"

"As expected." Chesterfield switched to a tone of voice appropriate to a father explaining the consequences of getting drunk to his teenage son. "When she shows up in a few days, not too much worse for wear, claiming to have been abducted by Spanish-speaking terrorists, I think he'll come to the realization that this is a very dangerous world indeed."

"What do you mean, 'not too much worse for wear'? You told me there wouldn't be any rough stuff."

"Don't worry. She won't get much sleep or food, but we're not going to beat her. The point is for the Senator to be grateful to get her back and realize it could be worse next time. That will maximize the impact the event will have on his view of the world."

Tyler nodded. "All right then. I can't say I'm terribly happy about this part of what we're doing."

Chesterfield assumed a professorial demeanor, with a touch of frustration. "I've already explained that. We're trying to do something good for the country here. If we're not careful, dissent will tear this nation apart. That's exactly what the terrorists want, for us to fight among ourselves so we won't have the energy or the resources to beat them into the ground. Why do you think this country has been at war for the last forty years? Why do you think so many of our former allies are falling into the hands of our enemies? The terrorists are winning! Our way of life is at stake here, Shorty. Anything we have to do to prevail is totally justified."

Tyler smiled. "You're right as usual, Pete. Full steam ahead."

Madison shut the computer off and looked at me for a reaction. For once, I didn't hesitate. "Bastards. Dirty fucking bastards."

She agreed with a nod.

"Listen!" Another element of what I had just heard struck me hard. "What I saw the first time was deceitful and devious, to say the least, but probably legal since these guys are official advisors. This is bloody kidnapping! Why don't you just go to the police? If you don't want to, give me the chip, and I'll go to the police."

She put her hand on my shoulder. "I thought about both those possibilities. I'm afraid it's impossible. First, another department of the Secret Service takes inventory of these chips frequently. It wouldn't take long to discover the theft. And that's exactly what it would be—theft of government property. You know what the sentence is for that." She looked at her hand as though she were about to lose it. "Besides, becoming a whistleblower is a dangerous business these days. Suppose I turn this chip in to the Washington, D.C. Metropolitan Police Department. They would just turn it over to the FBI. And who controls the FBI? The Attorney General. I can't prove the connection, but a career civil servant, a chemist in the Environmental Protection Agency, uncovered evidence last year that his boss' supervisor, the agency's Deputy Administrator, tampered with scientific evidence documenting the increasing threat of mercury contamination in our food supply. He sent a memo to the Justice Department suggesting that industrial polluters be prosecuted, then he vanished two days later."

I remembered. "Yes, Ben Taft. There was a short article in the paper about his disappearance. If I remember right, they said his body had been found in Pakistan. Terrorism was the alleged culprit."

"Domestic terrorism, if you ask me. But nobody is coming forward with any substantive allegations." Madison shook her head sadly but straightened her back. "In any case, I'm not ready to die. I've got kids to look after. Let's try to make your plan work."

"All right. I know you're out on a limb already. Part of the plan is making sure, if it goes down, you don't go down with it."

"I appreciate that. My kids appreciate that." I admired her ability to inject humor into a deadly serious situation. "Look, I'd better get back. We're going to have to keep our meetings to a minimum, maybe only one more between now and January. This room is secure, but your visits to the White House are a matter of public record. Somebody will get suspicious sooner or later if you come too often."

"Madison, if you have any misgivings...?" I didn't see how

she could, given what we had just witnessed, but she was a friend. I felt I owed her a way out.

"I had mixed feelings the night I showed you the first clip. The fact that they were being so secretive struck me as wrong. But I'm a glorified security guard, what do I know about government?" She waved a hand toward the computer. "Now I'm convinced. We have to do something. I just don't know if what you're proposing is possible." She placed the chip back in the file drawer. "Whatever happens, you be careful. Don't think they wouldn't go after your wife and your son if they thought it would advance their cause. I feel your passion, but the truth is, you are putting your family in danger as well as yourself."

"I think about that all the time. If I go through with this, and my actions cause them any harm..."

"I know." Madison touched my arm lightly. "All right. I'll walk you back to the side door, and you check out with the guard at the gate. Tell him you absolutely fell in love with the Oval Office."

Back on the street, I mulled over the situation as I walked toward my office to file the cursory but obligatory story about the lucky turkey. Apparently, my plan might work. Although composing the speech wouldn't be easy, that part didn't bother me. I had probably written a couple of million words in my life, and a few thousand more would not present a challenge beyond my ability. Yes, they would be the most important words I had ever written, but I knew that my convictions rested on a sturdy foundation; they would find expression. Madison was the ideal accomplice—well connected to say the least, growing in her understanding of the critical importance of thwarting Operation Capitol Hill, and a close personal friend. I had only known her a year when Chad was killed, but she'd made a special trip to the TDC to pay her respects. There is nothing more you can ask for than support during a personal crisis. Madison had provided it without being asked.

Two things still bothered me. The technology was questionable. Madison was looking into it, and there was nothing more I could do until she finished her investigation. Chesterfield was more problematic. He was bright enough to understand the need to take counter-measures against any and all potential threats to his grand scheme. I had to be cunning enough to implement my plan without him finding out.

CHAPTER FOUR

Thursday, November 22
Alycia prepared a Thanksgiving feast—cranberry sauce, green beans, gravy, pumpkin pie—everything but turkey, which was simply beyond our means. Matthew joined us, as he had no surviving family, and the four of us sat around the kitchen table draped with a decorative plastic cloth, stuffing food into our mouths as though we hadn't eaten for a week. Well, Devon didn't stuff himself. Alycia and I took turns feeding him carefully, but he seemed to understand it was a special occasion and charmed us with unusually loud gurgles.

Matthew went home shortly after dinner, coughing uncontrollably. Alycia wheeled Devon into his room for a nap, and I sprawled on the couch in the living room, observing the growing crack in the ceiling without really seeing it. I was half asleep by the time Alycia sat down and placed my head gently into her lap.

"Did you enjoy it?"

"You're a great cook, honey. I won't be able to eat for a week."

"We can't afford to eat for a week." Without looking at her, I knew she was smiling. She had probably been saving for a month, and future meals would not be sacrificed. I grunted to acknowledge her joke and snuggled up tightly. She put her head back against a cushion, and the slowing movements of her chest told me she only needed only about two minutes to collapse into a well-deserved sleep.

The first time I had experienced such bliss was on my third date with Alycia.

***

We met at Indiana University, in the charming little town of Bloomington. I was studying journalism as a graduate student, having graduated magna cum laude from Oberlin College with a major in English. She was a senior in the music department, a soprano looking for a career as a solo artist. One Friday evening, I found myself with nothing to do, all my assignments completed, facing a lonely weekend. Glancing through the student newspaper, I noticed an ad for a performance of Madame Butterfly the following night. The photo of her in costume captivated me—an exquisite face, saddened by the failure of her husband Lieutenant Pinkerton to return to Japan and love her again after a seemingly interminable three-year absence.

I had never seen an opera before. Still suffering from social phobia, I normally walked around campus from dorm to class to lunch and back, sticking pretty much to myself unless an assignment forced me to interact with people. I decided to skip the show. But as Saturday morning stretched lazily into afternoon, I picked up the paper again. Something about her thin cheeks and expressive eyes punctured my resistance sufficiently to generate reluctant activity. About five o'clock I traded my jeans and T-shirt for a freshly ironed shirt and a pair of casual slacks, not really knowing what the proper dress would be for this type of occasion, and went to the box office half hoping they would be sold out. A few seats were left in the balcony, and I bought one.

I glanced around before the performance began, happy that I didn't see anyone I recognized. Then the house lights went down, revealing a beautiful set and music so stunning it pinned me to my seat. Alycia sang "One Fine Day," the opera's most famous aria, with a passion that set me on fire. In my mind, I was on stage with her, listening to every beat of the heart that would never give up hope. Although I wasn't aware of it yet, I had fallen in love.

I went to the Sunday matinee too, and to my astonishment I found myself asking an usher for directions to the stage door. Then I mumbled an unnecessary explanation about wanting an autograph.

"On the north side of the building," she replied easily. "Give them about half an hour to remove their make-up."

Like I would have the courage to ask for an autograph! But half an hour after the performance, that's where I was, waiting for my butterfly. When she came through the door, in a group of three, all I could manage to do was shove the program at her and hope for the best.

"Did you like it?" she asked.

"It was...I was...You were...Yes, it was magnificent."

"Thank you." She took the program and smiled at me. "Do you have a pen?" Oh my God. Yes, she would need a pen, wouldn't she? I fumbled. A journalist without a pen, asking for an autograph. Classic!

She looked at her friends and shrugged playfully. "Help me out here, okay? I have an admirer." A pen was quickly produced from someone's purse, and she took it. That's when I first noticed the radar: the astonishing capacity she had to see past the veneer, to perceive beyond the purely visible. She looked at me, and I felt pierced. Pierced and naked. "Have you ever seen an opera before?" She tilted her head slightly.

I was captivated by every gesture, every nuance of motion. "Yes. Last night."

"I see." She thought for a moment, wrote something in the program, handed it back to me, and disappeared.

I was so thunderstruck I didn't even read it until I got back to my room: *I'm glad you liked the opera. It's one of my favorites. Alycia. 498-5523*

A week later, I gathered enough courage to ask if she might possibly consider having dinner with me. Two years later, after she threatened to leave me unless I proposed, we set a date to get married. By that time, Alycia had realized that her dream of being a professional opera singer was beyond her natural ability. She had a fine voice for community theater, but it wasn't strong enough for international stardom. So she got her educational credential and started teaching in high school, giving private lessons on the side. After the wedding, we moved to Youngstown, Ohio, where she got a job with the public schools and I worked for the *Chronicle*.

Chad was born a year later, on June 2nd. Alycia took the summer off, then went back to work in the fall. A year later I got an offer to move to Washington, D.C., to work the political beat for the *Daily Independent*. Alycia agreed somewhat reluctantly to give up the house we had just remodeled, and she found a job in Alexandria, Virginia, just across the Potomac River from my office.

Never in my most optimistic teenage moments would I have guessed that I would be so happily married. I grew to love music almost as much as she did. Alycia, in turn, appreciated the careful thought I put into my articles and the meticulous research I did to ensure complete accuracy. On a personal level, we just clicked, there's no other way to put it. We shared everything and enjoyed each other's company, whether we were talking, watching a DVD, resting quietly without a sound, visiting with friends, or sleeping comfortably and securely, wrapped in each other's arms.

Bliss continued until I went to France. My editor had asked

me to do an in-depth story on the reaction of the French people to the gradual dismantling of the American Bill of Rights. Alycia agreed it was a great opportunity, despite the three-week separation it would create, and we lingered endlessly over the last kiss before I boarded the plane for Paris.

We exchanged VOXmails daily and talked twice a week. But the translator the newspaper hired for me was a most pleasant companion, who had an insatiable curiosity about America and a figure as gorgeous as her native language. The first day we were together, I merely noticed that she was beautiful. The second day, I began to want to know more about her: married or single, what she had done with her life, what she wanted to do in the future. On the third day, I touched her shoulder when we talked and couldn't prevent myself from staring at the nape of her neck. Every day thereafter, I took another small step toward infidelity. She reciprocated just as gradually, rewarding my tentative advances without overwhelming the shy man pushing his way almost involuntarily toward adventure and disaster. By the end of the first week, I knew that conflict had been planted deep inside my soul. By the end of the second week, I knew that sin was inevitable. Still fighting the impulse, despite knowing I would lose the struggle, I held out until the last night. For all the agony I experienced, we slept together only once.

Alycia knew something was wrong about ten minutes after I got home. She had been looking forward to getting me into bed, and she succeeded. But my guilty conscience ate away at my confidence. She asked me if anything was wrong, and although I anticipated the consequences, I simply couldn't lie to her. Within the hour, she knew the whole story. She packed a few things and left.

I stayed in bed the next three days, calling in sick. I *was* sick. Mental anguish turned itself on me in an ugly fashion, creating periodic migraine headaches and almost constant stomach cramps. I cursed myself for succumbing to the temptation that threatened everything I valued in my life.

Alycia returned the fourth day, ready to resolve things one way or the other. I apologized profusely and begged her to forgive me, and she softened. We agreed that honesty would be the backbone of our relationship. There would be no affairs. There would be no secrets of any kind. Not ever.

***

My reminiscences had turned into dreams. When I woke up, my forehead was wet, and distress was carved into Alycia's face.

"You didn't sleep well. You haven't been sleeping well for two weeks." I sat up slowly, took a handkerchief from my pants pocket, and wiped away the sweat. "What's wrong, Roland? I'm worried about you."

Damn—I wanted to tell her, but how could I? If I proceeded with my plan, it would be dangerous for her to know anything about it. It would be a burden for her to act normally. If the authorities got wind of my scheme and detained *her* for questioning—a distinct possibility given the ruthless nature of the Vice President and the Attorney General—she would be far safer if she honestly knew nothing. If the plan succeeded, she could not be charged as an accomplice. Not accurately, anyway.

On the other hand, not telling her violated my sacred promise. How normal would I be able to act under the circumstances? I had no idea what the future would bring. What unusual trips or activities would I have to engage in to implement my plan? Would she suspect I was having another affair? There would be nothing else for her to suspect! The truth was too far-fetched for anyone to imagine. I began to wonder whether this secret of monumental significance would haunt me for the rest of my life.

I decided that some small fraction of the truth would be better than none at all.

"I'm worried about Jadon. I'm worried about the country."

"I know, sweetheart, but that's not new. Has something happened?"

"No." This was true, to a point. The major event wouldn't happen for another seven weeks. I looked into her eyes and saw concern, not suspicion. She looked back, and whatever it was she saw, it elicited a wise response.

"Whatever it is, you can talk to me about it. We promised."

Fearing that my eyes would reveal too much, I closed them and gave her a hug that I hoped would communicate what I couldn't put into words. I also hoped her radar would work, that it would bring her an answer—not the right answer, for that would be impossible, but at least an answer that would ease her anxiety. With Devon, she was used to reading non-verbal signals. I didn't know how long I could assuage her unease without coming clean, but I didn't know what else to do.

Alycia broke the hug off tenderly but firmly.

"Will you help me with the dishes?" she asked. The clatter of plates echoed my confused state of mind. For the moment, the issue would need to remain unresolved.

CHAPTER FIVE

Tuesday, December 4
With the technical feasibility of my plan still in doubt, certainty and skepticism alternated regularly. Duty to country won out when I was working and dreaming; duty to my family prevailed when I was eating dinner with Alycia and Devon, watching her cut his food, watching him watch her. What would happen to them if Tyler and Chesterfield discovered my plan? What would happen to me?

I wrote my editor a hand-written note, assuming our VOX-mail was monitored. I tried to sound as casual as possible: "Sid: I presume you'll want me to cover the Inauguration, as always. It is especially important to me this year. I'd also like some time for background research relating to presidential inaugurals generally. I think the manner in which fundamental liberties compare and contrast with the actions of this administration would make a great story, and the Inauguration is the perfect hook. I'd like to write a major analysis."

Two hours later I received a reply: "See me."

I didn't waste an instant getting to his office; my stomach would not have tolerated any delay. Sid was on the phone when I knocked on the half-open door. He waved me in and motioned toward the single chair opposite his small metal desk. His tie was draped over one of the OmniScreens, and the two top buttons of his dress shirt, open at the neck, revealed a thick mat of chest hair. It seemed to me, during his twelve tumultuous years as editor-in-chief, that every major story he had published had created another wrinkle on his face, resulting in a human sculpture with furrowed, richly textured skin—the kind that twentieth century photographers loved to shoot in black and white. One of the longest lines, extending practically from temple to temple, had made its initial appearance when South Carolina became the first state to endorse the 32nd Amendment to the Constitution in 2032. By July 3, 2035, when the legislatures of thirty-seven more states had pounded their nails into the coffins of free speech and freedom of the press, it had become a permanent fixture above sad yet resilient eyes.

I always felt slightly disappointed by the size of Sid's office. It wasn't worthy of the man or the position. Barely twelve feet square, it was hardly indicative of the power he wielded in determining what people read—at least the people who still read what Vice President Tyler had once referred to as a "lobby for lousy liberals." The small space contained all the technology the head of a major metropolitan newspaper could want, though: voice-activated editing, computerized layout based on story priority, and instant access to every news service in the world.

At least a dozen certificates and mementos hung behind Sid's desk. I knew he was especially proud of the large rectangular plaque recognizing his service in 2028 as President of the American Society of Newspaper Editors, which had been disbanded recently in response to governmental pressure. The side walls were reserved for aphorisms containing gems of journalistic wisdom, printed on parchment but inexpensively framed. My personal favorite: "There can be no liberty for a community which lacks the information to detect lies," attributed to Walter Lippmann. Sid himself had come up with "A tablespoon of intellectual syrup ruins the common man's flapjacks"—created in a moment of pique when he received a vitriolic letter from a reader who clearly misunderstood an editorial he had slaved over for days. Supreme Court Justice Hugo Black's opinion that "Only a free and unrestrained press can effectively expose deception in government" was displayed in a prominent location. I also liked the admonition cherished by journalists everywhere, attributed to the icon of the profession, Arthur Ochs Sulzberger: "Journalism's ultimate purpose is to inform the reader…and never to permit the serving of special interests." Through the most difficult of times, Sid had attempted to live by that maxim. I considered him one of the finest editors ever to hold that position at the *Washington Independent*.

He hung up the phone and got right to the point. "Roland, what is so special about this year's inauguration?"

Normally, Sid either approved my requests or denied them without much discussion. I wasn't prepared for his question, especially since I couldn't tell him what was really going on. With the maze of electronics in his office, I was certain it was bugged.

"President Hamilton is a friend of mine."

"I know that. He was a friend four years ago too, right?"

"Of course."

"Then what's the big deal?" Sid looked weary. The lighting was the same as always, yet the wrinkles stood out in relief from a slightly flushed face.

"I don't know," I stammered, searching for a justification that would sound convincing. "It's the first inauguration following the 250th anniversary of the Constitution. Wouldn't that be a good reason for an op-ed piece?"

"Normally I'd say yes. But these are not normal times."

"What do you mean?"

"I found out yesterday that the *Minneapolis Free Press* is going out of business." He wiped his forehead with a handkerchief, a habit he had acquired only a few months ago.

"Oh, Lord." The *Free Press* was one of only three newspapers left in the country not controlled by VOX. Besides the *Washington Independent*, the other was the *Berkeley Banner*. Gradually but steadily, following passage of the 32nd Amendment, the others had closed, forced out of business by either corporate takeovers or bankruptcies resulting from libel lawsuits filed by top governmental officials. The process had been just slow enough to prevent the average citizen from realizing that objective reporting was experiencing creeping cremation. I suspected that Pete Chesterfield and his gang were deliberately tolerating a tiny vestige of what had once been a thriving forum for public debate. Every time they were accused of bending the weakened First Amendment to their own political purposes, they pointed with delight to the few exceptions, ignoring the carnage of independent thought that generally characterized the last five years.

"And we're not far behind," Sid continued. "I got a call a week ago from the Attorney General."

"Chesterfield? Personally?"

"Lucky me." He chuckled. "Said I was skating on thin ice. Suggested I use 'discretion.' Implied our days are numbered."

"I'm sure nothing would please him more. What did you tell him?"

"You know me well enough to know exactly what I told him. I told him *his* days were numbered and that he should have used more discretion in dismantling the Bill of Rights."

That's the Sid I knew and respected. In a fight for freedom of the press, he was the man you'd want on your side. "Wish I could have heard it. Did he even attempt to debate the issue?"

"I wouldn't call it a debate. He used language I haven't heard since my teenage buddies and I were slopping pigs in Conway, Arkansas. But this is serious, Roland. Unfortunately, he probably has the power to make good on his threats. An op-ed piece from you that he considers inflammatory could be just the excuse he's looking for. Somehow he tolerates my tirades on the phone, but when the ink flies, he gets real sensitive."

"I don't intend to be inflammatory. As far as the Inauguration is concerned, the news article following the President's speech will be straightforward, as always. The op-ed, well, I don't know what it will say yet. That's why I want to do some research." I sat up straighter in my chair and offered a question I knew he would appreciate. "Do you think he considers the founding fathers inflammatory?"

I got the grin I'd hoped to see. "All right, you win. Do your research, and cover the inauguration." His mood changed suddenly. "Roland, I'll be retiring soon anyway. I was waiting for a good time to tell you, and I guess this is as good as any."

I had known Sid wouldn't be editor-in-chief forever. Still, I wasn't prepared, and with Operation Capitol Hill unfolding, he couldn't have picked a worse time. "Retiring, or being forced out?" We had the kind of relationship that permitted me to ask the question.

"Shit, Roland, if they tried to kick me out I'd be hollering and screaming. No, it's time to hang it up and enjoy life a little more. I don't think they've picked the new person yet, but whoever it is will have the same philosophy I do. You'll have a job come February."

It occurred to me that I'd like to have a country I could be proud of come February—but I couldn't say that. "I'm happy for you, Sid. You deserve all the relaxation you can get your hands on. But I'll bet you a thousand dollars you won't be able to stay away."

"I'm not going to take your money, son. Someone else will carry on."

"It won't be the same." I found it difficult to contemplate

the *Washington Independent* without Sid. "It won't be the same without you."

He walked me toward the door, offering a thump on the shoulder as encouragement. "Roland, sometimes I don't know why we work so damn hard on this thing anyway. What do we have now, five thousand readers, in a community of six million? Even if the government doesn't close us down, how does in-depth news compete with simple but compelling falsehood? How are we supposed to verify our sources, write coherently, and provide a forum for public discussion on an annual budget that VOX burns up in a day?"

It was a rhetorical question. "I don't know, Sid. Budget is not my department. I do know this. You believe in all the slogans that hang in your office. I hope whoever takes your place will believe in them too." He nodded and touched my shoulder reassuringly.

Back at my desk, I reflected on the meeting. I would have to get Sid a unique and meaningful retirement gift. But I had other things to deal with first. It was official. I would be at the Inauguration! Now the important question was whether to report the news or create it.

***

Freed from routine duties until the inauguration, I set out to convince myself that the crisis was indeed worthy of the aggravation it was causing me. I decided to reacquaint myself with the authors of the Constitution and the philosophers who had laid the groundwork for the powerful ideas on liberty that had fueled the Revolutionary War. I wanted to refresh my sketchy memory of the manner in which people throughout history had risen up against the tyranny of monarchs and dictators. Surely there would be Supreme Court decisions and legislative debates that would shed light on current events.

Being a Washingtonian, I knew there was no better place to research anything, particularly American history and the concept of freedom, than the Library of Congress. Taking advantage of the extensive on-line collection would probably not be wise, since such inquiries were almost certainly monitored. Besides, on those few occasions when I had visited the Library in person, I had reveled in the academic hush, the sight of intellectually curious people sitting at luxurious, hardwood tables with access to practically any document of any kind produced in the last three hundred years.

On December 6—one day before the ninety-ninth anniversary of Pearl Harbor—I ventured into the South reading room of the Adams building, one of three structures near the Capitol housing the gigantic collection of more than 250 million books, maps, photographs, newspapers, and journal articles. I stopped to read the inscription dedicating the room to Thomas Jefferson, along with a sentence from his prophetic letter to the Reverend Charles Clay dated January 27, 1790: "It takes time to persuade men to do what is for their own good."

The Library housed more than 35 million books, organized onto 600 miles of bookshelves. Even with my experience, it would take a long time to find what I needed. I approached the reference desk.

"May I help you?" a balding, kindly looking gentleman asked, looking up from a periodical. I described the information I was hoping to find. "That doesn't sound like too big a challenge," he replied. "Actually, I wish we had more patrons looking for things like that." He took a breath, as if to start another sentence, then thought better of it.

"Anything you could do to help would be greatly appreciated," I said.

"Right off the bat, I think you'd want to review the Magna Carta. Certainly the Federalist Papers. There are probably twenty or so key Supreme Court decisions that address various elements of the original Bill of Rights." He looked like a batter who had just been given the "hit" sign with the bases loaded. "How about major speeches on civil liberties by Martin Luther King Jr. and others who led the fight before...well, before. Also, there are some important articles in recent journals that I think you'd find interesting, and a few key books."

"That sounds like a good start."

"I'll put something together for you if you like. It will take me a few hours. Can you come back tomorrow?" He glanced at his watch. "I can have a stack of material ready by about ten in the morning."

"Of course." I turned and took one step away.

"Wait. We are required by the Patriot Act to enter your name into our database for a search of this magnitude."

"Oh, all right." It wasn't really all right, but I didn't relish the alternative, which would have cost me valuable time and probably resulted in a less productive search. "Roland Raines."

He wrote it down. "With an 'e' in 'Raines'?"

"Yes. Well, thank you. I'll see you tomorrow, then."

"Your name will be on the packet, in case I'm not here."

It was only 11:30. Satisfied that I had done everything I could, I decided to catch an early train home. Alycia would appreciate some unanticipated relief; I could take Devon to the park while she fixed dinner. Then I would begin my research the following day.

※※※

"Hello, Mr. Raines." The same man was behind the reference desk the next morning, but he seemed preoccupied. He caught my eye purposefully and offered an ominous glance, simultaneously waving his hand at a stack of paper on his desk about a foot high. "I suggest you start at the top and work your way down."

I wasn't sure what to make of the dramatic change in his demeanor. "Thank you. Looks like you've gone to a lot of trouble."

"Yes. It looks like a lot of people are going to a lot of trouble these days." He turned away abruptly, indicating that there was no point in pursuing the conversation. I retreated to a nearby table, leaving my jacket and my laptop where I could keep an eye on them, then returned for the research. I dumped the stack of material on the table, creating a dull thud that echoed throughout the nearly empty reading room.

Attached to the top article with a paper clip was a sealed, hand-written envelope. "Personal, for Mr. Roland Raines." I opened it immediately.

> *Mr. Gus LaVelle inquired about you. Wanted to know if you had given a reason for the research you are doing. In case you're not familiar with Mr. LaVelle, he's the Special Assistant to the Attorney General for Homeland Security Affairs. Apparently you are on some kind of watch list. I'm sorry, but I thought you should know.*
>
> *We enjoyed doing this research. There's a lot more. Give us another day or two and we'll have another stack for you.*

I refolded the note and inserted it back into the envelope, noticing that my hand had started to tremble. *Shit!* Well, it wasn't realistic to think that this kind of activity would go unnoticed. Had they discovered that I'd met twice with Madison, under unusual circumstances? My immediate impulse was to warn her, but there was no way to do that. She had clearly indicated we should keep our contact to a minimum. Madison had said she would need to check into the technical details. Had she asked too many questions? Had someone on the White House staff gotten suspicious? No, the note had said LaVelle was looking for information. He was fishing. He couldn't know. I put the envelope into my back pocket and made a mental note to destroy it before I got home. Then I turned my attention to the monumental task of reading and absorbing the documents in front of me.

Right on top was Volume I of *Historical Foundations of a Just Society*, by Gordon Richards, Professor of Economic and Political Theory at Georgetown University. Gordon had been one of my classmates at Oberlin College. I remembered him as bright and slightly eccentric, with a zeal for academic insight. We had lived on the same floor of Barrows Hall during our junior year. An image floated into my head—Gordon running into my room to share insights from *The Social Contract*, by Jean-Jacques Rousseau. "This guy is fucking brilliant," he had proclaimed, about twenty times a week. Frankly, it had gotten tiresome. All right, the man is brilliant. Get over it.

I began with the Preface.

> *The history of modern civilization is essentially the story of the never-ending attempt to conceive a form of government that approaches perfection despite the imperfections of the people who create it. There is no certain road to success in this endeavor; but the failure to travel any road in the desired direction inevitably results in human tragedy.*
>
> *The popular adage, "That government is best which governs least," provides no assistance. It suggests that the primary func-*

> tion of government is to stay out of the way. Then why have one at all?
>
> A more thoughtful solution rests on a simple premise: that government is best which furthers the natural purposes of mankind and complements the instinctive functions of the species. Indeed, any other form of government would be doomed to failure, challenged by the inherently unachievable task of countermanding the most fundamental behavioral patterns of its creators—known colloquially as "swimming upstream."

I smiled. This was vintage Gordon Richards, and exactly the kind of analysis I had been hoping to find.

> The task then becomes a matter of ascertaining what the natural purposes of mankind are and how they can be furthered by a self-imposed social order.
>
> Many philosophers and psychologists have suggested that the most fundamental purpose of the species is self-perpetuation. This translates naturally into an instinct for preservation among all individual members of the species. The concept is easily traced as far back as the 17th century, in which Thomas Hobbes wrote convincingly about the principle of self-preservation and its ramifications for individual members of the species. Also in the 17th century, John Locke referred to it as "the fundamental law of nature." The eminent 18th century philosopher Jean-Jacques Rousseau put it eloquently: "It is a contradiction in terms to say that any human being should wish to consent to something that is the reverse of his own good" (The Social Contract, p. 70). Similarly, the psychologist Abraham Maslow, in his famous hierarchy of needs, puts at the base of his pyramid the desire for food, water, and shelter, thus satisfying the most fundamental physiological requirements of the organism for staying alive.

He still loved Rousseau! I looked up briefly, resting my eyes. I wondered how many years it had taken Gordon to write this volume, and whether academicians realized how lucky they were to face deadlines measured in years rather than hours.

A man, dressed more formally than the average tourist, had seated himself about three tables in front of me. I was so engrossed in thought that I didn't consciously ask the obvious question: Why sit in a reading room with nothing to read?

> *While it may not be a "purpose" of mankind per se, it could hardly be denied that its members are by nature social creatures. The propagation of the species through sexual reproduction guarantees at least nominal contact with other members of the group. The complexity of raising a child with a long maturational process also ensures the formation of a social order of at least minimal scope—an order known as a family, normally characterized by extremely strong internal bonds of affection.*
>
> *Finally, common observations as well as studies in genetics reveal that members of the human species come into the world as diverse individuals, possessing strengths and skills—including those required for survival—in widely varying degrees.*
>
> *It follows from these principles that, absent any form of government as commonly defined, the human world would best be described as a disorganized collection of family units, each competing for the resources required for self-preservation, deriving such resources exclusively from the exercise of power. In such a world, while day-to-day survival might be achieved by those blessed with strength, speed, or cunning, it would be a constant struggle. There would no such thing as ownership of resources. Indeed, great effort would probably need to be expended merely to keep them long enough to use them, with the closest competing family unit under no obligation to pass up any viable opportunity to seize them for its own gratification.*

He was right. Without government, probably the most universally criticized institution in the country, there would be chaos.

Suddenly a woman in her early thirties sat down in the chair immediately to my left. Shoulder-length blonde hair gently tickled the top of a red dress that seemed more appropriate for evening wear than a trip to the Library of Congress. She carried only a small black purse. "That's quite an impressive pile of paper," she whispered, glancing at the stack of research on the table.

"Yes." I looked back at the book, but she seemed determined to interrupt.

"You've been concentrating on it very hard. I'm sorry, I just couldn't help noticing."

"It's not an easy read." *Who was this person, and why was she talking to me?*

"Is that so? Well, what is it that requires so much thought?" She edged her chair so close to mine that our shoulders nearly touched. "Do you mind if I peek?" Without waiting for a reply, she leaned over, practically resting her head on my upper arm. "Yes, that does look complicated."

She hadn't had time to read more than a single line. I moved my chair a few inches to the right.

"I'm sorry, I didn't mean to bother you. You just looked, well, a little lonely."

"I'm not lonely at all. Now, if you'll excuse me, I really want to get back to my reading."

"Of course." She pointed to a series of large decorative columns that separated the reading room from a second floor study area. "Well, I'm doing some reading too. Up there."

"Fine," I said. I watched her walk up the stairs. When I looked back, the man at the nearby table was gone.

Oh Jesus, what was that all about? Whatever it was, it wasn't good news.

It took an act of will to return to Gordon's book, but I was anxious to see where his logic was headed.

> *The question then arises, is such a world the best that can be envisioned? Does it contribute better than any other to the preservation of the species and its individual representatives?*

My eyes were passing over the words, but my brain was not comprehending. I flashed back to the lady in the red dress after every sentence. Had she been attracted to me as a stranger, or did she approach because she knew who I was? Why was she wearing that provocative outfit in the middle of the afternoon? Did the mysterious reader with no reading material have anything to do with her appearance?

Trying to finish was futile. I returned to the reference desk, balancing my laptop and the huge stack of paper.

The librarian looked up at me, bewildered. "You can't possibly have finished."

"Not even close. I'm afraid my concentration is shot for today."

"Did you see the book by Gordon Richards? I thought it might be especially relevant."

"I started the preface. Interesting stuff."

"Pretty powerful, in my opinion. A little wordy though." I couldn't help wondering how Gordon would react to being called "wordy"; he wasn't known for responding well to criticism. "He's already working on Volume II. Anyway, further down in your stack you'll find a good summary in a book review."

"Good, I'm sure that will be helpful. But I'm leaving for the day." I set the stack on his desk.

"No, no, take it all with you. We copied the articles for you, and they are yours to keep. The books are checked out in your name."

I gave him a tired smile. "Thanks. I'll be back for round two."

"We can go as many rounds as you want." What a great discovery—a reference librarian with a sense of humor.

CHAPTER SIX

Friday, December 7
Exhausted, my arms aching, I dumped the stack of books and articles on the kitchen table.

"You're not going to believe what happened today." Before leaving that morning, selecting my words carefully, I had told Alycia about my plan to use the Library of Congress for some research for my article on the Inauguration.

"Okay, I don't believe you," she said playfully.

"Do you remember Gordon Richards? From Oberlin?"

"You've mentioned him. Why?"

"He's written a book." I pulled it out of the stack and showed her the picture on the back.

"Well, how come you never told me how handsome he is? Looks like I married the wrong man." She gave me a hug.

"He might still be available," I joked.

"No, a guy like that is definitely not still available."

"Could be."

"Could not."

I never won these battles and decided to change the subject. "What's for dinner?"

"Nothing, until you move that pile."

I took everything into the bedroom, where it covered the small desk, and took off my shoes. The house seemed quiet, and Devon wasn't in his room.

"Where's Devon," I asked, returning to the kitchen.

"He's with Matthew. They're scouting for birds."

"Good." Every part of my body screamed for a nap. "I'm going to sleep a few minutes, okay?"

"No problem, more pasta for us."

I collapsed on the living room couch. Half an hour later, Alycia kissed me gently. "Come on, dinner's ready."

We talked over noodles and white sauce, embellished by a single slice of bread for each of us. We took turns cutting small bites for Devon. She said her day had been routine. I told her I had enjoyed the Library of Congress, leaving out the parts about Gus LaVelle and the lady in the red dress. "I can't believe I ran into Gordon's book. I started the preface. It's awesome."

"I'd rather look at his picture."

"Why settle? Ask him for a date." I had discovered that the best way to deal with Alycia's humor was to go along with it, extending it if possible to a logical but absurd conclusion.

"I told you, there's no way he's not married."

"I'll bet you a thousand dollars," I said, knowing she would find a clever retort.

"You don't *have* a thousand dollars," she replied. "Besides, how would you know whether he's married or not? You haven't talked to him in thirty years."

That ended it, or so I thought. After helping Alycia with the dishes, I retrieved Gordon's book from the bedroom and joined her on the living room couch. "Look, here's a VOXmail address for him. He's at the University of Virginia. I should congratulate him."

"Find out if he's married." She just wouldn't let it go.

"All right, smarty pants, I will. Right after I remind you that *you* are married." I pulled her to a standing position, hoisted her over my shoulder, and carried her to bed, knowing that her "Put me down, you brute" was only for show.

When we had satisfied each other, she slept. I got out of

bed and started reading the remainder of Gordon's preface, but it was too complex to digest at the end of a long, strange day. I did muster the energy to send him a VOXmail: *Gordon, started your book—loved it so far. Congratulations! I'm in Virginia too, let's get reacquainted. Curious about Volume II, any chance of a little peek in advance? Roland Raines, Oberlin Class of 2004. P.S. My wife thinks you're a hunk and wants to know if you're married! (Haha)*

By nine o'clock the following morning, he had replied. *Roland, great to hear from you. By all means, let's get together. Are you free next weekend? Bring the family, I'll send a car. Gordon. P.S. Your wife is out of luck. Been hitched eighteen years, two kids.*

"Sorry, honey, married with children," I informed Alycia.

"Told you," she replied, jokingly taking pleasure in being right as usual.

I answered immediately: *Sounds good. Really looking forward to seeing you again after all these years. Roland. P.S. Alycia is disappointed but says she wants to meet you anyway.*

***

I had just gotten settled at my desk in the newsroom the following Monday morning, intending to read Gordon Richards' book, when Sid opened the door to his office twenty-five feet away. "Raines, get your butt in here," he bellowed, exploding the quietly busy environment in which tomorrow's news was being molded. A couple of my colleagues gave me a "What did you do now?" look as I practically ran to his office.

"What's happening, Sid?" I asked, expecting bad news.

"The White House called. The President is going to Springfield, Illinois to give a speech. You're in the press pool." My relief, mixed with elation, must have been evident. Nervous, shallow breathing returned to its normal rhythm. "Well, what did you think it was?"

"These days, I'm afraid to predict. That's good news, though. I haven't been on Air Force One in a long time." Hamilton's advisors had reduced the size of the traveling press pool to three or four hand picked reporters and a single photographer. Working for a newspaper with an editorial slant they didn't care for meant I normally wasn't selected. Maybe Madison had planted a seed with Jadon. In any case, I was happy for the opportunity. Despite our friendship, I rarely saw the President and hadn't talked with him at any length for more than a year. "When do we leave?"

"You need to be at Andrews in an hour." The President would be flown to Andrews Air Force Base by helicopter from the White House. When he arrived, everyone else would need to be on board already. Sid handed me five one hundred dollar bills. "Here, take a cab. Pick up whatever incidentals you need on the way." He picked a tiny cell phone off the top of his desk and handed it to me. "Take this, too. We'll see the address on the OmniScreen, but maybe we can scoop the opposition and print what the President has for dinner before they do." Sid hated to be scooped. I stuck the phone, about the size of a book of matches, into my shirt pocket.

"Are we staying overnight?" Traveling with the President was a plum, but I wasn't anxious to be away from Alycia and Devon.

"They don't tell us things like that. It's only a two hour flight, so I doubt it, but just in case." He nodded toward the bills. When I didn't move, he feigned impatience. "Well, get going. If you're not there on time, they'll leave without you. And don't forget to write."

I smiled and ran at the same time, grabbing my laptop on the way out.

Andrews Air Force Base had become a fortress in response

to terrorist threats, real or imaginary, and security was especially tight when the President was traveling. Military jets screamed overhead as the cab drove up to the checkpoint and dropped me off. With my federal ID, my press pass, my face, and my palm print all matching, and my name on the list of approved passengers, I was cleared in about ten minutes. An Air Force van pulled up and transported me across the tarmac.

Jadon used a VOX 797 as his official plane. With a wingspan exceeding two hundred feet and a cruising speed of 750 miles per hour, it was an impressive piece of machinery. A wide white stripe accented the blue motif down the entire length of the fuselage. Large red letters centered in the stripe identified the aircraft unmistakably: *United States of America*. Despite my familiarity with the trappings of power, Air Force One never failed to send a shiver down my spine. The magnificent bird sat now, guarded by at least twenty military personnel with machine guns, waiting to fulfill its mission.

I entered through a rear door, directly into the press compartment. Twelve seats, upholstered in flag blue, were arranged in three rows, with a narrow center aisle. I took a window seat in front, figuring I'd have more legroom, and stowed the laptop underneath. A few minutes later, I was joined by a photographer from the *VOX Times*, a reporter I had never met before from the *Springfield Courier*, and Shrill O'Malley from VOX News. Shrill took the seat next to me.

"What a great day in the U S of A!" he exclaimed, extending a hand. "I don't know that we've ever met. I'm Shrill O'Malley."

I took his hand and shook it once. "Roland Raines," I replied, "*Washington Independent*."

"Is that a fact? Well, of course that's a fact, you're a journalist. News reporters always tell the truth." He chuckled, enjoying his joke just enough to make me feel uncomfortable. "Pleasure to meet you, Roland."

"Likewise, Mr. O'Malley," I said coldly, hoping he would get the message that I wasn't feeling conversational. He didn't.

"You know, I think I've read some of your stuff. I haven't the foggiest notion how you come about this attitude you seem to have, but hey, it's a free country." He chuckled again.

Lord have mercy, if he keeps this up for two hours, I'll be a nervous wreck. "In a manner of speaking," I replied. "Now if you'll excuse me, I didn't sleep well last night. I'm going to take a short nap." I tilted the seat back and closed my eyes. Fortunately, the reporter from the *Courier*, seated just across the aisle, chose that moment to ask Shrill his opinion of the new book that had just been published, *Dirty Rotten Lying Liars and the Lies They're Telling You About Their Oppenents' Lies*. It had already sold four hundred copies and was headed to the top of the "Best Intellectual Books of the Year" list.

The door to the press compartment was closed from the outside, and shortly thereafter I heard a helicopter. I roused myself and glanced out the window long enough to see Jadon step off, salute the uniformed guard at the bottom of the short stairway, and disappear toward the front of the plane. Moments later we taxied down the runway and floated into the air effortlessly. Once we leveled off at cruising altitude, the even motion put me to sleep.

I woke up with Madison tugging gently at my shoulder. "Roland, are you all right?"

"Oh. Hi, Madison. Yeah, just getting a little rest." I used the lever to bring my seat forward. Shrill O'Malley was chattering loudly two rows behind me.

"The President wants to know if you'd like to talk."

"Uh, sure." Alertness returned quickly, and I reached under the seat to get my laptop.

"You won't need that. It's not an interview. He just wants to say hello." She led the way forward, through a heavy door. Situated at the fuselage's widest point, the Presidential compartment had been configured into a full office suite. We passed a large forward facing mahogany desk, bare on top except for a red phone. The chair behind it sported a large Presidential seal embroidered into the headrest. Two side chairs with standard blue upholstery sat a few feet in front of the desk. At the far end of the compartment, about fifteen feet away, a Secret Service agent stood near another massive door. The other side of the aisle was appointed more casually. Jadon was sitting in an armchair looking out the window. Madison guided me to an identical chair facing the President.

"Mr. President?" she said, drawing his attention.

"Oh, thank you Madison. Roly, sit down, will you? I had a few minutes here and realized we haven't chatted in a while." Madison retreated to the rear of the compartment, near the door leading to the press room, and stood where I could see her if I looked over Jadon's shoulder.

"No, Mr. President, actually we haven't seen each other since your birthday celebration. And we didn't really get a chance to talk." *Actually, Mr. President, you were pretty well soused.*

"Hey, you can call me Jadon in here. It would help me feel like a real person. You know, sometimes I don't feel all that presidential."

I sensed immediately that Jadon needed to let his hair down, to have a conversation lacking global significance and the trappings of formality. "You *are* a real person, Jadon, everybody knows that. It's just difficult for most people to let go of the aura that surrounds the office."

"I know. Well, how is Alycia? How's the kid?"

"Doing well, thank you. Devon doesn't change much, except he's acquired a real fixation for birds."

"Kids get attached to the strangest things, don't they? My great nephew is only six, and he can name every kind of tree in the entire world."

I decided against explaining that Devon didn't see that many birds, or why. "How's Vanessa? Does she enjoy being First Lady?"

"Eats it up with a spoon. Wants me to go to Europe so she can hobnob with the royals and see all the castles and stuff."

"Why don't you?"

"I've suggested it. My advisors don't think it's a real good idea, with the war and all. The Secret Service isn't too keen on it either."

I decided to mix the slightest possible reporting with a largely social visit. "What's this trip to Springfield all about?"

"Believe it or not, it was Chesterfield's idea. Something about associating myself with Lincoln, building up to the Inauguration." I glanced at Madison, who shook her head slowly from side to side, as if to say "Don't go there." I guessed the agent at the other end of the compartment might not be in the friendly camp.

"Well, nothing's ever lost in being associated with Honest Abe. So, you'll give a speech?"

"Yes, right outside the Presidential Museum. You know, the Museum and the Library have both been there since we were kids, and I've never seen either one."

I wasn't sure that a trip down memory lane would be useful, but I decided to see where it would lead. "That was a long time ago. Santiago High School, home of the Cougars."

He looked out the window, seemingly lost in thought, then

turned back toward me. "You know, I enjoyed high school. I really loved football. Everything seemed so carefree then."

I didn't remember being especially carefree. "We still had tests to pass."

"Oh, I didn't worry much about tests." That could have meant a lot of things, but dredging up stories from forty years ago wasn't really what interested me at the moment. "Hey, you know, Roly, I'll never forget what you did for me my senior year. I'm really grateful."

I smiled reassuringly. "It was my pleasure. We had a pretty good time, didn't we?" I winked at him, and he winked back and smiled. "Hey, I hope you don't mind my asking. The speech you're going to give in Springfield—what's the gist?"

"I haven't seen it yet. But I'm sure it will be good, like all the others."

Madison avoided my look, forcing me to search internally for a reaction to this bizarre statement. The President of the United States was about to give an address, likely to be carried live on every OmniScreen in the country, with transcripts to be available within hours in every known language, and he hadn't even read it in advance! It was beyond careless—it was reckless, a total abdication of personal responsibility. Yet Jadon was totally unaware of his failure as a leader, accepting speeches from his advisors trustingly the way a little boy accepts ice cream cones from his parents.

"Yes," I said, knowing he would take it for agreement even though that wasn't my real intent. "Anyway, I'm glad to be along on the trip. Thank you."

"You're welcome, glad you were available. We'll have to do this more often."

It seemed like an invitation to conclude our visit. I stood up and excused myself. I couldn't resist commenting to Madison as we re-entered the press compartment. " 'It will be good, just like all the others.' Can you believe it?"

"Now behave yourself."

"Do you know yet...?"

She shot me a quick look of concern. "Not yet. Not here," she said softly.

I took my seat again. Shrill O'Reilly had fallen asleep, straddling adjacent seats in the second row. *Lord, thank you for small favors.*

Madison sat down next to me. "So, how *are* things at home? Generally?"

I glanced around the compartment. The photographer and the other reporter were both reading. But their presence, and Madison's clear warnings, told me she needed me to either speak in code or ignore Operation Capitol Hill altogether. "Devon is a delight. I love him a little more every day."

"Spoken like the caring father you are. And Alycia?"

I decided to be evasive but still give her a flavor of the situation. "Well, she has to have this *operation* toward the end of January, but the doctor hasn't informed her yet. Not certain it would be healthy for her to worry about. But she senses something and seems a little anxious."

"I'm sorry to hear that. I hope everything works out okay."

"So do I. And how is your family?"

Madison relaxed visibly. "Great. Julia's a senior, you know, applying to all the Ivy League schools. She'll get in, too, she's much smarter than her mom. Alan is not so academic. At sixteen, he has only one thing on his mind. My dad's kinda restless, hasn't quite come to grips with retirement."

"It's been more than ten years!"

"I know. But it's in his blood. He'll be okay, just needs a little more excitement in life than looking at soap operas all day." She glanced at her watch. "We'll be landing soon, I need to get back. Have a good time."

***

Twenty minutes later, the plane touched down in Springfield, Illinois. The President got off first, waving to a crowd of several thousand supporters but making no statement. Then the press crew disembarked. All four of us were shoved unceremoniously into a small black sedan, and we followed the Presidential limousine and several Secret Service escort vehicles, led by about fifty cops on motorcycles, directly to a hotel one block from the Abraham Lincoln Presidential Library and Museum.

We were informed that the speech would be delivered at three p.m. in the plaza separating the library and the museum. Speakers would be set up in the adjacent Freedom Park so the overflow crowd that was expected could hear the address. Of course, those of us in the press pool were guaranteed ringside seats. I checked into a room to freshen up.

With two hours to spare, I decided to wander outside until it was time to pass through security again and take my seat. The weather was about normal for this time of year in Central Illinois—clear blue skies, 55 degrees. I put a light windbreaker on over a sweater, grabbed my laptop, and took the elevator to the ground floor. Outside, a crowd was already starting to gather, milling around the park aimlessly. Presidential speeches always drew grandmothers and grandfathers, parents, and kids of all ages—kids who would be told their entire lives how they had seen President Jadon Hamilton, as if the event had been life-changing.

Suddenly, just behind me and to the right, I heard chanting. I turned and walked toward the source. About fifty feet away, the crowd parted, and I saw a group of four people wearing black robes carrying a makeshift casket, coming toward me. As they got closer, I was able to discern what they were shouting: "Hey Hey Ho Ho, where did my Bill of Rights Go?" I moved out of their path. The side of the casket had been painted with the slogan *Trial By Jury, R.I.P.*

Street Theater! Nobody had dared attempt it since the Vietnam War. This was a story!

Closely behind, another group of pall bearers chanted the same slogan. The casket said *Freedom from Searches and Seizures, R.I.P.* Then another: *Freedom from Self-incrimination, R.I.P.* The crowd parted to let them through. The children clapped, as though they were at a parade. Most of the parents observed silently, while a few jeered. Three more coffins followed: *Freedom from Cruel and Unusual Punishment, R.I.P.; Freedom of Speech, R.I.P.; Freedom of the Press, R.I.P.*

By the time the last casket had passed, the one in front had reached the edge of the park. All six caskets and their pallbearers lined up on the border between the park and the plaza where the President was scheduled to speak in less than two hours. Facing them, a line of soldiers had formed hastily, bayonets fixed, backed up by uniformed police and plain-clothes Secret Service agents. A man wearing a gold oak leaf on his military cap stepped forward with a bullhorn. "Disperse immediately!" he ordered. "You have no permit to assemble. This is an unlawful gathering."

The protesters had apparently been trained and knew what to expect. "Hey Hey Ho Ho, where did my Bill of Rights Go?" they chanted in unison, louder than before. I took a position off to the side so I could see everything.

"This is an unlawful assembly," the man with the bullhorn shouted again. "Disperse or you will be arrested."

The word "arrested" was apparently a signal. The protesters broke toward the Lincoln Library in full run—as fast as people carrying caskets *can* run. The presidential lectern had been set up at the opposite end of the plaza, in front of the museum, so security at the front door was minimal. The two local policemen assigned to guard it were quickly overwhelmed, and the protesters flew through unimpeded—all but the last. A shot rang out, and he fell on the stairs. Two colleagues just ahead of him saw what happened and retrieved him, dragging his limp body into the building.

All hell broke loose. The crowd in the plaza fled wildly in all directions. The militia took up positions in front of the library, weapons ready, but a stalemate was already upon them. Within minutes, a sign appeared in the front door, next to a gasoline can: *If you attack, we burn it down.*

TV crews scheduled to broadcast the President's speech turned their cameras onto the chaos in front of them. Shrill O'Malley stood on the steps of the museum, shouting into his microphone. "This is what anarchy is all about, folks. This is why we have *laws.* This is why the Bill of Rights was modified: people take advantage of freedom!"

Screeching sirens filled the air, and I could see the Presidential motorcade flee the hotel at a high rate of speed. There would be no speech today—at least not in Lincoln Plaza. My ride to the airport had just disappeared, but I didn't care. The real story was unfolding in front of me.

Normally I didn't carry a cell phone, so it rang about six times before I realized it was mine. I pushed the single button and yelled, "Hello."

"Roland, are you all right? This is Sid."

"Sid, you wouldn't believe what's going on here."

"Yes, I would. We're watching it on screen. How many people have been shot?"

"Only one, as far as I can tell."

"Are you okay?"

"Yes. As long as I don't have a heart attack. My ticker must be going 130 beats a minute."

"Settle down. Stay there and cover it. I'll contact Alycia and tell her what's going on."

"Of course. You couldn't drag me back if you tried."

A volley of shots rang out, and windows on the second floor of the library shattered. "Gotta go Sid. I'll be in touch." I pushed the button again and slid the phone into my pants pocket. Most of the crowd had dissipated. A police line had formed around the library, keeping curious on-lookers at a safe distance, but my press pass got me through. I searched for the man with the oak leaf on his uniform and found him huddled with aides at a makeshift command station. "Sir, I'm Roland Raines, from the *Washington Independent*. May I ask you a few questions?"

The man motioned at an aide, then pointed to me. The aide approached immediately and stepped in front of my face. "Can't you see we're in a crisis here? The Major is busy."

I held up my press pass. "I don't want to be in the way. I just want to know what's happening. Do you know who fired the shot? Was the protester killed? Is this an organized group?"

"I don't know anything yet. If you'll be patient, I'll try to find out for you." He looked like an overgrown kid, early twenties maybe, big ears sticking out of a brand new Army hat. "I'm Sgt. Conyers. I write for *Stars and Stripes*. I guess the Major will want me to act as press liaison."

"Roland Raines, *Washington Independent*. I was here to cover the President's speech. I'll appreciate anything you can do for me."

Conyers looked impressed. "Yes sir, let me see if I can get up to speed." He turned and headed toward the command post.

OPERATION CAPITOL HILL

For the first time since I'd spotted the lead coffin, I had a minute to think. But I had a lot more questions than answers. Who in the hell would pull a stunt like this? Was it an isolated group, or had some organized opposition sprung up for the first time since Civil War II? What did they hope to accomplish? Would they really burn the library down if they were attacked? Did this have anything to do specifically with the re-election or the inauguration? What impact, if any, would it have on Operation Capitol Hill—or my own plan?

Sgt. Conyers returned. "We've got telephone contact, sir. They claim that several of the coffins contain cans of gasoline. They are threatening to burn the library if we don't provide medical attention. Apparently the kid is alive. The bullet lodged in his right thigh. They've stopped the bleeding, but he's in a lot of pain."

"How are you responding?"

"The doctors at the hospital are on their way." Lucky for the protestors, it was standard operating procedure for an emergency medical group to be standing by whenever the President traveled.

"What's the kid's name?"

"Ryan Chesterfield, sir."

"Ryan *Chesterfield*?" Did the Attorney General have a son? No, more than likely, it was a coincidence. "Any other injuries?"

"A girl twisted her ankle running up the stairs. Nothing serious."

"Thank you, Sergeant. I need to check something here, would you excuse me?"

I pulled the phone from my pocket, pressed the button, and spoke hurriedly into the microphone. "*Washington Independent.* Newsroom."

Sid answered on the second ring. "Sid here. Is that you, Roland?"

"Yeah. Listen, the kid who got shot is Ryan Chesterfield. Not life threatening. A medical team is on its way. Does Pete Chesterfield have a son named Ryan?"

"I don't know, I think so. Hold on." I could hear him asking around. There must have been five or ten people huddled in Sid's tiny office. "We think so. Nobody knows for sure. I'll check and get back to you. What is this group anyway, some kind of underground? Shrill O'Malley is reporting that Civil War III has started!"

"I doubt it. But it's definitely a mess. I'll call again as soon as I get anything." I pressed the button.

Sgt. Conyers approached me. "The medical team has arrived."

Crisply delivered facts, to the point. Not a lot of time wasted. I appreciated his style—exactly what you want in a war zone. "Do you know who shot Chesterfield?"

"We're not releasing that information."

"Why not, Sergeant?"

"He has rights, Mr. Raines. We need to comply with military protocol. If he's guilty of anything, that will be determined in due course."

I decided that a philosophical discussion about irony was as inappropriate to a war zone as long-winded answers. "Do you know anything yet about what prompted this demonstration? Is this an isolated group or part of a larger effort?"

He started to reply but was interrupted by the Major about twenty yards behind him. "Sergeant, bring that journalist over here."

"Looks like you're going to find out first hand. C'mon." When we got to the command post, the Sergeant introduced me to his boss. "Major Lanning, Roland Raines."

Lanning had weathered skin and a deep, authoritative voice. "Hello, Raines. Are you willing to help us out here?"

"What do you have in mind?"

"The person in charge of this little band of renegades wants to make a statement. Doesn't trust me, doesn't trust anyone she knows. She wants to talk to someone who will get their message out. Then they'll give themselves up."

"What do I have to do?"

"Go in there and talk to them. Find out what the hell they want and take their statement. Put it on the goddamn Omni-Screen if you need to. The President called. He doesn't want any more blood spilled." Bless Jadon after all. The man may not be brilliant, but at least he's compassionate. Or maybe someone suggested that he call. Either way, it was a good thing.

"I don't know, let me check with my editor." I used the phone again.

"Sid here, go ahead Roland." When I had finished explaining the situation to him, he replied without hesitation. "Of course, if you can help diffuse it, by all means. Think of the scoop we'll have!"

"Sid, I'd like to do it. It could compromise my objectivity though."

"Roland, you've got a life and death situation there. Stuff your objectivity up your ass and go in there and talk to them." He was ten times the man I would ever be. "Oh, by the way, Ryan Chesterfield *is* Pete's son. His press aide confirmed it. Doesn't appear Pete is all that concerned. He was on the local news and acted like the kid had stubbed his toe."

"Pete's all heart. Okay, Sid, I'll keep you informed." I looked at Major Lanning. "Let's do it."

Lanning got on the phone immediately. "Hello, Sierra? Lanning here. I've got a journalist, a guy who was covering the

President. Roland Raines...No, I never heard of him either. He works for...who the hell do you work for again? Yeah, the *Washington Independent*...Yeah, sure." He took the phone away from his ear and cupped his hand over the mouthpiece. "Wants to talk to you. Leader is a gal, goes by the name 'Sierra.' Make it good, you're our best hope."

I took the phone. "Hello, Sierra? This is Roland Raines. I'm a reporter...No, I'm not CIA, I was in town covering the President's speech...Yes, I do believe in the right to protest..." Lanning gave me a dirty look, and I turned away. "Yes, I can get your statement in the paper....Of course it will be on the VOXnet too, unless they censor it....No, it's guaranteed, my editor already knows what's happening, and it's 100% he'll print what you want, as long as it's not libelous....The truth, it means you can't tell vicious lies about people....Of course you can express opinions....All right, happy to do it actually. Say, how's Ryan?...Good. All right, I'm giving you back to Major Lanning." I handed the phone back. "Make the arrangements."

Half an hour later I walked toward the front of the Lincoln Presidential Library, hands in the air, my laptop hanging from my side suspended by a strap over my shoulder. A young man opened the door as I approached, searched the computer case and frisked me when I stepped inside. "We're on the second floor," he said, satisfied that I wasn't carrying any weapons.

These were not exactly the circumstances under which I had envisioned seeing the library for the first time. The grand entrance was strewn with coffins, plywood painted black; some of the lids had been pulled off, while others lay on their sides, dumped hastily in the attempt to escape flying bullets. Blood stains marred the richly textured carpet on the stairway. At the top I was frisked again, then led into a massive reading room with shattered glass scattered on one side of the floor. On the other side, reading tables had been moved to permit the protestors to sit together. They had shed their robes and were now wearing regular street clothes. Two gasoline cans sat unattended on top of one of the tables. Ryan was lying on another table, being examined by the medical team; he was conscious, releasing an occasional scream when the pain became unbearable.

"Sit here," the man said, indicating a chair separated from the group by a good twenty feet. I watched him walk back to the group. They all appeared to be in their twenties, sitting quietly. I couldn't really tell from a distance, but from their facial expressions and body language I guessed they were experiencing emotional shock. The man spoke to a woman, who observed me cautiously, then approached.

"Mr. Raines. I'm Sierra." She was wearing torn blue jeans and a bloodied flannel long-sleeved shirt probably selected from the men's clothing rack. Blue eyes set off a thin face with high cheekbones and light brown eyelashes, graced by long blonde hair. She moved deliberately, as if she were consciously sending signals to her arms and legs, but I sensed that, in a state of relaxation, she would appear quite serene. "Thank you for coming."

"I hope I can help. How is Ryan?"

She pulled a chair up across from mine and sat down. "He needs to be moved to the hospital. We're arranging that now." She glanced back at the medical team. "How in the world could they open fire?"

"I don't know."

"Somebody's going to pay for this!"

I recalled my recent conversation with Sgt. Conyers. Maybe they would pay, and maybe they wouldn't. "Perhaps you can tell me what this is all about."

Sierra's rage dissipated, for the moment. "It's all explained in our statement."

"I understand you want it printed. That won't be a problem. But first, who are you? Why did you decide to do this?"

"It began quite innocently. We're all in Miss Crandall's American History class at Springfield Community College. Just a bunch of kids, really, some of us only going part-time. We got involved in a discussion about the Bill of Rights—as it read originally, compared with today. Some of the class members didn't think the changes were that big a deal. They said, in effect, you still have the rights, it's just that they're not guaranteed. This is the best of all possible worlds. People on the extremes of the political movements can't abuse their freedoms, making it more difficult for those in the mainstream to exercise theirs."

I nodded. She was articulate as well as beautiful. The cell phone rang, and I decided to ignore it. "Go on."

"Other class members disagreed," she continued. "They said, if the rights aren't guaranteed, you really don't have them at all, because they can be taken away. And they are most likely to be restricted when your need for them is vital."

"What did Miss Crandall have to say about this?"

"She believes in what she calls 'real-time education,' not just reading from a textbook. And she doesn't tell us what to believe. She suggested doing a little experiment."

I didn't want to be conned. "Threatening to burn the Lincoln Library down is a little experiment?"

"Oh, the gasoline cans. They're empty. A couple of the guys threw them in at the last minute as props. It was just a joke. We hid them inside one of the coffins. Of course, they did give our threat credibility once our lives were in danger."

I shifted in my chair, uncomfortable with what I was hearing. "So, let me see if I understand this. Your class was unsure whether you still had rights, like freedom of assembly and freedom of speech. So you organized a march through the park on the day the President of the United States was scheduled to give a speech, to see what would happen?"

"That's it, more or less. We had no idea anyone would get hurt."

"And what have you concluded?"

Sierra started to answer but was interrupted by the arrival of two EMTs with a stretcher. We both watched the medical personnel move Ryan off the table and roll him out of the room. Several of the students crossed themselves and bowed their heads.

Sierra wiped her slightly moistened eyes with her sleeve. "He's my boyfriend." For a second, it looked like she wanted to collapse in my arms, but then she pulled herself together. What a tough woman, I thought, doing a good job of juggling intense and conflicting personal emotions as well as leadership responsibilities with the group. "Well, they say he's going to be all right."

"I hope so."

Fire returned to her eyes. "Do they know who shot him?"

"So far, they're not saying."

"Bastards." She seemed to realize then that her anger would not solve any immediate problems. Some of the tension drained out of her face. "Anyway, we drafted two statements in advance, one in case we encountered no opposition, and the other in case…"

"May I see them?"

"The first isn't really relevant, is it? I'll share the second one with you. In light of what's happened, some of the students have been editing it. We've agreed to leave peacefully and take the consequences once it has been broadcast and printed." She motioned to one of her colleagues, who brought over a piece of paper. "Are you ready?"

"May I set my laptop up?"

"Sure, why not?"

I removed the laptop from its case and set it up as quickly as my trembling fingers allowed. "All right, please read it slowly. I'll just take a few notes, if that's okay, and I'd like to type the whole thing in afterwards."

Sierra read the statement.

> "The members of Miss Kelly Crandall's American History class at Springfield Community College debated the impact of the changes made in the original Bill of Rights over the last thirty years. When we found ourselves in disagreement, we decided to hold a mock protest to see what would happen. Half the class predicted that we would be allowed to express ourselves without incident; the other half predicted that the absence of a Constitutional guarantee would result in a crackdown by authorities.
>
> "We have unanimously concluded that the Bill of Rights as originally constituted is essential to the maintenance of American freedom. Without a guarantee founded in this country's most cherished document, it is apparent that dissent will be stifled by authorities nervous about the preservation of power, fearful of thinking that challenges their own, and overzealous in the pursuit of domestic tranquility."

"This next part has been added since the shooting," Sierra explained.

> "Never in our wildest imagination did we anticipate the tragic outcome of this experiment. We regret that one of our own was wounded, and we pray for his full and quick recovery. We apologize for the destruction of property, although we feel that appropriate ac-

tions on the part of the authorities could have prevented it. We accept full responsibility for our actions.

"Now, although it was not part of our original intent, we suppose that the experiment will continue. We anticipate being accused of unlawful assembly, as well as various other crimes. But in a larger sense, we are not the ones on trial. Fairness, justice, and the American traditions rooted in hundreds of years of careful thought and social experimentation—until recently—are on trial. We eagerly await the verdict."

I had started to take notes, anticipating the typical student essay full of tangents and filler, then stopped when I realized they had done their homework well. The sheer simplicity of the statement took me by surprise. I looked up at Sierra and spoke from my heart. "It's magnificent."

She attempted a joke. "We're all hoping for an 'A.'"

"You deserve more than that. You deserve a Congressional Medal of Honor."

"You'll print it then?"

"I promised, and I'll deliver. Let me call my editor now. Can you just leave this with me a few minutes?" Sierra nodded and rejoined her classmates. I pulled out the phone and got Sid on the line immediately.

"Roland, we're on deadline here. Why didn't you answer the phone? What the hell is going on?"

"This was a college class, Sid, doing a reality experiment that backfired." I told him the whole story. "And listen to this statement. This is what they want printed. You got someone there who can transcribe?"

"You're on speaker phone. There's about twenty of us, in the middle of the newsroom. Read it slowly, we'll get it down." When I had finished, he continued. "Jesus Christ, sign up whoever wrote that for an internship."

"Good idea. First, we'll have to see if they do jail time, or worse. Anyway, can you write the story from there, based on what I've told you? I'm kind of preoccupied here. I'll do a follow-up as soon as things settle down."

"Sure, no problem. What's with the kid? Ryan?"

"He's going to be okay. Already moved to the hospital."

"Find out everything you can. I'm wiring money to the hotel. Stay as long as you need to. I'm keeping Alycia informed."

"Okay, Sid, you got it."

"Nice work, Roland. We just scooped the shit out of VOX news."

I signaled to Sierra, and she returned. "Everything's taken care of. It will be in the *Washington Independent* tomorrow, and probably every other paper in the country the following day. Every other *respectable* paper, at least. The bloggers will have it in five minutes. The broadcast media will have no choice but to pick it up."

"Thank you." Her eyes expressed a combination of adult sincerity and child-like gratitude. "Now how do we get out of here without being shot ourselves? I want to go see Ryan."

That gave me an idea. "May I visit him with you? I mean, at least part of the time? I know you'll want some privacy. I'd like to get his perspective. You all have had a bad experience, but he's the one who got shot."

"Sure, I guess."

I was starting to feel powerful, and a strong desire to help the kids was beginning to develop. "Hold on, let me get the Major on the phone. Hello, Major Lanning?...Yes, things are taken care of on this end. The kids want out...Yes, there are a few conditions. Sierra and I are to be taken directly to the hospital to visit Ryan. Everyone is to be guaranteed safe passage to wherever they live...Yes, they understand they will be arrested and booked first, they are prepared for that…All right, I'll run it by Sierra, but I think that will work."

The evacuation took place peacefully. Sierra and I were taken directly to the hospital, but Ryan was sedated and unable to speak. A nurse informed us that they had taken one unfragmented bullet out of his thigh, where it had lodged near the femur after entering through the back of his leg. Blood vessels and nerves had suffered severe damage, but surgery had repaired much of it. He would be able to walk normally following rehabilitation. Sierra decided to come back to the hospital after she was booked, and I returned to the hotel, planning to return the next day. I called Sid again, then collapsed on the bed. Despite mental images fighting for space and attention in my brain, exhaustion took its toll.

I slept soundly until noon, then jumped out of bed, hooked my laptop up to the VOXnet, and brought the *Independent* up on the screen. The article appeared on the front page.

> *Springfield, Illinois*—An educational experience designed to resolve a community college classroom debate about civil rights turned ugly yesterday when national guard troops opened fire on a group of students demonstrating in Freedom Park, wounding Ryan Chesterfield, 23, son of the Attorney General of the United States.
>
> Members of Kelly Crandall's American History class at Springfield Community College chose the occasion of an intended speech by President Jadon Hamilton in Lincoln Plaza to carry coffins representing major concepts incorporated in the original Bill of Rights. Ordered to disperse or face arrest, they ran into the Lincoln Presidential Library. Chesterfield was shot in the thigh as he neared the front door.
>
> President Hamilton cancelled his speech and returned immedi-

ately to Washington, D.C. The White House has not yet released a statement.

A student leader identified only as Sierra, 22, explained that the class was doing a 'real-time' experiment to determine whether freedom of speech and freedom of assembly still exist as a practical reality despite passage of the 33rd Amendment to the Constitution. That Amendment significantly altered the long-standing First Amendment, which had provided those guarantees and others in the nation's founding document.

Isolated on the second floor of the Lincoln Presidential Library, the students demanded that a statement be distributed by the media. They threatened to burn the building if authorities tried to capture them—a threat that later proved idle when it turned out their gasoline cans had been used only as props and contained no fuel. The students' statement is printed immediately following this article.

A bullet was removed from Ryan Chesterfield's leg by a surgical team that had been assembled in Dirksen Memorial Hospital in case of a Presidential emergency. Chesterfield is currently listed in good condition. The person who opened fire has not been identified.

About two hours later, I walked past the guards into a small single hospital room, every square inch of which had been covered with plants. Ryan was alert. In fact, he was downright animated. "You must be Roland Raines," he said, as though I were famous.

"The one and only," I replied. "How are you feeling?"

"Like I got run over by a tank. But they tell me I'll survive." He was sitting up, with an IV running into his left arm and his wrist handcuffed to the bed frame. He smiled so broadly he might just as well have been at a hockey game. I inferred a vigorous sense of humor and an inexhaustible supply of positive energy.

"You lost a lot of blood. Before you got there, the carpet in the Lincoln Library was only white and blue."

"Just doing my patriotic duty, sir." He saluted, and we both laughed. He clutched his leg immediately with his right hand. "Oh, shit, that hurts."

"Why the handcuff? I thought we agreed everyone was to be arrested and immediately released?"

"Yes, released to parents. My parents live a thousand miles away."

"Shouldn't matter, you're no flight risk. I'll look into it."

"You don't have to."

"Do you mind if I sit down?"

"Help yourself. I've already seen our statement on the OmniScreen this morning. Nice work."

"It wasn't what you'd call a routine day at the office, but I was glad to help. Say, you sure have a gem there in Sierra."

"I'm a lucky guy." He looked toward his leg and seemed to enjoy the irony. "Yeah, she's pretty cool. Said you were cool, too."

I thought about laughing at his description of me as "cool," but then he'd laugh, and I didn't want to be responsible for any unnecessary pain. "She was here this morning, I guess?"

"Yeah, went out for a bite to eat."

"Good. Ryan, I don't want to overstay my welcome, but I wonder if I can ask you a few questions."

"I thought Sierra filled you in."

"She did, but I like to get two sources. Besides, you may have a slightly different perspective."

"Yeah, like being the one with lead in his thigh?"

"Among other things. How did this whole thing come about?"

"It was just a class exercise for American History. We

wanted to learn more about the Bill of Rights, first hand." He adjusted his IV. "I think I learned a thing or two."

"And that would be?"

"For one, those soldiers don't use blanks." He said it matter-of-factly. I even detected a slight smile. Here was a kid with every reason to be bitter, and so far there wasn't a trace of finger pointing or animosity. "Kind of ironic, don't you think?"

"What's ironic?"

"We've got men and women all over the world getting shot, trying to preserve the American way of life. I got shot trying to find out how much of the American way of life we have left."

The phone rang, and Ryan looked at it ambivalently, making no effort to answer. On the fourth ring, he looked at me. "Hand it to me, will you?" He put it up to his right ear. "Hello…yes, this is Ryan….oh, hello, Dad." I stood up, indicating I would be happy to leave the room if he wanted privacy, but he shook his head from side to side. "Yeah, I'm okay, just a single bullet apparently….Seems like it, so far, anyway, they didn't let me bleed to death….It was for school, Dad, nobody thought…" He listened for at least a minute, growing visibly more agitated. "No, she's an excellent teacher. She lets us think for ourselves." Another long pause. "*Your* plans? *I'm* ruining *your* plans?…Well, if the voters are that stupid." He moved the phone away from his ear about an inch. I couldn't understand the words, but it was clear Ryan was being subjected to a stern fatherly lecture. "I didn't mean to be disrespectful….No, you don't have to do that….All right. Goodbye, Dad." He dropped the phone onto the bed. The smile had disappeared.

"I'm sorry, I didn't mean to intrude into your personal life," I said.

"Doesn't matter. Everybody knows we don't have a good relationship."

"Sounded like he was pretty angry."

"To put it mildly." He retreated into thought. "Will you hand me that water?" I gave him a paper cup about two-thirds full. He drank slowly, then crumpled it and threw it toward the waste basket in the corner, missing by two feet. I waited. "Said he wanted to be President some day, and how would it look to have a kid arrested for protesting in public. About the Bill of Rights, no less." He adjusted the IV again, then used the button on the right side of his bed to raise his head a little. "Threatened to yank me out of college."

"I'm sorry, Ryan, I really am."

"Do you know him, by the way? You're both Washington big shots after all."

"I'm just a journalist. I know him only by reputation. Occasionally we're present at the same social functions, but we don't move in the same circles."

He nodded. The telephone conversation seemed to have depleted his energy. "I'm sorry, Mr. Raines, I'm getting tired, and this damn thing is starting to hurt. Would you mind...?"

"Not at all, Ryan, I appreciate the time you've given me." I stood up and took a step toward the door. "It looks like you're in good hands here." I found myself feeling very close to him. "Say, would you like to stay in touch? I'd like to see how you're doing every now and then."

My question elicited a slight raise of the eyebrows. "Why would you care?"

"Because you got hurt doing something innocent. It wasn't your fault. And you're a human being."

He shrugged. "Sure, if you want to."

I went back to my hotel room to write my personal account of the story. About half-way through, I realized I hadn't eaten in hours. Ordinarily, room service would have been out of the question, but the words were flowing and I didn't want to interrupt the train of thought by going out. I ordered a tuna on wheat and went back to the laptop.

Analysis and Commentary by Roland Raines. Springfield, Illinois—The United States Constitution found itself squarely in the crosshairs of a monumental struggle for the soul of this country yesterday, as members of the Illinois National Guard engaged college student protesters in Freedom Park adjacent to the Abraham Lincoln Presidential Library and Museum. Nothing less was at stake than the concepts for which the ragged Colonial army engaged the British Redcoats more than 260 years ago.

Once again, as they have so frequently during the history of the human race, peaceful methods of conflict resolution failed. Bullets flew, with one projectile fired by an unidentified soldier striking Ryan Chesterfield, son of the United States Attorney General, in the thigh.

As reported in this newspaper yesterday, the students were engaged in a test of the theory that civil liberties can co-exist with the gradual but inexorable removal of the guarantees to such rights in the U.S. Constitution. Their conclusion should reverberate throughout every freedom-loving household in every state in the Union and stand as a warning to the dark days awaiting this nation if the present trend continues.

Yesterday's events symbolize the polarization of political thinking that has reached dangerous levels in the last thirty years—thinking that places normally rational people in bizarre situations leading to irrational behavior. Twenty-four young people, whose previous transgressions against society have probably consisted primarily of using a fake ID to buy alcohol and smoking an occasional joint, will now have criminal records. Exactly what fate awaits them at the hands of school administrators and potential employers remains to be seen. Perhaps they were unwise to run into the Library;

other courses of action, equally effective at testing the system, suggest themselves. But they did run. If the test had been unnecessary, Ryan Chesterfield could be strolling through Freedom Park today, holding hands with his girlfriend Sierra, instead of being handcuffed to his hospital bed.

One soldier will live forever with the consequences of having shot a civilian in peacetime. We may never know what those consequences are. We may never even know whether he feels remorse. But he might, and he should. His bullet could have found any one of the protesters, and it could easily have been fatal. If none of the students happened to be his own son or daughter, then he is fortunate, because every one of them was someone's son or daughter, innocently pursuing a higher education in order to achieve the American dream.

None of this was necessary. In the grand scheme of things, the original Bill of Rights was working quite well. Zealots in search of their own personal vision have torn this country apart—attempting to justify preemptive war and the abolition of fundamental civil rights with distortions and scare tactics. Yes, there is insanity in the world; international terrorists and malicious citizens do exist. But we do not fight them successfully by living in fear and dismantling the basic structure of our society. The best defense against madness is not more madness.

What kind of future do Ryan Chesterfield and his fellow students face? Only time will tell.

I sent it off to Sid and glanced at the clock. I had missed the last plane back to Washington. I called Alycia and told her I'd be back the next day. As I lay in bed, with sleep a distant stranger, I couldn't help thinking about Ryan, the kid with the infectious smile and a quick sense of humor, whose mood had turned from contentment to depression because of a telephone call from his father.

CHAPTER SEVEN

Saturday, December 15
A large black limousine parked in front of our house.

"Who died?" Matthew called from his front yard.

"Nobody," I replied. "We're getting reacquainted with a college buddy of mine."

By the time Alycia and I maneuvered Devon into the vehicle and folded his wheelchair for storage in the trunk, a small crowd had gathered. Most of the children had never seen a gasoline-powered automobile. As we left the TDC, I refused to look out the window, not wanting to exchange glances with any more neighbors than necessary. Once we got onto the highway, Alycia and Devon quickly became absorbed in watching the passing scenery. I used the time to read the review of Gordon's book that had been provided by the reference librarian. With three days lost because of my trip to Springfield, I had only managed to finish the preface and the first chapter. I wanted to understand at least the essence of his logic as the basis for conversation. Skipping the biographical information, I skimmed until I found the following passage:

> *This volume draws heavily on Rousseau and other eighteenth and nineteenth century philosophers to construct a model of what many today consider an oxymoron: good government. According to Richards, individual members of society and the governments they create can and should form a symbiotic relationship that furthers an immutable principle of nature—the instinct for self-preservation.*

Governments of this nature are difficult to maintain, he claims, because they run contrary to the short-term interests of those who typically acquire power.

Richards describes the dysfunctional nature of the individual-governmental dyad when either side of the equation predominates. In the absence of government, society disintegrates into a constant power struggle between warring factions, thwarting the collaboration that would otherwise enhance self-preservation and improve the general quality of life. In the presence of a government that becomes too powerful and tramples on individual rights, especially the rights of the poor, society eventually disintegrates because tyranny always succumbs to revolution. Homeostasis is achieved only when checks and balances are institutionalized, preventing imperfect people from bending government to their own nefarious, self-serving purposes.

Volume I explores the manner in which the original Bill of Rights and the body of law that governed the distribution of wealth until the year 2000 contributed to a generally stable American society. In Volume II, scheduled for publication in 2043, Richards promises to discuss the impact of the dramatic changes we have witnessed during the last forty years.

I leaned my head back and closed my eyes. Yes, I definitely needed to find out what Gordon was planning to say in Volume II.

The driver slowed and pulled off the road. "Feels a bit bumpy, I'm going to check the tires," he explained. I hadn't noticed any bumps, and it occurred to me in passing that I probably would have, since I had been reading. It was one of those thoughts that comes and goes so fast, one of millions of pieces of information processed by our brains every second, that the bell signaling something significant doesn't have time to go off.

A minute later, the driver was back. "Everything's fine," he said, and I gave it no more thought.

After an hour, we slowed and exited the main highway, using a frontage road that served as the entrance to a series of large country estates. The driver turned right, onto a long, tree-lined approach to a circular driveway, then stopped in front of a two-story house that must have had at least twenty rooms. A man dressed in casual but neat slacks and a light pullover sweater waited just outside the large wooden front door. If I hadn't seen Gordon's picture on the dust jacket, I wouldn't have recognized him in a crowd of two.

"Roland Raines! Didn't you used to be about twenty pounds lighter?"

"Gordon Richards! Didn't you used to have hair?"

We laughed. "It's good to see you," he said. "Please come in."

With the driver's help, we set up the wheelchair, lifted Devon out of the limo, and passed through the gigantic doorway. Gordon ushered us into a sitting room, and a young lady in a uniform asked if we wanted drinks. Joined by Gordon's wife, we chatted a while, catching up on graduate school, jobs, and families. Suddenly, Devon got agitated, moving his arms in jerky circles and coughing up voluminous amounts of phlegm. It took me a few seconds to figure it out. "He loves birds," I explained, noticing through the picture window that three white ducks were following a trail of breadcrumbs.

"Oh, they come up from the pond about this same time every day. Why turn down an easy snack?"

"May we see? Up close?" Alycia asked.

Gordon's wife guided them outside, leaving the two of us alone.

"How about a tour of the rest of the house?" Gordon asked.

"Of course," I replied, trying not to sound over-eager.

We talked while we walked, and while the conversation consisted nominally of questions and answers relating to our work, my overwhelming reaction was surprise at the opulence of the residence. Evidence of craftsmanship was everywhere, from the finely carved wooden balustrades to the marble mantle above the fireplace. The grounds were exquisite; I especially liked the pond, dotted with lily pads. Large expanses of golf-course-perfect grass surrounded the house on all sides. From the second floor patio off the master bedroom, we observed Alycia and Devon feeding the ducks, assisted by Gordon's wife and two children. I began to feel strange and out of place. We were two people from similar backgrounds, both intelligent, both professionally successful, living lives at opposite ends of the economic spectrum.

The tour ended in Gordon's study, about the size of my living room, lined floor to ceiling with books. "Have you read them all?" I asked, indicating by my tone of voice that I considered it unlikely.

"No," he replied, sinking into an upholstered recliner and nodding toward its twin. I followed his lead, finding the luxurious leather and the elevating leg rests decadent yet relaxing. "Many are just textbooks, sent by the publishers to try to get me to use them in class. They're all essentially the same, a regurgitation of the obvious. But the original works by careful thinkers, yes. I've read those."

"You always liked careful thinkers."

Gordon started to answer but responded instead to a knock on the open door.

"I'm sorry, sir," the limo driver asked. "May I interrupt a minute?"

"What is it?" he asked, a hint of irritation creeping into his voice.

The driver hesitated. "Could I speak with you, please?"

Gordon stood and walked toward the door. "I'm sorry, Roland, this must be important. Look around if you like. I'll be back in a minute."

I took advantage of his absence to inspect the bookshelves more carefully. Although not labeled, they were organized into sections: philosophy, psychology, history, economics, anthropology, and political science. I pulled out a few volumes at random. They looked either totally unread or marked up extensively with marginal notes and underlines. There was a small fiction section as well.

When Gordon returned, he settled into his chair again. "Now where were we?"

"I was about to ask you something. I'm afraid I haven't gotten very far into your book yet. I had an unexpected assignment out of town. The review I read indicates you include some material on the distribution of wealth."

Gordon gave me a professorial look. "Yes, drawing to some degree on the thoughts of Andrew Carnegie. He talked about the importance of distributing wealth to society during one's lifetime rather than saving it and giving it all to your kids when you die. It's also important, politically, that the disparity between the rich and the poor not be allowed to grow too large, as this invariably results in social unrest."

I tried to hide my surprise, given the nature of the mansion I had just toured. "You cite evidence to support that, no doubt."

"Of course. Let me review a few statistics with you." Gordon picked up a copy of his book and opened to an appendix in the back. "This is from the U.S. Bureau of the Census. In 1968, Americans in the richest 20% of the population earned an average of 10.2 times as much as their counterparts in the lowest 20% income bracket. By 1994, that figure had increased to 13.6. By 2020 it was 16.3, and in the census just completed it is expected to exceed 20."

I did a quick calculation in my head. "So, in about 70 years, the disparity between the rich and the poor in this country has approximately doubled."

"It's more complicated than that, of course, but essentially that's a true statement."

"But if your thesis about social unrest is true, then there should be consequences. Right?"

"It's not just my thesis, Roland." He turned to a page close to the middle of the book. "In 2002, an article entitled 'The Social Wars' was published in France. It contained the following proposition: 'The great lesson of the history of humanity is that in the long term people will always revolt against worsening inequality.' "

I knew he didn't mind being challenged; it's one of the things I loved about Gordon and remembered fondly from our Oberlin days. "All the more reason to expect consequences. But we don't have riots in the streets. Where's the revolution?"

"Good question, but easily answered. Criminality can be a precursor to revolt. Why do you think it has become necessary to remove the constitutional barrier to cruel and unusual punishment? And the protections formerly included in the Bill of Rights regarding judicial impartiality and protections for people accused of breaking the law? Regardless of the rationale offered by those who supported these measures, the global reason—the macro-political reason—is that treating crime harshly has become the weapon of choice for those fighting to preserve the gross inequality we see around us today. One hundred years ago, this country spent more money defending its borders against external threats than it did fighting internal crime. Now that is reversed. Otherwise, you *would* be seeing riots."

I hesitated, unsure how far to press a challenge during a first visit. But his eyes were eager. "Gordon, is it all right if I bring the theoretical discussion down to a personal level?" He nodded. "Meaning no disrespect, don't economic and political concepts have to pass the test of corresponding to the real world, in order to be considered valid?"

"There's no need for reluctance, Roland. You know I'm delighted to see you again. If my theories don't stand up to your questions, then I'll change them." I should have known. It would take more than an intellectual challenge to step on Gordon's toes.

"All right, then. Your house here—perhaps I should say 'estate'—is magnificent. And it's your weekend home. My first and only home is barely big enough for three people. I live in a dark community where trees are rare. Sidewalks and streets fall into disrepair and are never fixed." I hesitated, but Gordon encouraged me with a quick nod. He loved the exchange of ideas the way most people love home teams that win championships. "People who live in TDCs struggle to keep their stomachs satisfied on a daily basis, and they are successful only sporadically. My neighbors and I depend on public transportation and our own two feet, while you send limousines to pick up your guests. But we are both college educated. Our wives are educated, and we have all worked hard at our chosen professions. Unless I'm missing something, the difference in our economic lives is all a matter of luck. Devon got sick and your daughter Sandi, the same age, didn't."

"So far, I can't disagree with anything you've said. And knowing you, there is a conclusion."

I smiled. "Of course there is. If I understand your philosophy correctly, a balance between rich and poor, between governmental power and individual rights, develops inevitably from natural principles. But that isn't what we have in this country today. Your analysis must be faulty on some level."

"Perhaps it's not the philosophy that's wrong, Roland. Perhaps it's the execution."

Good, I thought. We're getting into the material he is writing about in Volume II. "Would you elaborate?"

"Perhaps you didn't get far enough in my book to understand that the ideal society I describe is counter-intuitive. The ordinary person does not see the need to share wealth. Neither does the ordinary politician. In fact, opposing taxes is one of the surest ways to get elected."

"Yes, that fact hasn't escaped too many candidates for public office."

"My wife does very well as chief of pediatric nursing at National Childrens Hospital. I'm a full professor at a prestigious university. Together we earn close to a million dollars a year." He stood up and walked to the window, as though he were surveying his luxurious surroundings. "The property taxes on this 'estate,' as you call it, are only about ten thousand dollars a year. Frankly, I'm embarrassed." He turned and faced me. "Your description of our relative financial situations is painful but accurate. I know that it's inexcusable. But there's nothing I can do about it."

I was incredulous, and my voice reflected my skepticism. "Nothing you can do? Why don't you pay more in taxes than you're required to pay? Or donate huge sums to social service agencies?"

"We do contribute to a number of local agencies, and substantially in some cases. It makes a difference for them, but it doesn't change the facts you pointed out so poignantly. Besides, frankly, we enjoy our lifestyle. Why should we give it up if nobody else is willing to?"

I wondered briefly whether *I* would give it up, if the choice were mine to make. But it didn't matter; for me, it was strictly hypothetical. "For the reason you just stated—to prevent social unrest. Surely you are aware that we have already experienced a few instances of organized theft based in TDCs directed toward nearby gated communities. If this movement expands, does it not threaten your way of life, or at least that of your children?"

Gordon returned to his chair, using the leg rest and lying back comfortably. I was amazed at how easily he moved, how unnerved he was by a conversation that challenged his way of life. "You make a good point. But if we are the only wealthy people who choose to distribute wealth more equitably, the impact will be minimal. Therefore, there is little incentive for us to do it. Economists even have a name for this phenomenon. It's called the efficacy problem."

Déjà vu hit me between my eyes. Suddenly, I was back in my dorm room at Oberlin, debating with the young Gordon Richards. I was sitting on my bed, while he rocked on the back legs of the only chair in the room. Even in the intense environment of the small liberal arts college, he was unique, a multi-disciplinary man in an academically fragmented world. Sometimes I felt like I learned more from one free-for-all discussion with Gordon than I did from a month of class lectures. Frequently, I would head to the library immediately after we finished a conversation and check out one or two of the books he had referenced. I had learned the term "peak experience" in one of my psychology classes, referring to the feeling that accompanies an emotional high and the release of powerful pleasure-producing chemicals in the body. The truth is, I hadn't had too many. Gordon Richards was responsible for some of them, triggering a rush by pushing me to my intellectual limits.

"Roland, are you with me?"

"Sorry, I was having a flashback. Oberlin, junior year."

"Oh, Lord. I was just a kid."

"You were a pretty smart kid."

"Smart, maybe, not very wise. But I guess that only comes with age."

"And sometimes not even then." Tyler and Chesterfield came to mind. Especially Chesterfield. I made a mental note to call Ryan to see how he was doing.

"Back to the point at hand, if you're up for it." I nodded, and Gordon continued. "The efficacy problem. If we are the only people attempting to solve a social problem, we won't be successful. Therefore, we don't bother, to be blunt about it."

"So, if everyone else participated, you would gladly go along."

"Yes. But everyone else is not going to participate."

He sounded quite confident, and I was hard-pressed to disagree. Nevertheless, I challenged him. "How do you know?"

"Overwhelming evidence, Roland. There's a name for this, too. Economists call it the 'free rider problem.' Psychologists prefer the term 'social loafing.' In any case, what it boils down to is that many people who belong to groups will choose not to do their fair share because they perceive they can enjoy the benefits of group membership anyway. In small groups, members can be kicked out if they try to get a free ride. But there's no way to do that with society-at-large."

"So the fine balance that you describe can never really exist, is that what you're saying? People will neither understand what is in their ultimate best interest, nor will they engage willingly in the activities that create a fair and self-preserving society?"

"Almost, but not quite. If the situation were that somber, how would we have come as far as we have?"

"I've got to admit, Gordon, at this point I don't know." Sometimes I felt out of my element, debating him. He had barged into my room one day at Oberlin and posed a question. After an hour of probing and three days of mulling it over, I had finally understood what he was asking. I didn't have the answer, of course, but I remember being proud of being able to comprehend the issue.

"Leadership. Enlightened, enthusiastic, convincing leadership. Think back to the founding of this country. People were no different then. In fact, people have changed little since Biblical times—they can still be petty, thoughtless, and selfish, as well as generous and wise. The difference is that some eras of history are blessed with leaders who can, to borrow a phrase from Albert Schweitzer, inspire the 'unreflecting masses.' That's what the Federalist Papers did. Without them, we might never have had a Constitution."

I couldn't help thinking how close we were to not having one again, at least one resembling the original document.

"Let me quote you something, Roland. I've been reading Schweitzer extensively, in preparation for Volume II." Gordon retrieved a book from his desk and returned to his seat, holding the cover so I could read the title: *The Philosophy of Civilization*. A large number of pages had been marked with slips of white paper. "Yes, here it is. Remember that he's writing this in the early nineteen hundreds, around the time of World War I. But I think it's just as relevant today. 'Among mankind today both freedom and the capacity for thought have been sadly diminished.' I'm sorry. I wish I could be optimistic, but I see no evidence suggesting that I should be."

"And that will be the essence of Volume II—that we're on a downward path, and only leadership can turn the country around?"

"Yes."

"And do you see the necessary leadership coming from the current administration?"

"Roland, we're getting ready to go to war with Switzerland, of all places. We've been at war with one country or another for nearly forty years, using artificially generated patriotism as an excuse to stifle domestic dissent. Global warming is out of control, far beyond our ability to mitigate now even if we reduced carbon-based emissions nearly to zero. But we can't do that, because we've practically exhausted the world's supply of oil, so the segments of our society that can't afford nuclear power are using highly polluting coal. Health care for everyone but the wealthy is a cruel joke. Special interests control many of the key policy-making positions in the federal government, the result of political contributions and the most complete breakdown of ethical standards since Watergate." He paused for effect. "Does that answer your question?"

"And there's nothing we can do?"

"There's nothing *I* can do," he replied. "I fully expect that my great-grandchildren, if the human species lasts that long, will inhabit a very different planet."

"All for lack of leadership?"

"Yes, basically."

"It's not a very pretty picture."

Gordon pushed the leg rests down under the chair and leaned forward. "Roland, is there something about this visit you're not telling me? Why the sudden interest in distribution of wealth?"

"I explained that. I'm doing research for my article."

"That doesn't explain why you're being followed."

"I'm being followed?" I kicked the leg rests back under the chair and sat up straight.

"Yes. My driver says they weren't too subtle about it. They either wanted to be detected, or they were amateurs. A couple of kids in their twenties, apparently."

Things began to fall into place for me. First, the lady in the red dress at the Library of Congress. The driver stopping mysteriously, investigating bumps that didn't exist. Some sort of counter-attack was clearly in progress. But what could they know? Had Chesterfield found out that I was in the hospital room when he talked with Ryan? Nothing had been printed about that, and from what I knew about their relationship, it seemed unlikely that Ryan would have told him. In any case, was that a crime? I concluded that there was no way to account for the way a person with paranoid personality disorder thinks, acts, or behaves. Still, the stakes had obviously been raised.

But what should I tell Gordon? If he already knew more than he was letting on, then he wasn't on my side, and telling him anything would be potentially dangerous to me. If he knew nothing, only that I had been tailed, then telling him anything would be dangerous to *him*.

I had too much energy now to remain seated. I walked over to the window and gazed out momentarily, hoping for inspiration. "The government is paranoid these days, you know that. I go to the White House several times a year, at least. Maybe the Secret Service is on high alert."

"And the Secret Service would hire two kids to follow you driving a thirty-year-old Yugo with bald tires and rust spots the size of a soccer ball?"

"I really don't know, Gordon. I had no idea I was being followed. And I'm not a member of any TDC militia group planning to rob you. I'm sorry if this is making you uneasy."

He shifted in his chair comfortably. "I'm not worried about my family, or the estate. We are well protected. You were not aware of it, but you were screened for weapons electronically when you got into the limo. But I can't help wondering whether *you* are in danger, and if so, why."

"I work for a newspaper the government dislikes. I'm reading books the government disdains. I was involved, inadvertently, in the Springfield tragedy." I was warming to the task, convincing myself while I tried to make the actions of the kid spies believable to Gordon. "I visited the Hall of Rights in the Capitol recently and made my position on our entire political situation quite clear to the tour guide. Perhaps I shouldn't have been so explicit."

"Perhaps. In my mind, none of that justifies being followed."

"I'm not saying it's justified. But these are reasons our government can use these days. They don't need much of an excuse."

"Apparently not." He chuckled. "I suppose I'll have a Yugo following me to work on Monday."

"I'm so sorry, I didn't mean to bring any trouble with me."

Gordon stood up and patted me on the shoulder. "Not to worry. My driver can handle anything the kids can throw his way. Hey, I'm getting hungry, how about rejoining our families and getting a little lunch?"

"Sounds good to me. Hey, Gordon?"

"Yes?"

"I still love talking to you. I just wish we were still back in college, where...it didn't mean so much—where all we had to do was think, and let other people deal with the real problems."

CHAPTER EIGHT

Monday, December 17
My invitation to the annual lighting of the White House Christmas Tree had arrived the previous week. A special insert invited me to a reception in the East Room immediately following the ceremony on the South Lawn.

The event had almost been cancelled the previous year when a small-town liberal in North Dakota wondered too publicly how the country justified this kind of light bill when millions of Americans living in Trickle Down Communities could no longer afford electricity for their homes. Conservatives quickly rallied around the cause, claiming the tree was symbolic of the great principles of Christianity. A few of them sent in checks of a few million bucks each, and that squelched the rebellion.

I'd been to about a dozen of these ceremonies in the last twenty years, each one more religiously oriented than the last. If I hadn't had other fish to fry, I might have been concerned about the decreasing separation between church and state. Right now, that was the least of my worries.

Thousands of bulbs were scheduled to transmit their message of hope and peace beginning precisely at six p.m. I arrived early, around four o'clock, to ensure I would get through security in time. I encountered no difficulty. At least a thousand people stood shoulder to shoulder, gazing in anticipation at the dark fifty-foot Douglas fir. Right on schedule, the President pressed the button, and the guests "oohed" and "aahed" in unison. Against the backdrop of the famous South Portico, purposely darkened for the occasion, the perfectly shaped tree capped with its gigantic five-pointed star was quite a sight.

Inside the White House, Madison was waiting. She maneuvered me as usual into the basement. We passed the door we had used on previous occasions, entering instead another small room with nothing in it but three seemingly identical laptop computers and a miniature teleprompter sitting on a table. She wasted no time in getting to the point.

"It could work," she announced, a gleam in her eye squeaking past the usual professional veneer.

I wanted it to work—badly. "How?"

"What kind of laptop do you have?"

"VOX, 2340."

"Wireless option?"

"Of course."

"What's the range of the beam?"

"I don't know. Normally the monitor is only a few inches away."

"It's our only hope. Listen, here's what they plan to do. The President's teleprompter usually gets its signal through hard wiring from a laptop operated off-stage." She activated two of the laptops. One was already connected to the teleprompter with a short cable. Madison repositioned the other laptop so that a built-in wireless transmitter was pointed directly at a receiver on the teleprompter. I could see that the same words were appearing simultaneously on both devices. "The teleprompter has a wireless back-up in case something goes wrong." She unplugged the cable, and the speech kept rolling. "The back-up responds to two different frequencies, a primary for normal operations, and a secondary in case a national emergency occurs during a major address. The secondary creates a method of alerting the President to cut his remarks short without causing a general panic."

Madison turned on the third laptop, activated a different simulated speech, then pointed the transmitter at the teleprompter. The device promptly switched to displaying the words from the third laptop. "For security, the frequencies are changed every time the device is used. Tyler and Chesterfield plan to have an accomplice unplug the wire just before the President enters. They will see to it that the speech the President intends to give is replaced by theirs in the back-up laptop, and it will be beamed to the podium automatically."

"I'm not following. How does that help us?"

"The Secret Service is in charge of determining the operating frequencies for the back-up device located at the podium. I will ensure that the secondary frequency used for the Inauguration is the one your laptop uses. The teleprompter is programmed to project whatever message comes in on the secondary frequency, regardless of any other message it gets, on the assumption that it will be urgent. I will reserve a seat for you in the second row, close to the end on the right hand side, so you can aim your beam at the sensor at the base of the podium. All you have to do is be there and aim your beam properly."

It seemed a lot more complicated to me than she made it sound. "But all the other reporters have laptops too. What's to prevent someone else's beam from interfering inadvertently?"

"I thought of that. We'll just have to ban all other laptops." Her confidence was unshakable.

"Madison, you've obviously given this a great deal of thought, and I can't tell you how grateful I am. But how in the world are you going to arrange for me to be the only reporter out of several hundred who is permitted to bring his laptop to the Inauguration?"

"That's the one part I haven't figured out yet."

The idea hit me so hard it practically knocked me over. "Jadon owes me a favor!"

"What?"

"From high school. I did some things for him. He'll remember, he alluded to it on the plane. Tell him this is really important to me. Tell him I need the laptop with me to write the best possible article about his speech, that I'm looking for an edge on the competition."

"And if he doesn't remember?"

"Tell him 'love letters.' He'll remember."

Madison broke into a broad smile. "I'm not sure I want to know what this is all about. Some teenage prank?"

"It's not important. Just remind him that he owes me a favor."

"Okay, 'love letters' it is."

Thank God I decided not to blow him off forty years ago. What is it they say? What goes around comes around.

"One more thing, Roland."

"What's that?"

"I'm going to a lot of trouble to make this happen. It had better be a damn good speech."

***

That was my intent—to write a damn good speech. I spent the next few days reading everything in the pile on my desk and running the conversation with Gordon Richards back and forth in my head. It seemed to me there were still a few pieces missing. I also reviewed some of my basic texts on journalism, saved from my days at Indiana University. I had discarded the largest portion of my library when we moved to the TDC, but a few treasures remained. I found no evidence that any reporter who had influenced the event he was assigned to cover had won the Pulitzer Prize. Maybe I was after a bigger prize. Or maybe I was just delusional and would return to my senses before I got myself into serious trouble.

I returned to the Library of Congress two days later for what I hoped would be another gigantic gift from the reference department. They didn't disappoint me; another enormous pile of books and articles sat behind the desk with my name on it.

A couple of hours into the reading, I took a bathroom break. I hadn't quite finished my business when the door flew open, like it had been hit with a sledgehammer, sending the locking mechanism careening off the partition. A large man materialized in the doorway and stepped in as far as the tiny stall allowed.

"I'm Gus LaVelle," he said. He could easily have been a professional football player. Well in excess of six feet tall, weighing close to 250 pounds, he looked formidable except for the receding hairline that revealed a man past his prime. Nevertheless, he effectively blocked any hope I might have had of an easy escape. "I work for the Justice Department."

"Is that so?" I managed, not wanting to reveal the fact that I recognized his name. "And is it against the law now to go to the bathroom?"

"If I were you I'd measure my words carefully."

"I am, believe me."

"You don't catch my drift, punk. Don't be snotty or you'll walk out of here with a black eye or two, and there's not a damn thing you can do about it."

He spoke the truth. He was much bigger than I was, and probably trained in combat. He could hurt me if he wanted to and successfully lie about it with no repercussions. Besides, he had chosen the location for his battle carefully. In another situation, I might have been able to step away, maybe even run. He had me with my pants down. I decided to go along.

"How can I help you, Mr. LaVelle?"

"I'm not looking for help. I'm looking to give you a little

advice. My job is to protect the interests of this administration, and that's what I aim to do."

I suppose he meant "protect the interests of the Attorney General," but of course he didn't say that. He might not even know there was a difference. It's possible he didn't even know about the plot.

"You've been acting pretty strange recently. No belligerent columns in your shitty little rag newspaper. Hours of research hidden away in the Library of Congress. Visiting people you haven't seen in thirty years. What the fuck are you up to, asshole?"

Was Gordon in on this? Or were those kids who tailed me to his estate working for LaVelle? Probably the latter, I concluded. I hadn't told Gordon that I would be returning to the library.

"I don't have a clue what you're talking about. My editor has assigned me to cover the Inauguration, and I'm just getting ready to report on what I know will be a fine event. I want to give it some historical perspective."

"I'm going to give you some historical perspective, and you'd better listen good. The last time anybody hurt a President of the United States was when Ronald Reagan got shot, more than forty years ago." It was about sixty years ago, but at the time I was more concerned with his bulk than his brain and didn't particularly care that he was fifty percent off. "As an American citizen, you have the right to buy a gun, but if you did I'd know about it in about four seconds. And you'd never get within a mile of the President again, despite the fact that he likes you for some strange reason."

"We went to high school together."

"I know that. I'm a walking encyclopedia on Roland Raines, star journalist. I've read everything you've ever written."

No you haven't, I thought. You might have read everything I've published. But there's one little thing I'm working on that you haven't seen. I'm writing it, so far, only in my head.

"I'm warning you. We don't tolerate violence in this country. Whatever it is you are thinking about doing, if you step so much as an inch out of line, I will personally beat the shit out of you. Then I will personally transport you to the secret location where we lock up enemies of the state. Then I will personally take the only key that exists and pound it into oblivion with a sledgehammer. Do you get that, you little fart?"

"You're coming through loud and clear. I have no intention of harming the President."

"Well, listen to you. Since when did your intentions amount to anything anyway? You little jelly-bellied piece of shy shit. You think I don't know you've only fucked three women in your entire life?"

"That's not true!" I shouted, knowing that it was.

"Maybe four if you boinked your babysitter when you were twelve. But I doubt it. From what I hear, you don't have the balls to pick your nose in public." Ordinarily I'm a pretty rational human being. But at that moment, I hated Gus LaVelle passionately. "Now, about that pretty little wife of yours," LaVelle continued. "I understand you had a problem a few years back."

"That's none of your damn business."

"That's where you're wrong. I've made it my business. I made a special trip to France, if you must know. I met a nice translator there, working for the French embassy."

Shit! Just exactly how much did he know?

"You have an eye for attractive women, nothing wrong with that. But there are consequences." At that moment, I wanted more than anything in the world to wipe the sneer off his face with my fist. "You got lucky the first time. Your wife forgave you and came back. But will she forgive you again?" He pulled an envelope out of his back pocket and handed me a wrinkled photograph. It was a picture of me, with the lady who had leaned over my arm during my first visit to the Library, only the background had been changed to make it look like we were in a bar. Her lipstick had been enhanced, turning it bright red, and the dress had been doctored to reveal more cleavage. "Did you have a good time?" he taunted.

It's a good thing I was sitting down. I really wanted to slug him.

"Now listen good, you worthless piece of human garbage. You're being watched. My staff is all over you, like ants on a hot dog at a picnic. One false move out of you, and the little woman gets a copy of this in the mail. Understood?"

"So this is what it's come to. The Department of Justice blackmailing innocent Americans. Exactly what is it you think about when you say the Pledge of Allegiance? What do those words 'with liberty and justice for all' mean to you, if anything? Get your sorry ass out of this stall!"

"Go ahead, throw all the words at me you want. That's what you're good at—words. Just be sure it doesn't get any more serious than that. Consider yourself warned."

He turned and left, giving the stall door a hefty shove. It bounced off the side partition noisily. I ripped the picture into about a hundred pieces and flushed them down the toilet.

I wasn't in a very good mood when I got home. A VOXmail from Ryan didn't do a lot to cheer me up.

Hey, Mr. Raines, Ryan Chesterfield here. You remember me, right? LOL. Anyway, I'm doing okay, all things considered. Missed my final exams and have to do the entire semester over, but at least I'm able to walk.

> *Looks like the trial will be in early January. Most of the kids struck a deal and accepted light punishment—three months in jail, postponed until summer so they can finish classes. Can't say I blame them, but Sierra and I and four others are holding out. Don't know that we have much of a chance, but we just don't think we're guilty of treason. We hear Judge Jarred will be on the bench.*
>
> *Hope you're doing fine. Sierra says "hi." We truly appreciate what you did for us.*

Jarred. I thought I recognized the name, but details escaped me. I did a VOXnet search and came up with the following: Josiah Jarred, 49, appointed to the federal bench in 2037 by President Jadon Hamilton; elected District Attorney for Sangamon County in 2030 after serving in that office 14 years, with a 98% conviction rate; graduated University of Illinois law school 2016. He was Pete Chesterfield's classmate! Chesterfield had undoubtedly recommended him to Hamilton for the judicial appointment!

I replied to Ryan's VOXmail immediately.

> *Nice to hear from you and glad the leg is healing well. Jarred is a hard ass, you're not likely to get any breaks from him if he stays on the case. Went to law school with your dad, should recuse himself. Obvious conflict of interest. I commend you and Sierra and the other four, let me know if there's anything I can do.*

Treason? For a political protest that would have been peaceful except for a trigger-happy member of the National Guard? There wasn't much time left.

CHAPTER NINE

Wednesday, December 26

Fuck LaVelle anyway, why did he have to ruin the simple pleasure of looking forward to a warm hug after a day at the office? I did not think of myself as a vicious man, but the things I would have subjected that creep to given the opportunity would have made the operatives in the CIA's Clandestine Interrogation Department wince. In my imagination, every part of his body found itself used in a manner unfit for respectable members of the human race.

I had taken the second stack of materials from the reference desk to the newspaper office, spending a few hours every day gleaning a fact here, a quotation there, and more than a few powerful concepts from the best thinkers of the last three centuries. But my heart wasn't in it. It's difficult to lead a normal life when you're not sure your wife is going to be there when you get home from work.

When Alycia suggested that we go into Washington to spend New Year's Eve together, I readily agreed. Yes, it would be extravagant—we would have to cut back financially for a month to make up for it—but the notion of having some fun, taking a vacation from the routine that had become onerous with the pressure of an unacknowledged secret hanging over my head, was too tempting to refuse.

Matthew agreed to keep Devon overnight. We made room reservations at the VOX Hotel and scheduled a ten o'clock dinner at the Capitol Café on the eighteenth floor. Neither of us had ever cared for dancing. I figured we would finish dessert around eleven, then go up to the room and watch the OmniScreen until the glittering ball fell in Times Square at midnight. Then we'd usher in 2041 passionately, get a good night's sleep and—like most parents—be as happy to see our child the next day as we were to gain a brief respite from the constant responsibility the previous night.

We packed lightly, took the 4:15 p.m. train into Washington, D.C., and walked the mile or so to the hotel to save money. The woman at the registration desk greeted us pleasantly. "Just the one night, is that correct? One queen-sized bed?"

"Yes," I answered.

"May I see your ID's please?"

"You need to see ID?" Alycia asked, sounding a bit nervous.

"That's the only way you can get into the room, ma'am. Your palm prints will need to match the information that scans from your ID."

I was more familiar with security precautions than Alycia and pulled my wallet out without a second thought. "It's standard, honey, the city is on high alert."

The clerk scanned our ID's and handed each of us a key card. "Room 828. The elevators are to your right. Have a very happy New Year."

I waved off the eager bell captain, feeling guilty that I was depriving him of a tip he needed desperately, but we had no extra cash. Besides, Alycia and I had only one small suitcase each, which we easily carried ourselves. When we got to the room, I put my palm up on the sensor, and a green light came on immediately. Alycia did the same, and I heard the door lock click. When we walked in, the lights and the OmniScreen turned on automatically.

"Let's take a nap," I suggested.

"No, I want to go for a walk. With you." She said it firmly, deliberately.

We gravitated naturally toward the Mall, only two blocks away. Alycia pulled me toward the Lincoln Memorial, where a tour guide was speaking to a group of about twenty people. She sat down on one of the steps toward the bottom of the gigantic marble stairway and pulled me alongside. When she leaned over, my first impulse was to anticipate a pleasant nibbling at my ear. Instead, she whispered, "I'm being followed."

"What?" Were LaVelle and his troops escalating the battle? I didn't appreciate being confronted in the bathroom at the Library of Congress, but involving Alycia was out of bounds—exactly what I had hoped to avoid.

"Shhh. I'm being followed. There's an elderly man who always seems to be in the same place I am."

"Are you sure?" I whispered back. My nose was so close to her ear I could smell her freshly shampooed hair.

"I'm not positive, but I'm pretty sure. I've asked around, and nobody seems to know who he is."

My mind raced. Elderly? That clearly wasn't Gus LaVelle. "How long has this been going on?"

"A few days. I didn't really notice at first. Then it got more and more obvious."

It didn't make any sense. I understood why someone would follow her, of course—probably someone working for LaVelle. But wouldn't someone at that level of government know how to spy without being spotted?

"Why didn't you tell me before?"

"I wanted to be sure. But I spotted him again yesterday, and now I'm certain. I thought about telling you in the hotel room, but I didn't know if it was bugged."

"It probably was." I immediately regretted saying it, but it was too late. "What happens when you go home?"

"I don't know. He disappears."

"Maybe some kind of pervert."

"I don't think so. Honey, I'm getting scared. You're acting strangely, and now I'm being watched. Are you really in the CIA or something? Is journalism just a front?"

I laughed deliberately. "No, honey. I've never been to spy school. But if I had been, I wouldn't be able to tell you."

She considered this, and I could feel her head nodding slightly.

"I don't like it, Roland. I don't like it one bit."

How in the world was I going to respond without giving everything away? Was it close enough to the inauguration that it would be okay to tell her? No, I decided quickly, that would still jeopardize the plan—especially with her being monitored.

"Of course you don't like it, who would? That's damn scary. I'll look into it."

"But why would anyone follow *me*?"

"If there *is* anyone following you, I'll find out. Don't jump to conclusions."

"I don't like it."

"I'll find out, honey, promise. Have I ever let you down?" I realized immediately it wasn't the smartest question in the world.

"Once," she said, then stared at her feet.

"And that was the last time, you know that." I moved my head slightly and looked her directly in the eyes. "I am not having an affair. I love you." I said it with the self-assurance of an innocent man in the witness chair, accused of murder, trying to convince the jury to spare his life.

"I believe you. But find out soon, will you? It's getting so I don't like leaving the house by myself."

I nodded, took her hand, and kissed it. We walked back to the hotel, arm in arm. I couldn't tell what she was thinking. More than likely, she was totally confused. But her radar was telling her that I was faithful to her and that there was a good reason for my inability to explain my unusual behavior. She was giving me a chance to bring normalcy back to life. All I needed was two weeks. Then things would be normal again—or they would never be normal again.

It turned into one of the best New Year's Eves I have ever had. Temporarily, I was able to shove Gus LaVelle and his threats into the back of my mind and just enjoy being with Alycia. The dinner was scrumptious; I had a petite filet mignon that melted in my mouth. No wonder people used to eat a lot of beef! Alycia chose the salmon almondine with rice, topped by a delicious creamy white sauce. Sheer decadence. We both enjoyed Regis Philbin's commentary on the festivities in Times Square, where the glittering ball ended its fall right at the stroke of midnight. Then I made love to the most beautiful, patient, and trusting woman in the world.

***

I checked my VOXmail when I got home and found an up-date from Ryan.

> *Trial set to begin Monday, January 7. No defense attorneys permitted. We're just college students, what do we know about law? Got any suggestions?*

Alycia was reading over my shoulder. "You need to go help them."

I was relieved at her reaction. I *did* want to go, but I also feared for her safety. If anything happened to her I would never forgive myself. "With you being followed?"

"We'll spend a lot of time with Matthew. We'll be okay." She paused, apparently convincing herself of the argument that had already reached the tip of her tongue. "Besides, whoever it is, if he intended any harm, he's had plenty of opportunity."

I wasn't so sure, but I sensed an inevitability. "I don't know a damn thing about criminal defense."

"If you did, they wouldn't let you in the courtroom. You do *want* to go, right?"

There was no point in denying it. "It's a great story, honey. I'm the logical person to do the follow up."

She kissed me on the cheek. "You're the *best* person to do the follow up."

Sid was enthusiastic. I booked a flight for Saturday, January 5th, so I could spend some time with the kids before the trial, plotting strategy. All six of them crowded into my hotel room at two o'clock Sunday afternoon. Sierra and Ryan introduced me to the four I hadn't met: Soo May, a young lady right out of high school hoping to transfer to a four-year university after two years of community college; Carlos, a construction worker injured on the job, barely subsisting on Workers' Compensation benefits, trying to jump-start a new career; Tyrone, a lanky kid about six foot three inches, already kicked off the basketball team for engaging in "activities bringing disrepute to the College"; and Jennifer, a twenty-something mother of a two-year-old who wanted to become a teacher's aide.

"Miss Crandall said she'd be here, too," Ryan said. "She's usually late." The students shared a brief chuckle.

I was clearly out of my element. "What do you know so far, other than Judge Jarred will preside?"

"You're familiar with the 30th Amendment?" Sierra asked.

I nodded my head. Ratified in 2020, the sweeping act billed by its supporters as the "Freedom from Criminals and Corruption" initiative had decimated all the protections formerly enjoyed by criminal defendants.

"No more grand juries," Tyrone explained, as if he were demonstrating that he deserved an "A" in class.

"Don't try to get a criminal defense lawyer," Jennifer added. "And you can be jailed for refusing to incriminate yourself."

"No impartial jury," Carlos said, "and no way to force people to testify for you, even if they have evidence that you're innocent."

Miss Crandall was apparently an effective teacher. Sierra summarized. "The only resemblance this trial will have to the kind that used to exist is that it will be speedy and public."

From what I knew, she'd hit the nail squarely on the head. "And how do you think I can help?"

"We're not sure. Maybe the judge will let you advocate for us. Strangely, the fact that you're *not* an attorney could work in our favor."

"I suppose that's possible." Possible but unlikely. Nevertheless, I admired her innovative thought process. "What have they charged you with, other than treason?"

Ryan answered, clearly angered by the unfairness he perceived. "Trespassing and conspiracy to destroy government property. Unlawful assembly and disturbing the peace, both with special circumstances."

"Special circumstances?"

"Patriot Act IV," he reminded me, his voice turning bitter, "pushed through Congress by one Pete Chesterfield, Attorney General of the United States. Violating other provisions of the law with intent to create political chaos and provide aid and comfort to the enemy. Carries extraordinary penalties, you know."

"Life in prison without the possibility of parole," Sierra explained. "We're all pretty freaked out, if you want to know the truth."

"Of course, who wouldn't be? I admire you for standing up for your principles. All of you." I glanced around the room, observing somber faces representing a cross-section of America's ethnic diversity—common folks trying to provide for themselves and their families in a complicated world, caught up in a philosophical and political maelstrom not of their own making. An unintended consequence of the debate over civil liberties, resentment was replacing cheerfulness in these young people—too young in my opinion to be victims of the power struggles of older, supposedly more mature adults.

There was a knock on the door. Soo May, sitting the closest, glanced at me for approval, then opened it. "Hi, Miss Crandall." She looked at me. "This is Mr. Roland Raines."

I stood up and returned a firm handshake from a woman with red hair and a friendly smile, wearing khaki slacks and a blouse just a bit too elegant for the occasion. "It's a distinct pleasure, Mr. Raines. I appreciate everything you've done for the kids." I offered her my chair, but she waved it off. "The floor is just fine."

"So, what do we do?" Carlos asked.

I barely heard the question. I was concentrating on preventing myself from staring at Miss Crandall's narrow waist. "Well, what evidence do you want to provide in your own defense?"

Sierra answered. "We've thought about that. First, Miss Crandall is willing to testify that we were studying civil liberties in class, and our activities were an outgrowth of our discussions. They were not intended to disrupt the President's speech or cause any trouble. Some of the kids who agreed to plead guilty to minor offenses will say that the gasoline cans were just props, completely empty. As far as unlawful assembly goes, I suppose technically we're guilty, the way the law reads today."

"We would never have run into the building if they had allowed us to protest without threatening arrest," Ryan added. "And maybe I'd still have two good legs." Sierra put her hand on his knee.

"Do you think they'll ask you to testify against yourselves, or against each other?" I asked. My eyes wandered above Miss Crandall's perfect waist and fixed momentarily on her breasts. I tried to tell myself that it was subtle, that she hadn't noticed.

"We have no way of knowing," Soo May replied.

I tried to process the limited information available to me and came up blank. "Frankly, it sounds to me like the prosecutors hold all the good cards. I'll get to court early Monday and sit as close to you as possible. I strongly suggest, if you get a chance, that you challenge Jarred's impartiality. Normally, Ryan, having a friend of your father as the judge would be in your favor, but in this situation that seems unlikely. In any case, staying on the bench would be a clear violation of judicial ethics. And dress up a little for court—hair combed, no jeans. I'll see what else I can come up with between now and tomorrow morning."

The students thanked me and filed out, looking dejected. Ryan limped noticeably. Miss Crandall stood up as they left, then sat back down on the bed after the door closed. "Remarkable kids, aren't they?"

"Yes. Apparently they've enjoyed having you as their teacher."

"I'm afraid I've gotten them into a lot more trouble than they're ready for. If I could do it all over again..."

"You'd do the same thing," I offered, not knowing whether

it was true or not. "The kids are not blaming you. Far from it, they've gone out of their way to accept responsibility."

"Very noble, and very mature, but I could teach the class in a more traditional way, and they'd learn just as much."

"They'd learn just as many facts—maybe. Is that really what history is about?"

"Point well taken. That's what I keep telling myself, that people forget facts but remember concepts. Still, Ryan is limping, and I have to ask myself, 'Was it worth it'?"

"You're being hard on yourself. You didn't organize the protest, right?"

She stood up and smiled. I couldn't help noticing how white her teeth were. "Well, if you're not going to let me feel guilty, there's no point in my sticking around."

"All right, I'm ready for a nap anyway. I presume you'll be in court tomorrow?"

"Of course. I'm suspended, pending an investigation, so I have no place to be." She started toward the door, then turned around. "What are you doing for dinner, Mr. Raines? I hate to be the bearer of bad news, but the hotel restaurant here probably isn't up to Washington, D.C. standards."

"I haven't really thought about it yet."

"Well, there's a great Mexican place a few blocks away." It was an invitation, not a statement.

"I have to eat, I suppose." She didn't appear to be put off by my cool response, a futile attempt to delude myself into thinking that dinner with her would be motivated solely by the desire to fill my stomach.

"How about I come back around six, then?" I nodded, and she let herself out.

I lay back on the bed and closed my eyes. Just my luck, the students had to have a knock-out instructor. I channeled my thoughts back to the substantive issue at hand: the trial. The prosecutors *did* have all the good cards; indeed, they had a royal flush. They would call one or two members of the National Guard who saw the kids assemble with their coffins. Detectives would testify that they found the coffins inside the Lincoln Library, along with gasoline cans. *Empty* gasoline cans. How could we ensure that the Judge heard they were empty? Would it make any difference? Why hadn't the Judge recused himself from the case anyway? Eventually the questions faded into dreams.

Miss Crandall knocked on the door promptly at six o'clock, and we walked to the Mexican restaurant. I was careful to keep a proper distance. The food, it turned out, was nothing special; rice and beans is still rice and beans. The conversation, on the other hand, was delightful. She was smart, inquisitive, and liberal—a combination that would have drawn me in had it not been for the fact that I was already married, and quite happily. There are a few lessons in life you only need to learn once. It was just like she said—people forget facts but remember concepts—and I hadn't forgotten the consequences of infidelity. When I suggested that I could find my own way back to the hotel, she found it difficult to disguise her disappointment.

CHAPTER TEN

Monday, January 7, 2041
I woke up early and shut off the alarm clock, not due to ring for another hour. Breakfast in the hotel restaurant consisted of oatmeal and orange juice. Then I headed directly to the courthouse—a square-shaped, pleasantly landscaped building occupying an entire city block. Security was tight. I spotted only one local reporter, from his press badge; the OmniScreen crews had been banned from the courtroom. I was surprised by the number of empty seats, but the trial wasn't scheduled to start for another thirty minutes.

A man and a woman entered, placed heavy briefcases and a laptop on the prosecutor's table, and glanced around the room. He was short, neatly dressed, wearing glasses on a long, serious face. He checked the time on an elegant wristwatch with a gold band and a large circular dial. The woman, probably a little younger, wore a pale green pantsuit, with high heels and a string of pearls around her neck. She glanced at me suspiciously.

The man pulled his laptop out of its carrying case and set it up meticulously, except for the monitor, which lay folded on the table. The woman drew a pair of fashionable eyeglasses out of the same case and put them on, then walked about fifteen feet in front of the prosecutor's table. She looked around, as if she were testing whether this would be a good position from which to address the judge and question witnesses. The man swiveled the laptop so the beam pointed directly at his colleague, then pressed a few keys. She adjusted the glasses, looked deliberately at the judge's bench, the witness stand, and the defendant's table, then nodded to the man. She visually marked the spot where she had been standing, then took off the glasses and sat down again at the prosecutor's table. Then it hit me: they were using a portable teleprompter, similar to the one Madison had just described! The woman would appear to be asking questions spontaneously, but in fact she would be receiving prompts from her colleague. For all I knew, her entire opening and closing statements would be beamed to her glasses. I hadn't expected to see a demonstration of the technology that would be so important to the fulfillment of my own plan—a pleasant bonus to an otherwise disagreeable event.

The courtroom had filled in while I was watching the prosecutors. A few young people, presumably classmates of the defendants, huddled near the back. Miss Crandall mingled with them, carefully avoiding eye contact with me. I couldn't help but notice the stylish dress she was wearing, displaying her femininity as prominently as the courtroom environment permitted. A handful of adults chatted quietly—parents of the students, I assumed. One of the parents held a small child. I thought it might have been Jennifer's mother and her baby, but I didn't have time to find out.

The six defendants filed in a few minutes before nine o'clock and took seats behind a table, facing the front of the courtroom.

"All rise," the bailiff called. "Court is now in session, Judge Josiah Jarred presiding." Everyone stood in unison. Judge Jarred entered, cutting an impressive figure: about six feet tall, well-proportioned, salt-and-pepper hair, wearing a black robe just loose enough around the neck to reveal a carefully knotted red tie. After striding athletically toward the bench, he sat, and the bailiff called, "You may be seated."

The woman prosecutor rose. "If it please the court, we are prepared for trial in the case of United States vs. Chesterfield and co-defendants."

"Thank you." He glanced at the defendants. "Let the record reflect that all six defendants are present in the courtroom. In the interest of time, we will dispense with opening statements. Mrs. Haynes, you may call your first witness."

Ryan glanced at me, eyes wide and a question on his lips. "Now?" he mouthed. I nodded. He stood up, facing the judge. "Mr., ah, Your Honor, may I ask a question?"

"Please identify yourself for the record."

"Ryan Chesterfield, sir." Good, he planned to be respectful.

"And what is the nature of your question?"

"Are you friends with my father, sir?"

"I fail to see the relevance, young man. Please resume your seat."

Ryan stood his ground. "The relevance, Your Honor, is that the judicial code calls for judges to recuse themselves if they have a personal affiliation with any significant party to the case." Apparently he had watched a few reruns from "Miami Law."

Judge Jarred's face turned red, and his voice hinted at anger. "A little knowledge is a dangerous thing. Perhaps you are not aware that all judges now make such determinations for themselves, because only *they* know for certain whether a true conflict of interest exists. I suggest you sit down before you get yourself into serious trouble."

"Very well, Your Honor, but I would like the record to show that the defendants feel you cannot be impartial, and we officially request that you recuse yourself. If you do not, we will consider it grounds for an appeal." He sat down, and Sierra whispered something into his ear. Ryan glanced at me, and I gave him a broad smile.

"And who appointed you spokesman for the group?" the Judge retorted condescendingly.

Sierra stood up. "He speaks for me, and for all the others as well. Of course, we would welcome the opportunity to be represented by counsel."

"Perhaps you are not aware that criminal defendants rarely use legal counsel, Miss whatever-your-name-is." He glanced at his laptop. "Miss Sierra. If I decide you are entitled to it, then you are. In this case, you are not." I hadn't expected the verbal battle to get this heated, at least not so quickly. The students were doing well so far, but the process had only just begun.

"Under the Sixth Amendment to the Constitution, as originally adopted in the Bill of Rights, we *would* be entitled, Your Honor, and we request that the right be recognized in this courtroom."

"Request denied. May we proceed now?"

He didn't intend it as a question, but Jennifer interpreted it as such. She rose and stood next to Sierra. "Then may we be represented by someone other than counsel, Your Honor?"

Judge Jarred looked apologetically at the prosecutor's table. When his gaze returned to the defendants, his voice was harsh and unsympathetic. "Not that it matters, but who exactly do you have in mind?"

Soo May pointed to me. "Mr. Roland Raines is willing to represent us, sir."

"I see. And is Mr. Raines an attorney?"

"No, I don't believe he is."

"Then he is not qualified to speak in this courtroom."

Carlos stood up. "Look, Judge, excuse me if I don't talk this legal mumbo-jumbo very good, but it seems to me you just don't want us to have any help. Mr. Raines is a friend of ours. Since he isn't an attorney, you say he can't speak. If he was an attorney, you'd say he can't represent us. So how the hell are we supposed to present our case?"

The Judge picked up his gavel and pounded it on the desk. "We will have no swearing in this courtroom!" he yelled. "Any further outbursts of that nature, and you will be held in contempt of court."

Carlos was undeterred. "I'm already in contempt of this court, Your Honor."

"Whatever sentence you were going to receive, it has just been doubled." Jarred typed a few words into his laptop.

Tyrone rose defiantly. "Do you mean you've already decided we're guilty, and no evidence has even been presented yet? How fucked up is that?"

Jarred traded passion for quiet resolution, speaking so softly I could barely hear him in the first row. "Now you listen here. This insolence and disrespect must stop now, and I mean immediately. If it doesn't, you will all find yourselves displayed in your own personal pillories in front of this building, where you will remain until sun up tomorrow." Then, having exhausted his limited supply of delicacy, he thundered, "Now sit down!"

Sierra and Ryan glanced back at me, and I nodded for them to comply. Sierra tugged at Jennifer, and all the defendants sat down, one by one.

Jarred turned once again to the prosecution and spoke in an even voice. "You may present your first witness."

Haynes stood up, walked to the spot where she had tested her glasses earlier, and began. "The People call Major John Lanning."

I hadn't seen Major Lanning arrive, but as soon as his name was called he stepped forward, glided into the witness box as if he had been there a thousand times, and swore to tell the truth. Every crease in his uniform was perfectly ironed, and a lot more ribbons and medals were displayed than I remembered.

The man at the prosecution table pressed a key on his laptop. "Now Major Lanning," Haynes began, "where were you on the afternoon of Monday, December 10, 2040?"

"I was commanding a small unit of the National Guard, preparing to keep order during a Presidential address in Lincoln Plaza."

"And what happened on that fateful afternoon, sir?"

Lanning cleared his throat. "About half an hour before the President was due to arrive, a group of students barged through Freedom Park, which is adjacent to the Plaza, carrying black boxes that they were pretending were coffins. They had painted derogatory material on the sides of the boxes."

Sierra stood up. "I object to the word 'derogatory.' "

Jarred looked like he wanted to pat her on the head. "Young lady, if I decide to be real nice, I might let you object to a question. But you can't object to the answer. That wasn't even allowed under the Bill of Rights you claim to support." Sierra sat down. "Please proceed, Mrs. Haynes."

"Thank you, Your Honor. What happened next, Major?"

"I told the students to break up, that they were holding an illegal assembly. No demonstration permit had been issued. I told them if they didn't disperse, they would be arrested. Then they started running toward the front of the Lincoln Library."

Mrs. Haynes glanced at the defendants. "Now, I'd like you to look at the six people sitting at the defendant's table. Do you recognize any or all of them as individuals who participated in the demonstration in Lincoln Plaza?"

I'm not sure the Major's upper body shifted an inch during the entire proceeding. His head moved briefly in the direction of

Mrs. Haynes' gaze, then he looked back at her directly. "All of them, ma'am."

"Very good. Now, sir, did you have a telephone conversation with any of the defendants after they ran into the library?"

"Yes, I did."

"And what was the substance of that conversation?"

"I was told they would burn the Lincoln Presidential Library to the ground if their demands weren't met."

Mrs. Haynes paused and asked her next question as if the fate of the world depended on the answer. I couldn't help wondering: did she have legal training? Or was she an actress? "Did you take this threat seriously, sir? Was it your professional opinion that the demonstrators would in fact burn the Library?"

"I had no information to the contrary."

"Is that a 'Yes,' Major?"

"Yes."

She adjusted the glasses. "When members of your unit searched the Library after the defendants had been evacuated, what did they find?"

"They found two gasoline cans and quite a few pieces of plywood that had been nailed together in the shape of coffins."

"Did members of your unit inspect these coffins?"

"Yes, ma'am."

"And what did they see?"

"Slogans had been painted on the sides, things like 'Freedom from Cruel and Unusual Punishment, R.I.P.' Each casket made reference to a different provision of the original Bill of Rights."

"It would follow, then, that as the defendants carried these coffins through the park, they were exposing young children to these defamatory ideas?"

Bless her heart and soul, Sierra was on her feet. "Is it appropriate, Your Honor, for counsel to use the word 'defamatory'? Isn't she putting words into the mouth of the witness?" Jarred seemed amused. "Well, Miss, you may just have a point there. Objection sustained."

The man seated at the prosecution table typed madly while Mrs. Haynes stalled. After about five awkward seconds, she said, "I'll rephrase the question. While the defendants were carrying the coffins through the park, were any children likely to see these slogans and read them?"

"I can't honestly say that I knew who all was in the park, ma'am, but normally presidential speeches draw a large and diverse crowd. It would surprise me if there weren't any children. There certainly were in the plaza itself, where my unit and I were stationed before all the ruckus started."

"I'm going to ask for your professional opinion again, Major. As part of your training for the military, did you take any courses in American history?"

"Of course."

"And what is your view, in light of that study, about the role of protests, demonstrations, civil disobedience and the like, on the unity and solidarity that make this country strong, especially during wartime?"

"It's a slippery slope, that's what I think, ma'am. The old story applies—give them a finger, they'll take the hand. Allow a simple protest here and a small demonstration there, and pretty soon you've got chaos. In the best of times, I suppose we could afford the luxury of people thinking independently and drawing their own conclusions about complex issues, like war and terrorism. But we're engaged in a fight for our very way of life with people who don't give a damn about this country. We can't risk losing that fight so a few kids can have an educational experience."

Mrs. Haynes returned to her seat behind the table. "Thank you, Major. Your Honor, I have no further questions." She removed the glasses and set them down carefully.

Jarred looked bored. "Thank you, Major, you may step down."

I was on my feet before the Major had taken a single step. "There's no cross-examination?"

"Ah, Mr. Raines, is it?" Jarred said, ridicule escaping from every pore. "Another legal expert on behalf of the defense?"

"Yes, Your Honor. I mean, I *am* Roland Raines. I don't claim to be a legal expert, but doesn't someone get to cross-examine the witness?"

"The point being...?"

"The point being, sir, that the truth is discovered through a careful process in which *both sides* are allowed to probe for the facts."

"Are you suggesting, Mr. Raines, that Major Lanning is lying under oath?"

"I didn't say that. He is, however, testifying for the prosecution. Shouldn't the defense have a chance to...?"

Jarred cut me off, his ridicule turning to scorn. "*I* will say what the defense has a chance to do." He grabbed the gavel and pounded it. "Now sit down or you'll join your little friends out in front when this trial is over."

I wanted to argue with him. I felt like I let the students down. But Jarred had all the power, and pushing any harder would have risked my freedom—and along with it any chance to prevent Operation Capitol Hill from succeeding. I sat down.

"Now that's more like it." He closed the laptop and stood up. "I've heard all I need to hear. I'll have my decision in fifteen minutes."

Sierra was on her feet before Jarred had taken two steps.

"Excuse me, Your Honor, isn't the defense entitled to call any witnesses?"

Jarred answered standing up. "I didn't receive any witness list from the defense."

"We weren't asked to provide one. But we have a witness, and I think in the interest of fairness she should be heard."

"Fairness," he repeated, and seemed to mull the concept over in his head. Then, glancing at his watch, he returned to the bench. "I hope this won't take long, Miss Sierra. Who is your witness?"

"The defense calls Miss Kelly Crandall."

Miss America couldn't have made a more elegant entrance. Kelly Crandall was simply stunning. I tore my eyes away just in time to see that Jarred was also transfixed. The bailiff swore her in, and she took her seat in the witness box.

"Please state your name and occupation for the record." Sierra was clearly nervous, repeating words she had heard on countless occasions but clearly wondering whether they really belonged.

"My name is Kelly Crandall. I am Associate Professor of American History at Sangamon Community College."

"And what credentials entitle you to this position, Miss Crandall?" Sierra was apologetic.

"It's all right, Sierra, it's important for the record. I have a Ph.D. in American History from the University of Illinois at Champagne-Urbana."

"Thank you. Now, Miss Crandall, do you recognize the defendants, and if so who are they?"

"Objection, compound question," Mrs. Haynes blurted out.

"Sustained. Miss Sierra, you must ask only one question

at a time." Jarred glanced at his watch again impatiently. "But make it snappy, all right?"

"Oh, I'm sorry. Miss Crandall, do you recognize the defendants in this courtroom?"

"Yes, I most certainly do. They are...well, they *were* all students in my American History class last semester. Some of the best students I've ever had, frankly."

Jarred pounded his gavel. "Just answer the questions, please, there's no need to elaborate." His eye lingered on Miss Crandall just a bit longer than necessary before he turned toward the prosecutors and said in a loud stage whisper, "Amateur hour here. Be patient."

Sierra wisely ignored his insult and proceeded, gathering some measure of confidence. "And do you get to know your students fairly well, in your opinion?"

Mrs. Haynes was on her feet. "Just exactly where is this going, Your Honor? What is the relevance?"

I caught Jarred's momentary glance at Miss Crandall before his eyes settled on Sierra. "Young lady, I'm bending over backward here to give you an opportunity to make whatever point you're trying to get to. I understand you are not trained in law. But we can't be here all day." In fact, he *was* bending over. Jarred had started leaning just slightly toward the witness stand in order to get a more complete view of the impeccable Miss Crandall. I concluded that her beauty was the most important factor in permitting the trial to continue. The world works in mysterious ways!

Sierra took one step toward the Judge, perched more than five feet above her on the bench. It occurred to me that the trappings of power frequently included symbols of separation—robes, physical separation, claims of special knowledge or moral authority—all of which were in evidence in Jarred's courtroom but having increasingly little impact on Sierra. "Your Honor, isn't the context of our protest relevant? Don't you want to know what our motivation was?"

"Intent is not the issue, young lady. The Supreme Court decided that more than a hundred years ago. It's what you did that counts."

Miss Crandall turned slightly in her seat. "That's right, Your Honor, very impressive. The Sedition Act of 1798 made it illegal to even *intend* to defame the President, the Congress, or even the government generally. Fortunately, that sorry chapter of American history didn't last very long."

Jarred sputtered, apparently torn between the desire to get on with the trial and to prolong his opportunity to stare at Miss Crandall's breasts. "The witness will kindly limit her responses to direct questions," he finally managed, using a kindly voice so clearly gilded with sexual overtones that I wanted to be sick. Turning then to Sierra, he continued more gruffly. "Next question."

"Yes, Your Honor. Miss Crandall, why don't you just tell us in your own words what you tried to teach us about the Bill of Rights and how it applies to this situation."

"It's not easy to condense an entire semester into five minutes, but I'll try. Perhaps focusing on the First Amendment would be instructive. The lessons learned will apply to civil rights in general.

"Despite justifiable pride in the history of our country, the truth is that we have a checkered past in regard to personal liberties. The First Amendment as it applied to free speech was subjected to multiple attacks before its repeal, usually in the context of a foreign crisis, real or imagined. The Sedition Act of 1798 was followed by the Espionage Act of 1917 and the Sedition Act of 1918. When the Supreme Court started ruling these provisions unconstitutional, which it eventually did after generally supporting them in the beginning, people in power resorted to harassment, intimidation, and secrecy."

Mrs. Haynes was on her feet again. "I still don't see the relevancy. The free speech provision of the First Amendment has been repealed, as the witness clearly admits."

"I'll allow it, counsel, let's see where it's going. Please proceed, Miss Crandall. And perhaps you can provide just a little justification for these sweepingly critical statements."

"Of course. Well, in regard to harassment and intimidation, you don't have to look beyond McCarthyism in the 1950s—a full-scale attack on free speech based on fear and innuendo. For secrecy, consider the Nixon Administration, and frankly many others. The plain fact is that free speech and other civil liberties are sometimes inconvenient, especially to people in power, and they engage all the weapons at their disposal in stifling dissent when they perceive such actions to be to their advantage. One of the most dangerous of these weapons is the practice of equating non-conformity with disloyalty.

"There are a couple of things I want my students to have when they finish my class. First, I hope they understand that issues impacting society at large are rarely simple. Frequently they involve competing interests among well-meaning people. I encourage them to listen effectively, truly consider other viewpoints, and change their minds if the facts warrant. Only a fool thinks he is always right. I also want my students to understand the important role free speech, and its absence, have played throughout our history. It is a key to understanding many other aspects of our society, including the manner in which legislation gets passed, the role of the courts in determining the constitutionality of our laws, and the tolerance, or lack of same, exhibited by the majority toward the minority. So we discuss all these things in class, focusing on the continuing debates and application of the Bill of Rights as a case in point."

The gentleman sitting at the prosecution table stood up ponderously, as though he were about to produce an oration of historical significance. "Your Honor, we all have important things to do. How long must we listen to this drivel? The people of this country have discredited these so-called civil liberties through participation in the democratic process. They have, through entirely legal means, modified or repealed the entire Bill of Rights, and the fact that this witness holds the document in such high esteem does not change this fact one iota."

Jarred sighed. "I must agree with you. Miss Crandall, you must get to the point quickly now."

She continued. "Very well. I have always felt that, as an educator, my primary function is to help my students think carefully. In order to do this, they need facts, the ability to think critically about those facts, and an open-minded attitude that permits real time exploration of classroom concepts. Just one week before the incident in Freedom Square occurred, I quoted for them one of the most eloquent commentaries about civil liberties I know. In 1944, Judge Learned Hand stated, 'I often wonder whether we do not rest our hopes too much upon constitutions, upon laws and upon courts. These are false hopes; believe me, these are false hopes. Liberty lies in the hearts of men and women; when it dies there, no constitution, no law, no court can save it.' My students decided to discover whether liberty still lives in the hearts of men and women in the year 2040. I don't think they are pleased by what they are finding out."

"And neither are you, I take it," Jarred replied. "In any case, you've had your say. You are excused." Mrs. Haynes stood up, and Jarred waved her back to her seat. "There's no need for cross-examination here. And we can dispense with closing statements as well. I'll have my decision in fifteen minutes." He pounded the gavel, then left the bench so fast the bailiff didn't have a chance to tell everyone to stand up. I'm not sure I would have, anyway.

The students gathered around Miss Crandall as soon as Jarred disappeared, congratulating her and thanking her. Everyone gave her a hug. Then she walked toward me. "It was the least I could do," she said, "but we both know it was totally irrelevant legally. Jarred's going to throw the book at them. I hope you can help."

"I'm going to try." I watched her walk to the back of the courtroom. The students then surrounded me, asking for an assessment. "This was not a trial. This was a lynching." I put my hand on Sierra's shoulder. "And you, my friend, were magnificent."

"Can we appeal?" she asked.

"Let's find out what Jarred has to say when he gets back, not that I expect any good news. Any appeals court worth its name would order a new trial in a second. But it costs a ton of money to file. We'll have to investigate."

"I need to find a bathroom," Ryan said. The students scattered.

I stared at the side wall of the courtroom while the events of the last fifteen minutes circled in my head. I hadn't noticed it before, but letters had been attached in relief, about two inches high, spelling out "In God We Trust." By the time the students returned, I had come to two conclusions: in Judge Josiah Jarred, I could not trust; and God was on vacation.

The bailiff told everyone to stand. Such is the force of habit, and respect for the institution if not for Judge Jarred himself, that we all did.

Jarred took his seat almost hastily, as if he couldn't wait to pronounce sentence. He opened his laptop, pressed a few keys, then turned to the courtroom. "Defendants rise." They did. I found myself hanging on every syllable, fearing the conclusion yet wanting desperately to hear it, the way a parent waits when word comes from school that a child has been in an accident but the extent of the injuries are still unknown. "You have been charged with a variety of crimes against the greatest country in the history of the world, the United States of America. All of you are guilty on each and every count. You have shown reckless abandon for the safety of other people, for property of an invaluable nature, and for the concepts that make this country strong. You are not worthy to be citizens of this magnificent land. I am tempted to revoke your citizenship and sentence you to live the rest of your lives in exile, since you apparently do not value the benefits your privileged status here confers upon you. I would send you far enough away that you could not corrupt other young people with the ideas that have been planted in your heads as part of this so-called educational process." He paused long enough to scowl at Miss Crandall, then read again from his computer monitor. "However, in view of a certain phone call I received requesting leniency, you are all hereby sentenced to five years in the state penitentiary and probation for the rest of your lives."

I could see the students gasp for breath. Five years! How dare he? At the very worst, they exercised immature judgment during an educational experiment. Neither the library nor the country was in any danger.

Jarred continued to read. "I am taking the liberty of suspending the sentence of any defendant who shows remorse. Should any of you wish to take this course of action, you will do the following. One, you will sign a statement I have prepared disclaiming any belief that the amendments recently adopted modifying or repealing parts of the original Bill of Rights have in any way caused this country harm. Second, you will publicly apologize for conduct unbecoming a citizen of the United States of America. Third, you will promise never again to engage in political activity that reflects negatively on the established and duly elected government of the people. Should you make such a promise and break it, the suspension will immediately be lifted, and you will serve your time."

He stopped reading and turned directly to the students. "You will surrender to local police no later than 10 o'clock in the morning this coming Friday. I hope you appreciate my leniency in not taking you into custody immediately. Between now and Friday, you will either accept the conditions of the suspended sentence or put your things in order and prepare to endure the punishment you so richly deserve." He pounded the gavel. "Court is adjourned."

Jennifer immediately burst into tears. Soo May looked overwhelmed, unable to react immediately. Carlos and Tyrone scanned the room, with fear in their faces, apparently looking for their parents. Ryan and Sierra hugged.

I joined the group. "Let's get out of here," I suggested. "We can go to the hotel." The courtroom had taken on a stifling, distressing ambience.

We walked, mostly in silence, Ryan and Sierra hand in hand. The others stayed comfortably close to each other; clearly, a bond had developed.

Inside the room, their true feelings began to show. "If that asshole hadn't been wearing a robe, I would have knocked his teeth out," Tyrone claimed.

"I think he'd look good with his feet in cement, bobbing along the bottom of the Sangamon River," Carlos added.

"Five years!" It was difficult for Soo May to get her arms around that much time; she hadn't yet turned twenty.

Jennifer started sobbing again. "What's going to happen to my baby?" Sierra comforted her.

Ryan gritted his teeth and turned to me. "Well, what are we going to do?"

So far, my presence had not proved particularly useful. I felt comfortable making a suggestion, though. "First of all, I don't think you all need to feel obligated to make the same decision. Your circumstances are all different. Second, give yourselves some time. This is way too big for a snap judgment. Go home, talk about it with your family and your friends. Get a good night's sleep, if you can. How about we meet again tomorrow, ten o'clock?"

They readily agreed, and in a few minutes I was alone in my room. Despite emotional exhaustion, I felt obligated to file a story. I labeled it "opinion and analysis" and sent it off to Sid via VOX mail.

> *Springfield, Illinois*—*Six brave community college students received five-year prison sentences today at the hands of Judge Josiah Jarred in a trial that lasted less than an hour and demonstrated beyond any doubt that the Bill of Rights has been buried and forgotten.*
>
> *A visitor from another planet to this small courtroom in the heart of Illinois, Sangamon County, would not have seen a shred of evidence that the criminal justice system in this country cares one iota for fairness or truth. The defendants were permitted no legal counsel and no right to cross-examination. The word "jury" was never spoken. One gets the impression that, had the Judge not already determined the outcome prior to hearing the first witness for the prosecution, he would have coerced the defendants into testifying against themselves, or against their colleagues, with refusal resulting in the kind of punishment that until recently had been banned from the so-called civilized world.*

This entire process started when the students exhibited curiosity about the impact recent Constitutional amendments have had on our society. Now, ironically, they have their answer.

The Judge made it possible for the Springfield Six to avoid incarceration and lifetime parole by renouncing their beliefs. Think Galileo, succumbing to the teachings of the Church that the sun revolved around the earth. It remains to be seen how the young people will respond to this challenge.

I undressed and slipped into bed, falling immediately into a shallow, troubled sleep.

I woke up to the incessant ringing of the telephone at six o'clock in the morning. It was Jennifer.

Although she barely managed to talk between sobs, I figured out that she wanted to see me before the other students arrived. We arranged to meet for breakfast at eight thirty.

"Thank you, Mr. Raines," she said, after ordering eggs and toast. She had pulled herself together marginally and put on almost enough makeup to mask a face darkened by regret and despair.

"It's my pleasure. How can I help you?" I was hoping desperately that I could. So far, events seemed nearly out of control, beyond my ability to influence.

Jennifer looked down into her lap and whispered, "I don't think I can do it."

"You can't do what?"

"I can't go to jail. I can't leave my baby for five years!" She started crying again, then dried her tears with a napkin.

"You don't have to. The Judge told you how to avoid prison."

"But how can I do that to my friends? What kind of traitor does that?"

"Do you know that they won't make the same choice?"

Her look made me feel ignorant. "You don't know them very well, do you? They'll go to jail. They won't do all that stuff the Judge said."

"We'll find out soon, I guess. But they don't have a two-year-old."

Breakfast arrived. After the waitress left, Jennifer continued. "No, they don't. But they'll be sacrificing five years of their lives, just the same."

Several brainstorms hit at once. "What's your baby's name?"

"Deena. She was in court with my mom."

"And what kind of life do you want for Deena?"

She hesitated, apparently not expecting a philosophical question. "I don't know, just a normal life I guess. School, friends, the chance to be whatever she wants to be."

"And doesn't she need a mom to help her be what she wants to be?" Tears appeared again. She nodded. "Jennifer, unless I'm missing something, your class was focused on the things that used to make this country great. One of those things was the right of different people to see the world differently and to express their views—to be individuals. You have every right to decide to stay with your daughter. I think your friends will understand."

She considered this. "I can't go to jail."

"No," I said softly. "It's your decision. But I don't think you should go to jail, either."

We finished breakfast in silence. The waitress sensed an intense conversation and stayed away, although I saw her glancing in our direction. She got a big tip.

Other than Jennifer, Sierra was the first to arrive. She paced the ten feet between the bed and the window continuously, full of nervous energy. When everyone was present, flopped onto the bed or seated on the floor, she made an announcement: "We'll go on a hunger strike!"

"We'll do what?" Tyrone asked. I couldn't tell if he didn't understand the idea or if he understood it all too well.

"We studied it last semester. You remember Gandhi, in India. James Connolly, in Ireland. Taco Bell tomato pickers in California less than forty years ago. Maybe we have to go to jail, but we can make our point."

"Haven't we already made it?" Soo May asked.

Ryan picked up the argument. "No, I'm not sure we have. Aside from Mr. Raines, the national media didn't even cover the trial. We're still unknowns…unknown soldiers." He liked the phrase and smiled at me.

"We're not soldiers, we're students," Carlos said. "We tried to learn something, and now we're learning the hard way. What's all this about making a point?"

"Two days ago, I would have agreed with you," Ryan explained. "But you saw that sham of a trial yesterday. I don't think either of the alternatives Judge Jerk-off presented to us is the right answer." He stood up, favoring one leg slightly, but displaying an air of confidence. "I'm starting to like this protest thing."

Carlos looked at the clock on the night stand. "Where's Miss Crandall? Did anyone invite her?"

"I did," Jennifer said. "She didn't seem too enthusiastic. Said we were in good hands."

"Well, I wish she was here."

"What exactly would a hunger strike accomplish?" Soo May asked, bringing us back to the point at hand.

Sierra had apparently given the matter a lot of thought. "It calls attention to the complete lack of justice we experienced yesterday. And for all we know, it's the same thing that happens in that courtroom *every* day." She addressed Carlos specifically. "I agree, we're students. But we're also citizens. And if we don't protest, after what we've seen, then who the hell is going to?"

Tyrone turned to Jennifer. "You're pretty quiet, Jen. What do you think?"

She had comes to grips with her decision. "I can't go to jail. I've got my baby to think about. I'm not going to abandon her. And I'm not going on a hunger strike." She looked at each of her friends in turn. I was so proud of her. "I am a student. And a citizen. But *first*, I'm a mom."

Sierra raced over to embrace her. Everybody else did the same, and tears flowed freely. I went to the bathroom and brought a box of tissues. "I wasn't sure you guys would understand," she said.

Sierra still had her arm around Jennifer's shoulder. "Of course we understand. I'm ashamed I didn't think of it that way myself. I got kind of wrapped up in my anger."

"Do you want me to leave?" Jennifer offered.

"Hell no," Carlos said. "You may be the only sane person here."

Everyone laughed, but the light-hearted mood only lasted a few seconds. "What do you think about it, Mr. Raines?" Sierra asked.

I didn't know much about hunger strikes. The reporter in me took over. "If I were you, I'd be asking a lot of questions before I made a decision like that. What kind of physical impact does it have on your body, and how long does it take before it becomes dangerous? And what exactly would you be trying to accomplish? Judge Jarred probably doesn't care whether you live or die."

"I looked it up on the Internet," Sierra replied. "There are two different kinds. You can do water only, or you can use dietary supplements and have other liquids, like juice and soup. You have to take precautions, like not moving around a lot, to conserve your energy."

"That won't be difficult if we're in jail," Tyrone observed.

"You have to avoid getting too hot or too cold, because you lose your ability to regulate your body temperature. In about ten days, your bones start to weaken. Permanent damage to muscles starts about the fourth week. Brain damage begins about the fifth week." Despite the factual nature of her report, her voice showed an understanding of the immense burden of such an undertaking.

"The point is, we won't have to do it that long. It's a protest, not suicide," Ryan added.

Carlos was skeptical. "How do you know how long we'd have to do it? Mr. Raines writes a few stories for his big city newspaper about a thousand miles away. Maybe the local media cover it, maybe they don't. I agree with Mr. Raines, the Judge doesn't give a damn, and if we die of starvation he'll celebrate the fact that the government won't have to feed and house us for five years."

Ryan was respectful but adamant. "Nobody has to do this. But count me in."

"Me too," Sierra said.

Soo May shook her head from side to side.

"Not me," Carlos said. "The Judge is an asshole, but I don't get starving myself."

All eyes drifted toward Tyrone. "I don't know. I'm not clear on what it accomplishes."

"Let's work on a statement," Sierra suggested.

Jennifer stood up. "I'm sorry, I'm just not comfortable

hanging around, since I'm not participating. You guys know I'm with you in spirit, and I'll help if I can."

Soo May and Carlos took advantage of the opportunity to leave also, following a long round of hugs. A lot of adults could learn something from these kids, I thought: you can have a conflicting opinion with a person and still be friends. Civil disagreements don't necessarily lead to civil wars.

"Let's go downstairs," Ryan suggested, addressing Sierra and Tyrone. "Maybe Mr. Raines will help us edit when we're done."

I nodded. "Yes, of course. But you need more than a statement, you need a purpose and a proposed resolution. What exactly do you want to happen? Sierra, you've studied this. Think back to Gandhi and the others. They always had a demand, and if the demand was met, they ended their strike." She nodded. "I'd like to get back home this afternoon if I can get a flight. Why don't you come back in a couple of hours, and we'll see where we are."

"You're not going to cover it?" Ryan's voice revealed panic. "Without publicity, we're dead."

"I'm covering it. But I have a wife and a child. I'll stay in touch, and I'll come back if I need to. You may not have to go as long as you think."

I booked a flight departing five o'clock for Chicago, with connections to Dulles International arriving after midnight. Public transportation would be shut down by then, and I wouldn't get home until six or seven in the morning. Still, I preferred that to staying in Springfield an extra day.

Sierra, Ryan, and Tyrone returned about an hour later, energized by their work. "Okay, what do you think?" Sierra asked, reading at a rapid pace.

"Throughout history, hunger strikes have been used by

courageous individuals as the weapon of last resort against overpowering forces that are morally, ethically, or legally repugnant. Given the gross miscarriage of justice that occurred recently in the courtroom of Judge Josiah Jarred, we the undersigned feel we have no choice but to engage in such an activity. Beginning Tuesday morning, January 8, 2041, at six o'clock, we will eat no solid food until we and our three other co-defendants are granted a fair trial on the charges brought against us in connection with our demonstration in Freedom Park last month. On the advice of a family doctor, into whose care we entrust our lives, we will accept daily vitamins and juice.

"We do not engage in this activity lightly. We understand it will be painful, harmful, and potentially fatal. But we are not guilty of any transgression against society that justifies a prison term of five years. To succumb without protest would also be fatal, emotionally and intellectually. We firmly believe that a jury of our peers, hearing evidence from all appropriate witnesses, with the truth revealed through cross-examination by competent counsel, will reach a verdict of 'not guilty.'

"Until such time as this trial takes place, whether we be in or out of prison, we will protest unfairness with the only weapon still at our disposal: a commitment to the death for principles we believe in, with the American people the ultimate judge of the validity of our cause."

It was hand-written on two pieces of hotel stationary, and all three of them had signed their names. Sierra handed it to me solemnly. "The people can only judge if they know what's happening. That part is up to you."

I tried to talk and discovered a lump in my throat about the size of an apple. I felt privileged to be in the same room with these...kids. That's all they were, and perhaps it was fortunate. Another few years under their belts, and they might have become practical realists. "It's very impressive," I finally managed, "and you will have my total support. I'll submit this statement for publication in tomorrow's edition. We'll carry an up-date on your condition every day." My mouth went dry and my mind went blank. I just wanted to hug all of them—so I did.

CHAPTER ELEVEN

Friday, January 18, 2041
The VOXmails from Springfield were not encouraging. The kids had basked in novelty and notoriety the first two days. Their statement, and my background articles, had gotten some national attention, and their pictures had appeared in the local paper, but Jarred was unmoved. He reminded them that, for a mere $250,000 in legal fees, they could file an appeal; in the meantime, they would have to report to jail. And they did, continuing to refuse solid food of any kind. The information flow slowed considerably then, as they were allowed only one communication each out of prison every week, but I could tell that things were bleak.

Upon returning home, I had reacquainted myself with the details of my personal situation. Gus LaVelle was undoubtedly having me followed. I expected he knew every detail of my involvement with the kids in Springfield. Alycia was also being followed and didn't care at all for my inability or unwillingness to let her know what was going on. I experienced sheer hell every day. Migraine headaches arrived promptly about nine o'clock in the morning, put into check by three extra strength aspirin, only to return with a vengeance in the middle of the afternoon. I tried to delve into the second stack of materials from the Library of Congress during my few peaceful hours, but I couldn't concentrate well enough to absorb any new information. By six in the evening I was emotionally exhausted. I ate very little for dinner, feigning interest in the conversation Alycia initiated, helped her with the dishes, then went to bed. Gus LaVelle appeared in my nightmares more than once, balanced by an occasional appearance of the calm, professional Madison. Sometimes I dreamt that I opened the front door of my house, expecting to see the usual weed-strewn lawn and cut up sidewalk, but instead finding the elegant grounds of Gordon Richards' estate, complete with pond and ducks. Every morning I woke up soaked with perspiration.

I was not prepared to play for stakes this high. Journalism had been my highest professional aspiration. All I had ever wanted was to report important news accurately, succinctly, and with a little good fortune, a touch of grace. Unlike Jadon, who had gravitated to the front of the cameras, I had always preferred staying behind them. The idea of writing a political speech, much less an inaugural address, had never entered my consciousness. Now it seemed that the country demanded it—the integrity of the Constitution demanded it.

I loved Alycia and Devon with a fervor that bordered on obsession. Yes, I had strayed once, and every cell in my body had regretted it ever since. I had won them back with the truth and a promise never to stray again, and now all that was in jeopardy. Why couldn't I just tell Alycia what was going on, explain the incident with the lady in the red dress, and get on with life? I traced the logic I had used innumerable times to convince myself that doing so would put her in danger. Chesterfield and Tyler were determined to abolish Congress. They had already demonstrated that they would stop at nothing to achieve that goal. Their spies had apparently not discovered my plan. The inauguration was only two days away. They would be frustrated. What would prevent them from abducting Alycia and torturing her for information? If she knew, then she would try to protect me and hold out as long as possible, causing them to inflict unbearable pain. If she didn't know, they would figure that out, and torturing her would be useless.

How long would Alycia tolerate being followed? So far, she had given me space, trusting that it didn't involve romance and that I had the connections necessary to bring it to an end. But what would happen if LaVelle followed through on his threat to show her that ridiculous photograph? LaVelle! Every time I thought about our confrontation in the bathroom I felt my temperature rise. Was he right about my not having the guts to do anything but put words on a page? I thought not. But I hadn't actually implemented my plan yet; until I did, there was a chance that his assessment was correct.

Alycia interrupted my reverie. "I'm going out for the milk. Will you be okay?" That's the kind of woman she was—concerned about her husband when *she* was the one being followed. I wanted so badly to restore normalcy to our little household and devote more of my energy to the wonderful wife I was starting to feel I didn't deserve.

"Yes, we'll be fine. I'll get Devon dressed."

"I'd buy some piece of mind, too, but I understand he's sold out." It wasn't like Alycia to be sarcastic. Yes, she was caring, but events were wearing her patience thin.

I went into my son's bedroom and heard the back door close behind Alycia. "Well, good morning, young man," I said, seeing Devon lying in bed, eyes alert as usual. "How are you feeling today?"

He answered with a gurgle. I went to the closet, picked out some clothes, and held them up. "How about these?" He nodded enthusiastically.

"All right, up we go." I lifted him to a sitting position, took off the top of his pajamas, and gave his upper body a sponge bath. "Say, Devon, there's something I've been meaning to ask you. I've got a bit of a dilemma on my hands." I knew he didn't understand. Still, I enjoyed posing the question, pretending without believing it that an internal monologue had become dialogue. He looked at me, his face indicating that he was enjoying the sound of my voice but wasn't hearing any of the few questions to which he knew the answer. "Some very bad people are getting ready to make a big power grab, and I'm the only person who can stop them. But it's dangerous, and I don't know what will happen to me if I do it. They might not let me live with you and Mommy any more."

I put his shirt on, then removed his pajama bottoms and continued the sponge bath. "I've got this friend, Gordon, you remember him, don't you? The man with the duck pond. What do you suppose he would do if he were in my shoes?" I wiped some drool off Devon's chin and the clean shirt I had just put on. He continued to gurgle pleasantly, as if he were asking me what we were going to have for breakfast. "Yes, I guess you're right. Gordon is just waiting for Armageddon, enjoying himself in the meanwhile."

Putting Devon's pants on was a little trickier than his shirt. He had learned to hold his arms up to make the latter a little easier, but he didn't have the strength to move his lower body off the bed. I had mastered the technique of lifting his legs up, one at a time, and slipping on his underpants, followed by the pants. "Now, Jadon, he doesn't have a clue what's going on. I can't ask my friends for advice. These days, you just don't know who's listening behind the wall. And I can't involve your mom—not just yet."

I lifted Devon into his wheelchair, and he became more animated. He knew what came next: Cheerios, and the almost-daily walk to Laffer Park. "So, what do you think I should do, son?" I paused for the answer I knew he could not give me. Then it hit me—whether I wanted it or not, I had been thrust into a leadership role, the kind Gordon had spoken about. I was alone in the polling booth of life, choosing between action and inaction, between courage and impotence. The buck stopped with me, and there was nothing I could do about it.

Alycia returned and set the milk on the kitchen table. "I'm home."

"Okay, we're ready." I really enjoyed bobbing for Cheerios that morning. But I hesitated taking Devon to the park. I didn't feel up to it. My plan required that I spend the last day before the inauguration at home, composing on the keyboard the speech that I had been attempting to write in my head. There was only one day left before that happened, but the speech was still a jumble of ideas. I considered myself reasonably talented at the process of synthesizing large amounts of information and reducing the product into small bites understandable to the American public. Normally I would write things down, then edit extensively. In this situation, I couldn't risk that. Once I committed the speech to written form, there was no way I was going to let the laptop out of my sight. So I was forced to organize the ideas and come up with the language in my head, and it wasn't working. The concepts wouldn't arrange themselves into logical order. The language that would have to be convincing, eloquent if possible, simply wasn't coming to me. What a horrible time to experience writer's block!

I decided to give Devon an abbreviated walk, then go to Washington. Sometimes a change of scenery helps clear the mind. In the process, I could return the borrowed materials to the Library of Congress.

"I've got to return this stuff," I said to Alycia, loading the books that needed to be returned into one of the canvas bags she used to carry groceries. I kissed her goodbye and walked to the train station, picturing her unhappy face all the way.

Fortunately, I saw neither LaVelle nor the lady with the red dress at the Library of Congress. The reference librarian who had been so friendly during my first visit was there. I thanked him profusely for his help. "Glad to be of service," he replied. I walked up 2nd Street to East Capitol Drive, then turned left toward the massive dome. Maybe walking through the Capitol would inspire me. After all, it might not be there forever.

I started in the National Statuary Hall, then migrated through the Cox Corridors, where some of the words of the nation's wisest statesmen were emblazoned in stone. It didn't take me long to locate my favorites.

"The greatest dangers to liberty lurk in insidious encroachment by men of zeal, well-meaning but without understanding." Louis D. Brandeis.

"The nation behaves well if it treats the natural resources as assets which it must turn over to the next generation increased, and not impaired, in value." Theodore Roosevelt.

"Our government conceived in freedom and purchased with blood can be preserved only by constant vigilance." William Jennings Bryan.

"Bring it on." Historians anxious to preserve the legacy of the 43rd President had insisted that he be represented in this hall. These were the three most famous syllables George W. Bush had uttered in his remarkable presidency.

"Mr. Raines."

I looked around and saw the young lady who had guided my tour in the Hall of Rights a few weeks ago. "Karen?"

"Yes. Thank you for remembering. It's good to see you again."

"Likewise," I lied. "I hope everything is going all right."

"Oh, yes. Thank you."

I starting walking away but had taken only a few steps

when she called after me. "Mr. Raines, might I and a couple of my colleagues buy you a cup of coffee?"

I turned around. "I don't know, for what purpose?"

"Well, during the tour you seemed frustrated, not only at the changes in the Bill of Rights but in the whole direction this country is taking. You had a general malaise that I'm not comfortable with, and I don't think I did a very good job of explaining why you shouldn't feel that way. I…we…I'd like another opportunity. Please?"

I began to see a certain poetic irony in the situation. It didn't seem to me that this meeting was coincidental. Karen was probably a spy for LaVelle and Chesterfield. One or more of her colleagues might be as well. Their real objective would be to assess my state of mind two days prior to the inauguration. It's unlikely they would know what their bosses planned to do, but they could report their observations, and LaVelle and Chesterfield would decide if I posed a danger to the implementation of their plan. I could use them for my own purposes. I could convince them that I was harmless, just a man who loved words and ideas but abhorred violence. Not only that, it would give me a chance to string the ideas I had for the speech together into some logical order.

"All right, Karen, I guess I can spare a few minutes."

Awkwardly silent, we walked to the public cafeteria, where three other twenty-something tour guides appeared magically without benefit of overt communication. Karen retrieved a cup of hot tea without asking me if I wanted anything, then explained that she and her friends were all members of Young Americans for Homeland Security. They were doing a year's internship in preparation for careers in the federal civil service. Paul, neatly groomed except for a pair of tennis shoes that had seen too much tennis, supplied me with a cup of coffee and sipped one himself, doctored with so much sugar I was surprised he didn't soar off his chair. Celia, all of about five foot two, wearing earrings so ostentatious I could barely look at them without laughing, preferred hot chocolate. I suspected immediately that she spent more time at the manicurist than in the library, a notion that was soon confirmed. Zachary, a tall blond who obviously hadn't heard about the depletion of the ozone layer and its consequent impact on the danger of being outside too much, downed a combination carrot and orange juice in about thirty seconds. When I remarked that he looked like a surfer, he confirmed it readily and said he grew up in California. "California or West California?" I ventured, and he shot me a look that would have disemboweled a charging gorilla. "California, of course." Evidently the hard feelings associated with Civil War II had not been extinguished on the West Coast.

"Well, Karen, I don't have much time. You said you wanted to talk?"

"Yes, and thank you for the opportunity." She gave me a smile worthy of a model in a toothpaste ad. "You are an important man, Mr. Raines, a respected journalist and friend of the President. I'm disappointed that you disapprove so vehemently of the progress this country has made over the last thirty years or so, and even more disappointed that I couldn't change your mind."

Unintentionally, I presumed, Karen had given herself away. I had said nothing during our tour of the Hall of Rights about being a friend of the President. She had been briefed.

Celia jumped in. "What exactly is it that you don't like, Mr. Raines?"

I tried not to be condescending, but I'm not sure I succeeded. "What is it you want me to like? War? Poverty? Civil liberties disappearing like they were chocolate covered strawberries at a summer picnic?"

"You're angry, aren't you?" Karen asked.

"I don't think the country is living up to its potential." She seemed disappointed in my reply. Probably in her first year of spy training, I guessed, and expecting her target to reveal secrets while the tea was still hot.

"It's the best country on the face of the earth. Always has been, always will be." Apparently history had not been Celia's best subject.

Paul was more rational. "Why don't you explain to us what you mean?"

"All right. Let's start this way. Has anyone here been involved in athletics?"

"Surfing is a sport," Zachary said, somewhat defensively. "Besides, I've also studied martial arts."

"I ran track in high school," Paul volunteered. "I did the 440 and the mile."

"Track provides a much clearer example," I said. "Paul, how did you know whether you ran a good race?"

He looked at me quizzically. "I either won or lost." Then, apparently giving some consideration to the possibility that I might be a moron, he added, "If I won, that was good. If I lost, that was bad."

"Okay. And how did the winner know whether he ran a good race?"

"I don't follow."

"Isn't it possible that the winner was simply better than his competitors on that particular day, but ran a poor race compared to what he was capable of? Even more to the point, could he really claim to be a good runner if his best time was considerably slower than the school record, or maybe the world record?"

"Yeah, man, like there are good waves, and there are great waves!" Zachary struck me immediately as contradictory. He had proposed a reasonably intelligent analogy, yet he spoke like an idiot.

"Yes, something like that," I explained. "There are standards against which we can measure our performance. It's true in athletics, in the working world, and in academia. So why shouldn't there be standards for how well our country is doing?"

Celia looked down at her nails, spotted an imperfection, and clicked her tongue. "That's silly. We have the finest, most powerful country on the face of the earth. Everybody knows that. What standards could there be?" I couldn't help wondering where they found her and why she had agreed to be a Washington, D.C. tour guide when she would obviously rather be polishing her nails. If she was CIA or FBI, they were either scraping the bottom of the barrel or recruiting recent graduates from acting school.

"Let me propose a few, and you see whether you agree. If you do, then we can talk about whether or not we're achieving them."

"Fair enough," Paul said. "Hey, this could be fun."

Karen gave Paul a look I couldn't immediately interpret, but I'm pretty sure it didn't indicate agreement. "Aren't we getting off track here? You visit government buildings the way bank robbers case their targets before they hold them up. I'd like to know why."

She was definitely a spy. But if Tyler and Chesterfield couldn't muster a higher caliber agent than Karen, I didn't have much to worry about. So there was no reason for me to bail out of the conversation. Besides, I liked the way my arguments were coming together—finally.

Paul came to my rescue. "Karen, why don't you give the man a chance to say what's on his mind?"

"All right," she said. "But I think we're wasting time."

"You're the one who invited me here," I reminded her. "If you don't want to continue, I can be on my way."

She backtracked hastily. "No, that's not what I mean. Please." I almost felt sorry for her.

"All right. We were talking about standards. Do you believe that every generation of Americans should leave the country better off for the next generation, or is it all right for the current generation to make a mess and let their children pick up the pieces?"

Karen seized on my terminology. "How do you define 'mess'? Isn't that a pretty ambiguous term to be throwing around in the context of a serious discussion about national policies?"

"Good for you, Karen, I agree. I used the term loosely to get the discussion rolling. How's this as a first approximation? Our children should enjoy the same standard of living we enjoy, or better. Their world should be at least as secure physically, or better. They should enjoy the same modern technology, the same health care, and the same pleasures of the natural world, or better."

"In other words, if my kids want to surf, they should be able to," Zachary chimed in.

"Among other things, yes," I said. "And will they?"

"Depends on the oil spills, dude, which way the wind is blowing, you know?"

Paul became thoughtful. "My parents told me they used to take vacations using their own personal car. They could go anywhere they wanted to and buy as much gasoline as they needed. I can't do that."

"And why can't you?" I prodded.

"There isn't enough gasoline."

"And why isn't there enough gasoline?"

"It pretty much got used up. The current supply is reserved mostly for the military and for civilian emergency vehicles."

"And why did it get used up?"

"I think you're going to tell us," Karen quipped.

"If you're interested, yes. Have you heard of automobile fuel efficiency standards?" Silence around the table gave me the answer I expected. "I guess not. Fifty years ago or so, vehicle manufacturers were required to produce cars that achieved certain mileage standards. But they wanted more immediate and larger profits, so they lobbied the government to exempt certain kinds of vehicles. Then, in 2019, they secured legislation that exempted *all* vehicles. Cars got bigger, profits soared, and gasoline supplies dwindled. Now practically everyone uses mass transportation, which although workable is hardly a step up the economic ladder. And everything made of plastic, which uses petroleum as a raw material, has gone up in price due to the shortage. Do you think that meets the standard of leaving the country better off for the next generation?" I thought I had made the point rather well.

Karen struggled. "One example doesn't prove anything."

I was just getting started. "Zachary, out there in California, do people like to go hiking? In the mountains, I mean. Yosemite, Sequoia, national forests, places like that?"

"Ain't too many forests left."

"My point exactly. Do you know that in generations past, people could go on long backpacks, or camp out on weekends, enjoying the natural beauty of forests that had never been cut by a logging company?"

"No way, dude. I mean, Mr. Raines."

"Yes way, dude." I hadn't used that word in over 30 years, but it felt natural, especially given the company I was keeping. "The government decided to let the timber companies cut down as many trees as they wanted. They even built roads on public land to help them do it. Now we've got twice as many people in the country as we had then, and half the recreational area for them to enjoy. How's that for watching out for the next generation?"

"Who wants to go hiking anyway?" Celia asked.

A logical question from a person who doesn't want to put her nails in jeopardy.

"All right, one more example, and then we'll move on to another standard. How good are our public schools today?" It was a rhetorical question. "Are the buildings modern? Are the teachers well qualified? Are there enough textbooks for all the students?"

"It depends what school you go to," Paul replied.

"Good point, Paul, and one we can return to later if time permits. What about the average school?"

"I'd have to say no, from what I've heard."

"And what have you heard?"

"It depends who you believe." I was starting to like Paul, even if he was a spy. He seemed to have a knack for intellectual analysis. "According to an article you wrote a few years ago, we can't afford them. Most of our taxes are going to pay off the national debt. There isn't enough for current services. Not just education, either. Public health clinics are just about non-existent. Foster parents are going unsupervised because we can't afford social workers. People with mental illness and developmental disabilities are roaming the streets." As an afterthought, he added, "At least, that's what you said in your article." Paul had apparently been briefed as well, and possibly in greater depth, taking advantage of his greater intellectual ability.

"That's exactly what I said. And the national debt is high because...?"

"I don't know the details. Apparently deficits became the rage in the early twenty-first century when President George W. Bush cut taxes on a trial basis, thinking it would help the economy. Then they were made permanent a few years later. When President Sassenbruger took office, he terminated the income tax by executive order. The country just kept borrowing. Civil War II put the country even deeper into debt, and the international community threatened to cut off our credit unless we started paying the money back. But by that time, we owed about a gazillion dollars, interest rates skyrocketed, and we went into financial shock."

I was about to compliment him on his analysis when Karen cut me off. "I need some more tea, Paul. Aren't you ready for another cup of coffee?" Her eyes indicated she strongly preferred an affirmative answer, and they both left the table. I engaged Celia and Zachary in small talk, watching Karen and Paul engage in an animated conversation in my peripheral vision.

When they returned, I continued. "You're doing very well for not knowing the details, Paul. You must have gone to some good schools."

"I'm lucky, my parents sent me to private schools."

"I'm happy for you. But let's get back to the point at hand. Is this an example of a generation of Americans looking out for the best interests of their children?"

Zachary looked at me vacantly. Karen and Paul exchanged glances but said nothing.

"It's all bullshit," Celia blurted out suddenly. "My family has a car, and we can afford all the gas we want. If we want to go hiking, we'll fly to some country that still has forests. Nobody in my family is a foster child, and if we need medical care, we just go see a doctor. And as for taxes, about the only thing we pay is sales tax."

"Well, thank you for a wonderful segue, Celia," I said. Zachary looked confused. "That's transition to you," I said, winking at Paul. "Celia has given us an opportunity to examine another standard. And that is whether the current gap between rich and poor in this country is a healthy state of affairs. Does it benefit the country? Is it fair?"

I hoped I'd be able to remember all this when it came time to commit the principles to the written page. I also hoped I'd be able to translate them from casual speech to more formal, more presidential, language.

"Rich people deserve what they have," Celia stated. "They worked for it, they earned it, and I don't see a problem with them keeping it. If poor people want to be rich, they should just work harder."

"So the reason people are poor is that they're lazy?"

Karen intervened. "They're not necessarily lazy, Mr. Raines. Sometimes they're just less talented, and it follows that their labor will be worth less. Do you believe in paying people more than they're worth, just to promote a more egalitarian society?"

"Good question, Karen." Paul's voice offered surprise and grudging respect.

"The simple answer is 'No,' " I replied, "but we are doing a disservice to the issue to leave the discussion on this superficial level. First of all, we have determined that Celia's family is wealthy. May I ask how this fortune was accumulated?"

"My grandfather started a technology company in the 1980s, and it was very successful. He owned 10 percent of the stock in the company when it went public, and my mother was the sole heir when he died."

"I see. And what does your father do for a living?"

"He doesn't work. He doesn't have to. I'm just doing this..."

she swept her head disdainfully around the room…"because they want me to. 'Real world experience,' they called it."

I hoped she was acting, although I had no evidence to support that hypothesis. Otherwise, she was a real bitch-in-waiting who would make some lovesick guy very unhappy one day. "So, correct me if I'm wrong. Your father is wealthy, without having to work, because his father-in-law was successful in business."

Celia crossed her arms defiantly but didn't respond. Paul accepted the facts not in dispute. "Sounds right to me," he offered on her behalf.

"Celia, don't get me wrong. I'm not implying there's anything wrong with that. But tell me, were any inheritance taxes paid on your grandfather's estate when he died?"

Celia looked up from her nails. "What's an inheritance tax?"

It suddenly occurred to me that, in a strange way, Devon's disabilities were blessings in disguise. He would never be subjected to the spin that passed for common political wisdom in most of the schools and the mainstream media. He needed no excuse not to understand essential elements of our national heritage.

"Through most of American history, wealth was taxed when it passed from one generation to another. A portion of the estate went to the government, to help provide the essential services that made it possible for people to accumulate wealth, and for the next generation to enjoy it. The tax was phased out beginning with the administration of George W. Bush, then eliminated altogether in 2016."

"And for good reason," Karen offered. "That money was taxed once when it was earned, and it was unfair to tax it again."

"Another specious argument advanced by people who dislike taxes," I countered, surprised at the vehemence I was allowing myself to express.

Paul turned to Zachary and said "That's 'false' to you, bro," then winked at me.

I winked back. "First of all," I continued, "we don't know for a fact that it was taxed the first time. Corporations have all kinds of legal loopholes that permit them to avoid paying taxes, even when they make a lot of money. But aside from that, money is frequently taxed more than once. In a few states, people still pay income tax. When they buy things using the money they keep, they pay sales tax. When they own real estate, they pay property taxes. When they pay people to provide goods or services to them, those people pay income, sales, and property taxes again on the money they earn. The important question is not how many times money is taxed. The question that should be asked is, 'How much money is legitimately needed to provide the services most people think are the appropriate responsibility of government, and given that amount, what is the fairest way of raising that revenue without destroying the incentive to work?'"

"I want to go back to an earlier point," Karen ventured. "You said that inheritance taxes went to the government to provide services that made wealth accumulation possible. Celia's grandfather was smart, ran his business successfully, and reaped his reward. I don't see that the government had anything to do with it."

"Well, let's ask Celia. Did your grandfather have an actual physical location where he ran his business?"

"Of course." She seemed slightly more engaged in the conversation, now that it revolved around her.

"Was this location used by homeless people to congregate? Did the employees feel free to burn it down if they had a disagreement with management? Could people use the goods and services of the company without paying the invoices when they arrived?"

"I wasn't there, obviously, but I suppose the answers are all 'No.' "

"And did the employees use public roads to get to work?"

"I guess so. What does that prove?"

"It proves that your grandfather was the beneficiary of an organized, stable society, guaranteed in effect by a capable government. His property was protected by the police. He was willing to engage in commerce because money had permanent value, not subject to the wild fluctuations common in countries with domestic discord and frequent revolution. And he could spend his money on things he considered valuable, useful, and enjoyable, because others received the same basic protections and were therefore willing to manufacture useful products."

Paul glanced at Karen and grinned at her slyly, apparently thinking I wouldn't detect the non-verbal cue. "In other words," he offered, "if government sanctioned by the people had not done its job, there would have been economic chaos. There might even have been political chaos, in which case money would probably have been worthless, because in a lawless society, the only things that count are power and immediate access to food and shelter."

"Exactly." Whatever game he was playing, it suited my purposes for the moment. "Have any of you heard of Oliver Wendell Holmes?"

Paul and Karen looked at each other vacantly. Zachary made a stab at it. "A detective of some sort?"

I couldn't help but smile. "Well, Zachary, your answer does show you've done some reading. But I'm not referring to the fictional detective *Sherlock* Holmes. The man I'm talking about served for thirty years on the U.S. Supreme Court, from 1902 to 1932."

"And what possible relevance could he have to this conversation?" Karen challenged.

"Quite a lot actually. He once referred to the act of paying taxes as 'purchasing civilization.' That's the point I'm trying to make. Maintaining a peaceful and organized society costs money, and the people who benefit should be willing to pay their fair share."

Paul countered. "We have a peaceful and organized society now, with minimal taxes. Your argument fails the reality test, I'm afraid."

"Actually it doesn't. The reason you think taxes are minimal is that wealthy people pay very little compared to their capacity. Working people carry the burden for the most part, in both obvious and subtle ways." Karen's face registered strong disagreement, and I decided to bring the issue to a head. "Is it, in fact, not a form of stealing to expect the benefits of a stable government without paying for them?"

"Stealing? *Stealing?*" Karen couldn't get her arms around the concept.

"Two people go into a restaurant. One has a bowl of soup. The other orders a fabulous six-course meal. Should they pay their own bill, or should they switch, so that the person who enjoys the full dinner pays for the soup, and vice-versa?"

"You've lost me," Paul confessed.

"We have two classes of society today, Paul, as distant from each other as they have ever been in the history of this country. Essentially, we have a wealthy class living a life of leisure, unless they choose to work, and another class living in poverty, without social services considered essential as recently as fifty years ago. Yet the poor pay a much higher percentage of their income and their assets in taxes than the wealthy. A good case can be made that the rich are stealing from the poor."

"All right," Paul admitted, looking a bit guilty and glancing at Karen sheepishly. "If that's true, and I don't necessarily agree that it is, then it would be slightly unfair."

"Slightly unfair, Paul? Some people live in gated enclaves, with homes averaging 4,000 square feet and more bathrooms than residents. Others are confined to Trickle Down Communities built on old hazardous waste sites, with a population density ten times that of the cities of the late twentieth century. Some people attend fine educational institutions, like you. Others go to schools starved of essential resources, fifty kids to the average classroom. Some people receive the finest medical care available, from skilled medical professionals, and have access to all the modern drugs. Others are lucky to be able to afford a nurse, and the only drugs they take are the ones available over-the-counter. How long can this last before people rise up in frustration and anger?"

Paul summarized. "So your point is, sooner or later the economic and political disparity we see today will cause people with nothing to lose to come knocking on the doors of the wealthy, with or without guns."

I leaned back in my chair, feeling triumphant. "That's it in a nutshell. History shows that it's inevitable."

Karen seized on the opportunity. "So you're a revolutionary?"

I thanked her silently for giving me the opportunity to implement my primary strategy. "Not at all, Karen. I am opposed to violence. I try to convince people with words and logic. And the logic leads us to the conclusion that this country is on the wrong path. The majority today see their interests as paying less in taxes, accumulating as much wealth for themselves as possible, and basically not giving a damn about what happens to the rest of the population. People with a slightly more enlightened view support social causes in which they have a personal interest, but it's not enough. If they could be convinced to view the world more strategically, they would see that such behaviors will eventually become dysfunctional, destroying the very society they intend to preserve."

"And has that time arrived, Mr. Raines? Are you preparing to destroy society as we know it?"

It was pretty blatant, but I admired her for asking the question directly. I could see her "spy evaluation" now: "Has potential. Deeply committed to the cause but lacking in subtlety. Recommend further coursework in the use of nuance."

"Not at all, Karen. We're engaged in debate here, an exchange of words and ideas—not bullets. What I'm saying is, we have one last chance, and it goes by the name of leadership. That's why the Presidency has been called the 'bully pulpit.' People hang on every word the President says. He has the power to bring out the best in people or the worst in people. I know this is ancient history for all of you, but I think of Abraham Lincoln, Franklin Roosevelt, Winston Churchill, Martin Luther King Jr. People who inspired their natural constituency to the highest possible calling, whether it was war against tyranny or war against discrimination. The only thing this administration and most of its immediate predecessors have declared war on is the Bill of Rights."

"Ah, full circle at last." Karen sighed.

I glanced at my watch. "And just in time. I really should be going." Then, to my own surprise, I added, "I've enjoyed this. I wish you all the best of luck." Spies or not, they were all people.

Karen had one final question. "I admit you made some good points, Mr. Raines. But where did you get all this from? I've never heard anyone talk about this stuff before. Did you just make it up out of your head?" Confirming my earlier suspicion, I concluded that Karen's training had skipped over the more esoteric aspects of my background and my columns. *Roland Raines light*, I thought.

"Actually, Karen, I didn't. A great deal of it comes from a famous American historical document. Would you mind if I quote it to you?"

"If you have time."

"For this, I have time. Here it is: 'WE THE PEOPLE of the United States, in order to form a more perfect Union, establish Justice, insure domestic Tranquility, provide for the common Defense, promote the general Welfare, and secure the Blessings of Liberty to ourselves and our posterity, do ordain and establish this CONSTITUTION for the United States of America.' Have any of you heard that before?"

Nobody had.

***

I got home about six o'clock, hoping dinner would be on the table. I was tired and hungry from all the walking. My conversation with Karen and her friends had drained me emotionally, although I retained some lingering satisfaction from being able to put together some reasonably powerful arguments. The house was silent, and I found a note on the kitchen table.

> *Honey, bad news! Matthew has disappeared. I took Devon over early this afternoon and found his house ransacked. I don't understand what is happening. Clearly something has been eating at you, something massive and important. Whatever it is you are involved in, it is destroying our lives. I have the feeling you would have told me if you could, yet I can't imagine what it is that you can't tell me. Unless...*

I am choosing to believe that you wouldn't let that happen again. It wouldn't explain Matthew's disappearance, and if I'm being followed, it wouldn't explain that either. But I am left with lots of questions and no answers. I'm afraid. Devon and I are going away, somewhere I hope we will be safe.

Honey, please understand that I trust you. But I can't live any more with this uncertainty and sense of helplessness. Please take care of yourself. When I have figured out what to do, I'll contact you.

I love you. Alycia.

I read the note four times, then sat down at the table and cried. I tried to get up ten minutes later and collapsed in tears again. Then a feeling started to come over me, starting in my chest, and extending eventually from my head to my toes. I would do this thing. There was no longer anything to lose.

CHAPTER TWELVE

Saturday, January 19
One day before President Hamilton's second Inauguration, I got up about six o'clock in the morning and went straight to my laptop, where I composed the piece that I had been struggling with in my head for more than a month. The previous day's conversation with the young spies had actually been helpful. I finished about one in the afternoon, following several hours of careful editing. Then I drafted a separate document: a brief description of Operation Capitol Hill.

From that time on, I never let the laptop leave my sight, nor did I get on-line. I printed four copies of each document and inserted them into separate envelopes marked "Personal and Confidential." One I addressed to Sid at the *Washington Independent*, another to the Editor-in-Chief at the French newspaper *Le Monde*, the third to the Ambassador from Canada, and the last one to Ed Martin.

I fixed myself a late lunch and felt more lonely and depressed with every bite. Then I packed a small overnight suitcase and gave the tiny bungalow one last look before walking out, checking about three times to be sure I had my ID, my press pass, the laptop, and the four envelopes, as well as my suitcase.

On the way to the train station, I entered the post office, finding Ed Martin behind the counter as always.

"Have a few things to mail, Ed," I said as nonchalantly as I could under the circumstances.

"Sure thing, Roland."

"Could you overnight these for me?"

"Wow, important business, huh?" he remarked, weighing the envelope addressed to *Le Monde*.

"Yeah, kinda. They all weigh the same."

"I'll take your word for it. But don't think that means I'm gonna believe you have a straight flush next time you bet a hundred dollars." I laughed. "Hey, this one's addressed to me."

"Yes, it is. Put postage on it anyway. I want it to be officially mailed."

He looked at me as though I had just bet a million dollars on the chance of drawing an inside straight. "I've always known you were kinda wacko, Roland, but this one takes the cake. What gives?"

I gave him the most somber look I could muster. "Ed, this is no poker game. This is serious business. Do me a favor will you? Make sure these other envelopes get out of here safely. And don't read yours until tomorrow afternoon. Lock it up somewhere."

He shook his head from side to side grudgingly, clearly wondering when and why I had taken complete leave of my senses. "Whatever you say, Roland. It must be important if you're willing to pay two hundred dollars for it."

"Trust me, it's worth that and more." I pulled four fifties out of my pocket and walked out, leaving him with a puzzled look on his face.

I walked rapidly to the station a block away. The 5:50 to Washington, D.C. was right on time. Stepping onto the train, my shoe squeaking against the sterile indestructible metal platform, I couldn't help thinking about that famous quote from Neil Armstrong: "That's one small step for man, one giant leap for mankind." That's the way I felt. I just happened to be the man history tapped on the shoulder this time when an extraordinary act was called for, an act that would reverberate around the world—if it succeeded.

I had played every detail of the plan in my head a thousand times. The only question mark was whether the beam from the laptop would be strong enough to activate the sensor on the President's podium, but I had no way of determining that in advance. Consequently, my mind wandered, and I found myself looking out the window. The full moon hung over the eastern horizon, providing just enough light to make out the deserted highway, the overgrown shoulders, and the rusted speed limit signs long since robbed of their original purpose. As the train hurtled down the median, propelled magnetically at 150 miles per hour, I remembered clearly the ceremony that had closed what used to be known as US Highway 91, attended by almost every prominent politician within a two-hundred-mile radius. "A watershed in the history of environmental protection," the Governor of Maryland had pronounced. "Clear evidence that the government is concerned with saving lives," Vice President Hal E. Burton had intoned, implying that he personally was responsible for the decrease that would occur in the number of automobile accidents. The truth was, residents of TDCs were simply not allowed to drive anymore; there wasn't enough gasoline to go around.

Did the man in the moon look sad, or was it just my imagination? There wasn't any question that *I* was sad. I had just been through an entire day without seeing my wife and my son—and I had no idea when I would see them again. My focus returned to the task at hand. I patted the seat of my pants to ensure that I had my wallet. I did. I resisted the urge to take it out and verify that my photo ID was in it. It would be. That ID and my Federal Press Pass would get me through security. The laptop would be examined thoroughly, but it would pass, just as it always did.

Softly, but with authority, the OmniScreen embedded in the seatback in front of me reported the news, with the headlines scrolling across the bottom. **"Pope Pius XIV to provide invocation at Inauguration."** That's not really news, I thought; pictures of the Pope leaving Rome two days before had been played incessantly. Clearly this Inauguration would be wrapped in the Bible as well as the Flag. **"Beef production decreases in Alaska; temperatures soar to unprecedented levels…Secretary of the Interior denies global warming responsible."** Nothing new there either. Global warming or not, I hadn't had a hamburger in seven years. Not that I didn't like beef; but who can spend a week's salary on one meal? **"Switzerland suspected of manufacturing weapons of mass destruction and training terrorists…Imminent threat forces national security to remain at highest possible level…Attorney General orders all citizens with Swiss heritage to report to FBI for questioning."** Last year it had been Iceland. **"NFL considers Los Angeles for expansion team. Only two potential sites remain under consideration."** Now *that's* news. Just last week it looked like negotiations had stalled again.

The train slowed as it approached the station. I thought I detected an increase in the anxiety level of the passengers as they gathered their briefcases and purses and prepared to disembark. Did they dread the increased security that always gripped Washington during the Inauguration as much as I did? Maybe I was just projecting my own feelings onto them. I grabbed the laptop and my small suitcase, checked again to see that the Press Pass was hung around my neck, and waited for a lady with short brown hair to get off. We both headed toward the main station.

A new checkpoint had been added, just inside the gate. "I'll need to inspect your suitcase," a grim-faced guard said. When he found only a change of clothes and a few toiletries, he closed it and handed it back to me.

"And what is that?" He nodded toward the computer case, his hand hovering just above his service revolver.

"I'm a reporter. I'm allowed to carry my own laptop and mini-monitor."

He considered this at length. Apparently the subject had not come up in his training program. "Is that a fact? Something wrong with the public kiosks?"

"No, nothing at all. Sometimes I have to work in places where there aren't any."

"Turn it on, please." He motioned toward a counter-top at his work station.

Sweat poured from my armpits. The guard had the authority to confiscate the computer on the spot if he suspected anything unusual, and I had no back-up plan.

I removed the CPU from the small pocket, then unfolded the keyboard. The CPU slid easily into the slot provided and snapped into place as the connectors matched up. The "Active" arrow lit up green. I looked at the guard. "Okay?"

"Let's see the monitor."

Just my luck, I had to get someone who was obsessively thorough. *Please, let him not want to see every single document.* My fingers trembled slightly as I pulled the monitor out and set it up just beyond the keyboard, ensuring that the wireless receiver was positioned correctly. In a matter of seconds it displayed the customary greeting: Welcome to Windows 2040.

"All right," the guard said. "You can turn it off."

I clicked on "Start," then "Shut Down," but the logo only blinked. After a few seconds, a message came up: "You have performed an illegal operation." I just about wet my pants.

"Damn thing," I managed through gritted teeth.

To my relief, the guard laughed. "Happens to me all the time. Go ahead."

I replaced the laptop in the case and silently prayed that it would get through the next 24 hours without crashing. After that, it wouldn't matter. I had walked about three steps when the guard called out again. I don't think he saw the "Oh, shit!" form on my lips.

"You covering the Inauguration?" he asked.

"Yes, I am. The President and I have been friends since high school. He personally invited me to attend."

The guard closed the distance between us ominously and eyed my press pass. "What's this mean, 'Zone 1 permitted'?" he asked.

"It means I can get as close to the President as I want. The Secret Service knows me well, and they trust me."

"Well, lucky you. So I guess you voted for the guy?"

"I'm just a reporter, I don't discuss my personal points of view." Of course I did, under the right circumstances, but this was neither the time nor the place.

"All right. Carry on."

I turned and walked away, deliberately adopting what I hoped would appear to be a normal gait. I wanted to run like hell.

I felt better once I was clear of the station. Despite the presence of military jeeps at most of the intersections, manned by Marines with bayonets fixed, my heartbeat returned to a rhythm resembling normal. I didn't like the idea of having to walk the fourteen or so blocks from the station to the hotel, especially in the dark, but a taxi would have been prohibitive.

Compared to the train station, security at the hotel was

routine, almost indifferent. The guard glanced at my press pass and waved me through.

"Hello again, Mr. Raines. I have your reservation." I was surprised that the registration clerk remembered me but figured he just had an especially good memory. "How was your stay on New Year's Eve?"

"We enjoyed it, thank you."

"I'll have to ask you for your ID again. I'm sorry."

"It's not a problem."

He swiped it, then handed me a key card. "Have you seen the Mall tonight? The Washington Monument is lit up splendidly."

"No, I came directly from the train station." My intention had been to go directly to my room.

"It's really spectacular, Mr. Raines." He glanced at the clock behind the counter. "And fireworks are scheduled in about fifteen minutes."

"I'm sure it would be worth seeing. I'm a little tired, though."

"Well, you really shouldn't miss it." I looked at him skeptically, wondering why it seemed so important to him that I go. "I'll have your things taken up to your room, and they'll be waiting for you when you get back." Before I could reply, he struck a bell sitting on the counter, and a man in uniform appeared. "Would you take Mr. Raines' things up to Room 843?"

The suitcase was practically removed from my hand by force. I surrendered it in order to hold onto the laptop, a far more important item. "I'll keep this with me."

"If you wish, sir," he answered brusquely. I began to feel as if I were being assaulted.

"I *do* wish." Reconciling myself to a quick trip to the Mall and promising myself an early bedtime, I walked toward the exit, noticing along the way someone who reminded me of Karen, the tour guide at the Capitol. I only saw the back of her head, though. It probably wasn't her, I decided, and if it is, I don't want to talk to her anyway. I headed straight for the Mall. Six blocks away, I approached the Lincoln Memorial, beautifully and tactfully lit. The view from the top of the stairs at night would be stunning, I thought; it would require only a few extra minutes to take in the impressive sight of the Washington Monument and the Capitol, lined up almost perfectly.

Once I got to the top, I was drawn out of habit to the sides of the Memorial, where the words of Lincoln's Second Inaugural Address were inscribed. *"Fondly do we hope—fervently do we pray—that this mighty scourge of war may speedily pass away,"* I read out loud.

"With malice toward none; with charity for all," a nearby voice added, coming closer to me during the recitation.

"Paul! What a coincidence." First Karen, then Paul? Was this really a coincidence?

"Indeed. Isn't this magnificent?" He continued reading. *"With firmness in the right, as God gives us to see the right."* He hesitated. "I suppose you know it by heart."

"Parts of it, yes. *'Let us strive on to finish the work we are in; to bind up the nation's wounds; to care for him who shall have borne the battle, and for his widow, and his orphan—to do all which may achieve and cherish a just, and a lasting peace, among ourselves, and with all nations.'* I believe it's his best speech."

"I've heard some people say that." He sounded distracted, unprepared to engage in the kind of discussion I knew he was capable of having.

"You don't agree?"

"I haven't studied it enough to offer an opinion."

"I see. Well, I certainly didn't expect to bump into you again. I enjoyed our little chat in the Capitol cafeteria."

"It was very instructive." He looked away momentarily, then met my eyes, and I sensed something burning brightly within. "I wonder whether you'd want to visit the Jefferson Memorial with me. I haven't seen that one in a long time."

The Jefferson was actually my favorite, not extravagant in size, but inscribed with words I considered to be both powerful and prescient: *"I have sworn upon the altar of God eternal hostility toward any form of tyranny over the mind of man."* I probably would have wandered in that direction anyway. "All right, why not?"

He seemed relieved.

Just as we turned around and started walking down the steps, a fireworks display started, originating at the base of the Washington Monument. The sky lit up in a brilliant tribute to the Inauguration, with bright flashes of light bursting even higher than the tip of the giant obelisk. We paused and watched. It was gorgeous. The noise made conversation difficult. We walked silently down the massive stairs, bearing right toward the eastern edge of the Tidal Basin where the Jefferson Memorial was located.

We were about two hundred yards away when I noticed something wrong; the Memorial wasn't lit. Fifty yards away, I saw military vehicles parked in the semi-circular driveway. Twenty yards away, the light from the fireworks display had diminished considerably, but it was possible to see from the glow of the moon that a barbed wire fence was being erected around the entire structure. A gigantic crane with a wrecking ball dangling from a long cable loomed ghostlike above the horizon. "We'd better go back," I said. "It's pretty clear someone doesn't want visitors tonight."

"It's okay, let's investigate," Paul urged.

I stopped. "I think I'll go back to the hotel."

"No, I insist." His voice changed completely, acquiring a

steely authoritative tone, and I felt a gun barrel in my back. "Just keep walking, around to the back, up to the water's edge." *Oh fuck! Why didn't I just go straight to my room?* Not having much choice, I did as he instructed. "Wade in ankle deep and turn around."

I complied, while my mind raced uncontrollably. "Paul, have you gone completely loony? What the hell is going on here?"

He stayed on dry ground, standing about five feet away. "Well, Mr. Raines, what's going on here is that we are getting ready to dismantle the Jefferson Memorial. And you are getting ready to abandon whatever little plan you have in mind to turn this inauguration into either a circus or a disaster."

I cursed myself for believing that I had been successful in convincing the spies at the Capitol that I was harmless. "I have no such plan. And what's the problem with the Jefferson Memorial?"

"Jefferson has been overrated as a statesman. He deserves a lesser place in history, and this memorial is no longer appropriate."

My brain began to settle down, clicking into survival mode. I figured my chances improved the longer we talked. The fireworks provided natural camouflage for a gunshot. Maybe I could engage him in conversation long enough for them to finish the show. Then I would come up with another plan. "Jefferson? Overrated? He wrote the Declaration of Independence! He was our third President, and one of the smartest we've ever had. He was a champion of free speech, pardoning the people who were convicted under the Sedition Act of 1798 that made criticizing the government a crime. He was one of the prime supporters of the Bill of Rights!" I quickly corrected myself. "The *original* Bill of Rights."

"Precisely. And did you know that Jefferson came very close to being a traitor to our country?"

"Really?" So far, so good.

"He advocated overthrow of the government he helped create. He encouraged people to rebel."

I knew what he was referring to from my reading at the Library of Congress. "Are you talking about his letter to James Madison? *'A little rebellion now and then is a good thing.'* I hardly think that qualifies him as a traitor."

"It is being quoted today as justification for criticizing the current administration."

"And you don't think Jefferson would have approved of criticizing the administration?"

"Maybe he would have. That's why he's overrated."

Despite the fact that my life depended on it, I couldn't think of a suitable reply. "Please don't kill me" were the only words that reached my lips, but it didn't appear they would find a receptive audience.

Then, suddenly, a tall figure streaked toward Paul from behind, pulling both his ankles backward simultaneously and knocking him face down onto the ground. His arms moved instinctively to brace the fall, and the gun discharged, but the bullet hit the ground harmlessly. Paul started scrambling to his feet. He had barely gotten onto his hands and knees when the person behind him unleashed a powerful snap-kick to his groin; the curved part of his ankle, just above his foot, caught Paul squarely, practically lifting him off the ground. Paul doubled over in agony. A follow-up kick to his ribs rolled him over onto his back. After a sidekick to his face and a vicious stomp on his ankle, Paul curled up into a little ball and tried to rock the pain away.

If I'd had any sense at all, I would have used the few brief seconds of respite to run like hell, or at least step out of the Tidal

Basin onto firm ground. Instead, I just stood there, mesmerized. It was like a scene out of movie, only the pain was clearly real.

"You never know when a little Kung Fu will come in handy."

"Zachary!"

"Are you all right, Mr. Raines? That was a close one."

"What the hell is going on here?"

Zachary glanced over his shoulder. The memorial stood between us and the soldiers. "Paul and Karen are working for Gus LaVelle. Celia and I are Secret Service trainees, pretending to work for LaVelle. We were instructed to watch out for you." The surfer dialect had disappeared.

I stepped forward out of the water, finally. "I don't get it. Why did you both act so dumb?"

"The less the opposition knows about you, the better." Paul groaned loudly and started to move. Zachary gave him a pathetic, condescending look that would have wilted a 250-pound wrestler. "Move one more inch and you get it in the balls again." Paul curled up again meekly. "You need to go directly to your hotel room now. Triple lock the door and don't let anyone in, unless you hear two knocks, followed by a pause, followed by two more knocks. That will be Celia. She won't bother you unless it's absolutely necessary. I'll take care of this guy and make sure he stays out of commission a few days."

My feet didn't move.

"Go!" Zachary's forceful command cut through my confusion, and I half walked, half ran, back to the hotel. Celia was seated in the lobby and looked up briefly as I passed, giving me the slightest possible nod of her head.

I took the elevator to the eighth floor, found Room 843, and pressed the palm of my left hand onto the key plate on the door. Nothing happened. My heart began to pound. I knew that the signal was being sent to the Homeland Security PalmPrint Database. Had LaVelle revoked my clearance? Were the computers overloaded? If entry was denied, I'd be answering questions from the house detectives all night, or worse. My brain flashed on what had happened two years ago to one of my colleagues when a faulty transmitter had sent incorrect information from the door at a fast food restaurant. He was half-way through his VOX Fries when a swat team arrived, arrested him, charged him with Conduct Unbecoming an American Citizen, and interrogated him for three days. Fortunately, the error was eventually traced to a transistor manufactured in Iraq, where quality control had not yet achieved desired standards.

Finally, a small green LED came on and I heard the door lock click. I walked in, expecting the lights to come on automatically as usual. For a split second the room remained pitch black, and I held my breath. *Oh please, maybe the circuits are just overloaded because of the Inauguration!* The OmniScreen switched on, and a couple of cheap-looking directional lamps pointed toward the ceiling bathed the entire room in indirect light. I exhaled. Then it dawned on me: LaVelle hadn't bothered to revoke my clearance. He thought I would be dead.

I secured every lock on the door and placed a chair under the knob for good measure. I didn't know if it would keep anyone out, but at least I'd hear them coming. The room was merely functional: a single dresser, topped by a small mirror; a desk outfitted with a high-speed computer connector; and an end table with a telephone. The lack of luxury didn't bother me, considering the alternative I had just narrowly escaped.

I set the laptop on top of the desk, stepped out of my wet shoes and socks, hung up my clothes for the next day, and flopped onto the bed. "News, volume up" I said to the Omni-

Screen, which sprang to life. Just my luck; I had arrived in time to catch Shrill O'Malley.

"Tonight, on the eve of this historic Inauguration, I am pleased to have the opportunity to interview two of this nation's most prominent political figures—the minority leader of the United States Senate and the Secretary of Defense.

"Welcome, Senator Bell. Thanks for being on the show. Now, I know you worked against the re-election of President Hamilton, but 62% of the electorate voted for him. Why do you think the people have so seriously repudiated your position?"

"Actually it was 52%, but…"

"Senator, you can quibble about a few percentage points if you want to, but the fact is that the vast majority of the American people don't give a rat's ass for your position on the important issues of the day. How do you even justify earning your large income at taxpayer expense?"

I couldn't help wondering where Shrill had earned his journalism degree—if he had one at all. He had certainly read an entirely different set of textbooks than I had.

"The constitution…"

"Well, that raises an intriguing question," Shrill interrupted. "During the last twenty-five years, we've seen a number of amendments to that document, with excellent results. You have opposed all of them. I'm amazed you don't just quit and go back to your small-town hardware store and sell deadbolts to little old ladies too timid to protect their homes by buying a gun."

"Actually, it's thirty-two years. But I'm offended by…"

"Well, of course you are, you've been offended by the truth during your entire career. This country is marching forward, and you and your little band of malcontents are doing your level best to drag the political process through the mud at every conceivable opportunity."

"Are you going to let me...?"

"You're not going to use this program to spread your vindictive hatred toward everything that's American. You have the floor of the Senate to do that. Since you've abused that privilege, the American people will take it away from you, one way or the other. In my humble opinion, this country would be much better off without Congress debating every single expenditure the President wants and delaying implementation of his domestic and foreign policies."

"That's the purpose..."

"No, your time is past, Senator. And speaking of time, we have to move into the next segment of this program. Thanks for coming in. By the way, I'm glad your wife was found safe and sound."

I was glad I hadn't eaten dinner.

"Now I'm pleased to have as my second guest the Secretary of Defense. Thanks for being on my show. You must be terribly excited on the eve of this historic Inauguration."

"Definitely, Shrill, it's a great day for America."

"Indeed, who isn't thrilled by the re-election of this president! There is a palpable sense of excitement pervading the entire nation, especially here in Washington, D.C. Tell me, Mr. Secretary, do you know which Inaugural party the President will go to first? I can't tell you how many people have asked."

Talk about a softball question—that one floated up to the plate fat as a grapefruit.

"I'm not really certain. Besides, even if I knew I couldn't tell you for security reasons."

"Well, I think the Canadian Party would be the right one

to start with. We don't want to lose the one ally we have left in the world, now, do we? Oh, you know I'm joking. But seriously, there have been rumors of some unusual activity around Secret Service Headquarters. Can you tell us anything about that?"

"Security is tight, and the Swiss Embassy has been evacuated. That's all I can tell you."

"Well, of course it has. This president would never allow any terrorist activity to interrupt such an historic event. Tell me, is it true that a total travel ban has been imposed into and out of the states of Massachusetts, Minnesota, and Western California?"

The Secretary looked uncomfortable. "I can neither confirm nor deny."

"I'm sorry, I didn't intend to put you on the spot, Mr. Secretary. Please forgive me. Just one more question, if I may. Do you have any idea what the President will say in his Inaugural Address?"

"Yes, I've seen a draft. I don't want to steal his thunder, but it's fair to say he will continue to promote the policies that have made his first term so successful."

Like hell he will, I thought.

"I'm sure it will be inspiring, like all of his speeches have been throughout his splendid career as a public servant. Well, we're just about out of time. I hope you'll be a frequent guest on this show during the next four years."

"It would be my pleasure."

"You know, the backbone of any democracy is a highly educated electorate. We here at VOX News feel like we are doing our fair share of bringing Americans a balanced information diet that results in a stronger and more unified nation."

"Indeed you are. We are fortunate to have talented journalists like yourself adding to our security by ensuring that our citizens know what's going on in the world."

"Well, thank you. Now, ladies and gentlemen, we present today's 'All-American Question,' the series we started four months ago that measures the opinions of community leaders like yourselves and uses the results to formulate public policy. What could be more democratic than that? Today's question is 'Given the fact that a few members of Congress continue to obstruct the President's international and domestic agenda by offering public criticism, thereby giving aid and comfort to our enemies at home and abroad while brave American military personnel are losing their lives in the Wars for Freedom, should we continue to permit the minority to make deceptive and despicable statements on the floor of the House and the Senate that are immune from legal censure and disciplinary action, as provided for in Section 6 of Article I of the Constitution?' If you've purchased a VOXBox and attached it to your OmniScreen, please vote now. We'll be back with the right answer immediately following this commercial break."

I decided to end the misery by getting to sleep early. Tomorrow would be a long day. I pulled the shade on the single window down as far as it would go, knowing that an inch of access to the outside world would remain. It was the law; you weren't permitted to shut yourself off completely. Whether the authorities actually used this narrow "privacy gap" (my term, one I never used in public) to spy on people, or whether it was merely symbolic, I really didn't know. What I did know is that the breach permitted enough light, filtered by the blowing leaves of a climate-confused tree, to cast shadows on the ceiling. I flopped into bed, feeling lucky to be alive, yet dreading my uncertain future.

Two hours later, I turned onto my back again, trying to find a relaxing position. But nothing I did ended the relentless procession of images that left me doubting the wisdom of my mission. Searching for meaning and insight in a world that seemed more confused by the absence of Alycia's warm body and caring embrace, temporarily overwhelmed by the enormity of my mission, my mind leapt off the bed and intertwined itself with the whispers of the leaves on the murky ceiling. The long line in her forehead suddenly detached, and I watched in amazement as it reconfigured itself into the face of her mother, a woman whose caring smile magically dissolved even the most intense depression. She had lived with us the last three years of her abbreviated life, unable to afford nursing care after an untreated flu damaged her brain. These two incredible women, Alycia and her mother, had loved each other the way people do in the movies—unabashedly, boldly hugging at the oddest moments, bereft of secrets. If my wife was bitter that no doctor had been available in her mother's TDC to prevent this avoidable tragedy, she said nothing to me. But the line in her forehead formed shortly thereafter and never went away.

Now the small wrinkles in the corners of Alycia's mouth floated off independently, and an outline of Devon's face appeared on the ceiling. I loved this boy. Challenged by demons not of his own choosing that had ravaged his brain and stunted his growth, he persisted in the pursuit of happiness far beyond the capacity of others who considered themselves more fortunate.

Get a grip, I told myself, and the faces disappeared. But I started to cry. How can I leave these people, my family, the people I depend on to give my life meaning? What will they do, how will they feel, if I don't come home? Will I really be making their lives better if I go through with this? I don't know, I just don't know. I'll decide in the morning.

CHAPTER THIRTEEN

Sunday, January 20. Inauguration Day
About seven o'clock, I reached over and turned off the alarm clock, set for eight, and gave in to my racing neurons. After a quick shower, I dressed, then glanced in the mirror. Despite the lack of rest, excitement stared back at me. I hung the press pass around my neck, checked my wallet for the photo ID, picked up the laptop, and walked into the hallway, leaving yesterday's clothes and the suitcase behind. It had taken me an hour to get ready. Four hours to go.

I picked up a newspaper on the way to the hotel restaurant. The front-page stories, like the eggs, were bland and lifeless, as if the cook and the editor had conspired to tranquilize my senses with uniformity and convention. I turned to the sports section: **Off-season Trade Makes Cubs a Contender.** In their perennial search for a World Series berth, the team from the Windy City had just agreed to pay $300 million to a pitcher with a 105 mile per hour fastball. At that speed, he could only throw twenty or so pitches, but, according to the manager, "having a closer in the bullpen will bring us the championship we so richly deserve."

Sipping a cup of coffee, I settled into the "National Affairs" section. It was devoted mostly to Jadon Hamilton and his second inauguration. Nestled close to the bottom of page two, I noticed a brief article about some protesters in Boston who had taken a small ship into the harbor the previous day and thrown copies of the revised 4th amendment to the Constitution into the bay. This was all the Secretary of Homeland Security needed to declare a State of Emergency under Section 3 of Patriot Act VI, forbidding protests nation-wide until after the swearing-in. An eight p.m. curfew was imposed in every state except Montana, where people generally didn't stay up that late anyway, and violators were carted off to whereabouts unknown to be interrogated. "I take my job as head of the Inter-agency Task Force on Prevention of Domestic Terrorism very serious," the Secretary was quoted as saying. "If anybody thinks they can disrupt the peace in Washington, D.C., he had better think again." I belched, not certain whether it was elicited by the bad grammar or the bitter coffee.

Page three featured the winner of the National High School Conformist of the Month Award. Under the picture of a young man from Mississippi dressed in a white shirt, a red tie, and a blue suit, flanked by his proud parents, the caption read, "I can't honestly recall any original idea I've had during my entire high school career. I just believe whatever I'm told." The article went on to explain that this youngster would be eligible at the end of the year, along with the other monthly awardees, to compete for a full four-year scholarship to Bob Jones University.

Also on page three, below the fold, an article on the 21st National High School Essay Contest caught my eye. Entries were limited to 150 words, which recent research demonstrated equaled or exceeded the average American's tolerance for serious reading. Each essay had to address the general topic "America: the last quarter century." Judging the contest were Professor Jon Ashcraft from the University of Missouri, Tim Delaid, Lieutenant Governor of Texas, and Phil Wulfuwitz, Acting Governor of Iraq. Third place went to an entry entitled "Drawing Congressional Districts in Texas Using Scientific Method." Second place went to "Bill of Rights…or Bill of Wrongs?" The grand prize, earning the proud winner a summer internship at the George W.

Bush Presidential Library in Crawford, Texas, was entitled "Why Dissent is Unpatriotic." President Hamilton smiled broadly for the photograph with the three top contestants, who had been invited to the White House to receive their awards.

Page four was dominated by an in-depth interview with the Vice President, in question and answer format.

> "Starting first with an international issue, what do you think the repercussions will be of the United Nations voting to move its headquarters to Brussels?"
>
> "I really don't think it matters a great deal. If the European Union wants the damn thing, they can have it. That real estate will be worth a fortune to some lucky developer."
>
> "Mr. Vice President, moving into domestic affairs, I'm told that many public schools in the Trickle Down Communities are closing their doors for lack of funding. Does it bother you at all that people living in the TDC's won't be able to get a basic education?"
>
> "First of all, I wish you'd use the official name for these places. You know as well as I do that they are designated by the legislation that created them as 'Temporarily Disenfranchised Communities.' Nobody wants American citizens to live in these conditions permanently. We just need a little more time for the tax cuts to strengthen the economy. It would probably happen a lot sooner if the vocal minority would stop throwing political jabs at the Administration and just spend their money like they're supposed to so the corporations could create more jobs.
>
> "Secondly, I disagree with your assumption that the closing of the public schools prevents people from get-

ting an education. These people can be home-schooled. There's no reason to keep those expensive buildings open, especially when the local school boards insist on air-conditioning them. The kids need to learn not to let 120-degree temperatures affect their ability to study."

"Sir, if I may, a few people reading this article might wonder why it's so important for federal government offices to be air-conditioned if we don't have enough energy to provide it for our children."

"First of all, let's present the whole truth. The constant liberal media spin on the news grates on my nerves. Only sixty percent of the children in this country attend schools that aren't air-conditioned. The other forty percent—that's almost a majority, you know—enter modern temperature-controlled buildings, and every student has a set of textbooks, a desk, and a touchscreen. Secondly, comparing the importance of our federal workforce to children living in TDC's is a little far-fetched, don't you think? The mission of federal employees is nothing short of the preservation of our way of life for future generations, and we need resources to do that."

"By 'resources,' do you mean taxes?"

"No, of course not. We're borrowing the money. Our national debt is only 38% of gross domestic product, easily within the capacity of our economy to handle."

"Mr. Vice President, regarding this country's chronic shortage of energy, do you think if we had been more prudent a couple of generations ago we could have avoided this crisis? Why was it necessary to consume our limited supply of fossil fuels so rapidly, and why did we not develop alternative sources of energy sooner?"

"You're missing the point entirely here. There's still enough energy for the people who can afford it. It's the law of supply and demand, a basic principle of economics. Besides, drilling for oil provided jobs for hard-working Americans, and they used the income to support their hard-working American families. What could be wrong with that?"

"Mr. Vice President, I have heard that some Congressional leaders are worried about the mounting debt. They want to re-institute the income tax."

"Over my dead body. The President stated his opposition to the income tax very strongly in his speech to the Young Americans for Homeland Security in Topeka last summer. I don't know if I should say this, but those Congressional so-called leaders had better get their act together or they may find themselves to be irrelevant in a few years."

"What exactly are you implying, sir?"

"I'm not implying anything. I'm just saying that the decisions that need to be made by this government are too important to be left to a group of people who troop in here every year from hundreds or thousands of miles away without the foggiest notion of what's really good for this country. Their debates, especially in regard to international affairs, prevent us from presenting a unified front to terrorists, who are motivated by this internal dissension and consequently implement even more heinous acts. The President feels that we need patriotism, not pandemonium."

"Sir, along this line, you and the Attorney General have both been exceptionally critical of Congress the last few months, even though your party is in control of both houses. Do you not think, even though you disagree with what the minority members have to say, that it serves a useful purpose to have a spirited debate over the critical issues facing our country?"

"I thought we settled that when we modified the First Amendment. Of course there's a place for dissent, but not public dissent. People can think anything they want, but openly criticizing the policies of our government provides aid and comfort to our enemies, of whom we have many. Congress merely provides a soapbox for loudmouth liberals from the states that lost Civil War II to harass the legitimately elected government of the United States. We'd have them shot in the public squares of their own districts if not for Section 6 of Article I of the Constitution, giving them legal immunity for their speeches while Congress is in session. I think it's reasonable to ask whether Congress still plays a useful role in our governmental structure."

"One more question, sir. Do you expect the President to make any changes in his staff or the Cabinet in his second term?"

"No. The President is lucky to be surrounded by the highest caliber advisors ever assembled in one central government. He hasn't given a moment's thought to changing any of them."

"Thank you, Mr. Vice President."

I left the newspaper on the table next to a $20 tip,

checked to make sure I had everything, and exited through the hotel's revolving door. Forty-five more minutes had passed. I had plenty of time for the two-mile walk to the Capitol.

On the way, I was asked for my ID six times. Three separate guards checked the computer. Clearly the Secret Service was taking no chances today. By the time I got into the Rotunda, it was 10:00. I didn't need to be in my assigned seat until 11:00. At 11:30 dignitaries would start appearing on the platform, barely twenty feet away, in reverse order of prestige. At precisely 11:50 President Jadon Hamilton would be escorted to his seat by a bipartisan Congressional delegation. At 11:52 the Pope would offer an invocation. At 11:57 the national poet laureate would offer a selection composed specifically for the occasion. At noon, the oath of office would be administered. At 12:02 p.m., Jadon would begin to read the speech drafted for him by his staff. Or so he thought.

I decided to head toward the press section and get settled into my seat, even though I had an hour to spare. Today of all days, there was no reason to take chances. It would be important to observe the preparations for a few minutes before the beginning of the ceremony and set up my laptop properly. I walked up a flight of stairs, thinking it would be a simple matter to exit through a set of double doors onto the West Balcony. I was wrong; a long line snaked toward the door marked "Press," with an extensive security checkpoint clearly the culprit.

I got in line; there was no alternative. 10:07. I stepped to the side and counted eleven people in front of me. Two minutes apiece, twenty-two minutes. No problem. It's a good thing they were checking credentials and not measuring vital signs; they would have detained me faster than you can say "freedom of the press."

The line didn't move. Some bozo in front apparently didn't

have all his papers and was causing a fuss. Five minutes later, they resolved his problem, and he got in. One step forward. I felt like I was at the post office. Then I noticed that the lady in front of me was carrying a laptop similar to mine. Alarms went off in my head. If the restriction on laptops had not been formalized or circulated properly, there might be electronic interference. On the other hand, if the restriction was being enforced but she hadn't heard about it, she would protest, causing the line to move more slowly. An eternity of long minutes ensued. Finally, she got to the head of the line.

"Ma'am, you are not permitted to have a laptop at the ceremony."

Whew! One problem solved.

"Why is that?"

"It's a security precaution."

"How could a laptop computer possibly be dangerous? What am I going to do, throw it at him?"

"Ma'am, I agree it's unusual, but it simply isn't allowed today."

"Well how am I supposed to take notes?"

"Our concern is the safety of the President and his guests. How you take notes is your business." The guard was polite but unyielding. "We'll be happy to check it for you and return it after the ceremony."

"My editor is going to be furious." But she relinquished the machine.

The guard turned his attention to me. "ID?" I took out my wallet and showed him my Federal ID card. "Press pass?" It was hanging around my neck, plain as a politician at a Texas Bar-B-Que. I held it up for him to see more clearly. "All right." Then he noticed the carrying case for the laptop. "What's in the case?

"Laptop, and monitor."

"Sir, did you not hear the conversation I just had with the lady in front of you?"

I stood as tall and straight as I possibly could, hoping that a confident act would mask my inner terror. "I did hear it. I have special permission."

"Nobody informed me."

My left leg started trembling. "I'm sure there's a directive. It was cleared all the way to the top."

"I'm in charge of this security station, sir, and it wasn't cleared with me."

I was running out of time. "I respect that, sir. It was cleared with the President. It was cleared with the President of the United States."

"Is that a fact?" I could see he was starting to regard me as a trouble-maker, possibly a nutcase.

Ignoring my leg, which had starting shaking visibly, I spoke as calmly as I was able. "Sir, I know you are just doing your job. But President Hamilton and I are friends. The Chief of the White House Security Detail personally arranged this for me. If you don't believe me, please call her. Madison will confirm everything."

Don't ever tell me that name-dropping doesn't help move bureaucracy. My use of Madison's name, and her correct title, had the desired impact. "Just step aside, then, so we don't hold up the line." I moved two feet to the right. The guard motioned to an assistant, who approached. "This guy here..." he eyed my press pass again—"Roland Raines, claims that the President authorized him to bring his laptop. Check it out, will you?" The other agent stepped away immediately and began speaking into an invisible microphone.

Had there been some last-minute change in plans? Had the opposition discovered what we were up to and taken counter-measures? People who experience near-death situations talk about how time seems to stand still. I swear, I was able to count the nanoseconds. In reality, it probably took less than a minute for the assistant to flash the thumbs up sign.

"All right, Mr. Raines, looks like you've got pretty good connections. Enjoy the ceremony." He seemed relieved that he had remained professional throughout the ordeal.

"Thank you," I said, and stepped outside. Ten minutes to spare. I found the seat marked "Reserved for Roland Raines" exactly where Madison said it would be, in the second row. From experience, I knew that everyone in the first row would be plainclothes security from one branch of the government or another. I set up the laptop but left the monitor in the case. It was too early to turn it on, but I mentally practiced directing the output laser toward the podium from which the President would deliver his speech. A small device at the base of the podium was barely visible, and I assumed it was the receptor Madison had indicated would be there. Further back on the rostrum itself, I saw Madison, dressed smartly in her Secret Service outfit. She glanced in my direction briefly and let her head nod. I turned the laptop on. We were ready.

A few minutes before the procession began, every chair in the front row filled quickly—except the one directly in front of me. That seemed strange, but fortuitous; I didn't have to worry about the laser beam penetrating some lady's hair. Suddenly, disaster! I saw it coming ten feet away—Gus LaVelle was headed toward the empty chair, all six foot three of him. He sat down, completely blocking the path of the laser. And this was no coincidence. He turned around and snarled. "I don't know who your guardian angel is yet, punk. But you and me are going to have a nice little chat when this is over."

I considered asking the people next to me to change places,

but LaVelle would no doubt have followed suit. I thought about holding the laptop up over my head during the address, but that would be foolhardy as well as awkward. The people behind me would complain, which would cause a commotion, and LaVelle would turn around to see what was going on.

Then I did what anybody else in my situation would have done: I panicked. I glanced toward the podium and caught Madison's eye again. She must have seen the fear, because she looked puzzled for a moment. There was just enough of a pause for her well-trained, think-under-pressure brain to figure it out. Her face brightened, and she turned her head slightly. I saw her lips move. Thirty seconds later, LaVelle pushed what looked like a hearing aid a little tighter into his ear using his index finger. Then he got up and left, giving me a look in the process that I interpreted to mean, "If you so much as lift your ass off that chair, I'll carve you into a million pieces and feed you to the bears at the Sassenbruger Zoo."

That was just fine by me. I had no intention of lifting my ass off the chair. All I wanted to do was aim my harmless laser beam at the President's podium. And now it was possible. *Thank you, Madison!*

Shortly thereafter, the procession started. The Pope entered first, followed by the Ambassador from Canada, the only foreign dignitary in attendance. Selected members of Congress came down the center aisle, followed by members of the Cabinet. In black robes, justices of the Supreme Court walked solemnly toward the front. The Vice President, smiling ear to ear, whispered to the Attorney General as he sat down. Finally, the President himself, escorted by additional members of Congress and his personal staff, took their places.

The ceremony started with the Pope's invocation, offered in perfect English:

"Heavenly Father, we look up to you today from a weary country, with hope in our hearts for salvation for all its leaders and all its citizens. We pray for a multitude of blessings on a people beset with hardships not of their own choosing.

"Father, for more than forty years, this nation has fought the demon of terrorism. You have provided allies from time to time, but mostly these brave Americans have soldiered unaided. Hundreds of thousands of grieving families have looked to You in sadness, recognizing that You have chosen to recall their sons and daughters and asking that their loved ones be not taken in vain.

"Today we ask again for a world where brothers and sisters of all nationalities and all faiths can break bread in harmony.

"Our Lord and Savior, we ask for Your assistance in balancing the resources of the good Earth with the enormous demands placed on it by a growing population. Give us the wisdom to be economical in the utilization of Your blessings. We rejoice in the bountiful deposits of coal You have provided to keep Americans warm in the winter and the infinite sunshine of the other seasons.

"More than two hundred and fifty years ago, You helped the founders of this nation create the Office of President of the United States. Lord, it is an awesome responsibility. We pray for your blessings upon the man about to assume that Office for a second term. We ask that You bring him the wisdom to represent the citizens of his nation in a manner befitting their glorious history. We pray that You will give strength and courage to his advisors. May all the leaders of this large and diverse nation forsake the trivial for the grand and abandon personal glory for the greater good of all.

"Finally, our Father, we pray that You will bless the speech this President is about to make. Just as You bless food to the nourishment of our bodies, sanctify this speech to the nourishment of our minds. Provide inspiration this day to the man chosen to lead this country. Show him the way, that he may show those who follow him the way.

"These blessings we ask in the name of the Father, of the Son, and of the Holy Ghost. Amen."

While the Pontiff was offering his prayer, I was offering my own: "Please, Lord, let the laser beam be strong enough to project the signal from my laptop to the podium."

The invocation was followed by a long boring poem that made no sense at all, at least to me. Finally, the Chief Justice administered the oath of office to Jadon P. Hamilton, who looked splendid in a dark blue suit. The Chief Justice sat down, and President Hamilton prepared to address the nation.

Everything came together in that next instant. More than forty years ago, I had reluctantly accepted the role of ghost-writer for high school football star Jadon Hamilton, who was full of lust but lacking the words to express it. That friendship had given me access to the White House, where I met Madison, a conscientious Secret Service agent with access to a dark secret. A long career as a journalist, with an interest in American history and public affairs, had prepared me for the role of undercover presidential speechwriter. My words, *my thoughts*, on the American spirit, were about to be delivered verbatim by a man practiced in the art of reading fluently words he had never seen before and didn't bother to understand.

President Hamilton cleared his throat. I pressed the "Enter" key on my laptop.

"My Fellow Americans: An ominous wind blows across this nation today, threatening to dissipate the last vestiges of the ideals that once made us great. Our purple mountains are shrouded in fog; amber waves of grain feed our bodies but not our minds;

prevarication, manipulation, and obfuscation are crowding out truth and freedom from sea to shining sea."

Chesterfield was the first to notice. He looked at the Vice President, whose own cheery demeanor of the past few moments had turned to horror. The Attorney General glared at the Chief of Staff, who shrugged his shoulders in disbelief.

"These crimes against America are being perpetrated by basically decent people whose judgment has been clouded by personal ambition and self-delusional fantasy. They are not criminals; they are not terrorists. They are educated men and women who have succumbed to the beguiling notion that they alone understand the nature of our complex world. They have been trained by some of the best institutions of higher learning, and by popular culture, to believe that they possess some type of inimitable inspiration, uniquely equipping them to steer the ship of state through the unknown waters of the next one hundred years. But they are wrong. They are seriously misguided. And unless they are confronted, they will lead this country into a blind alley of history."

Panic set in among the President's advisors. They shuffled their feet, as if they wanted to run forward and tackle him, preventing him from reading whatever it was that had taken possession of his teleprompter. But the address was being carried live on OmniScreens all over the country and being translated simultaneously for viewing around the world. It was too late.

"How do I know such things? Have I too been smitten by delusions of omniscience? I will tell you how I know. I have learned, in my privileged fifty-eight years on earth, that daily decisions are best guided by the principles of the ages. When we are facing the right direction, it is natural to step in the right direction. It feels comfortable; we do not experience a gnawing at the soul. I have studied the principles of the ages, especially those espoused so eloquently by those who struggled with the conundrum of government more than two hundred and fifty years ago. And I find our current state of affairs to be inconsistent with those great principles.

"What are these doctrines that should guide us, and what must we do to abide by the wisdom they would teach us? First, we must recognize that the affairs of government are conducted by people, who bring with them to the noble undertaking not only good intentions but also human frailties. The advanced electronics of the late twenty-first century were unimaginable even one hundred years ago; yet they have left the human mind as vulnerable as it was a thousand years ago. Looking up to our parents from their kneecaps, we assume what they tell us is true; we learn to filter information through the lens of personal experience—theirs and ours. What information we accept we do not always process. What we process we do not always act upon properly. What we act upon, in egregious cases, may be to our own advantage rather than the advancement of the general welfare; public service may be a disguise for the fulfillment of unmet and unrecognized personal need.

"Knowing all this about human nature, we should not and must not ignore one of the most basic principles in the history of our great nation: the separation of powers. Our Constitution, a document that deliberately established three co-equal branches of government, with an intricate balance that has served us well, is in danger. While we nominally celebrated its two hundred and fiftieth anniversary recently, people were already devising legal means to subvert the essence of its genius. I tell you now: should there be any attempt to regulate, manipulate, or mitigate the power of the Congress of the United States, or the judiciary, I will fight it with every cell of my being."

This phrase elicited scattered applause from the members

of Congress on the podium, quickly silenced by a stern glance from the Vice President.

"Secondly, a free and universal public education should be the birthright of every American. To allow only those already privileged to attend the best schools demeans the natural talents of those not born to wealth and shields the nation from the ideas and inventions that, given proper opportunity, might spring from their fertile imaginations. Lest I be misunderstood, by education I do not mean the mindless memorization of facts and figures that has overtaken our institutions of formal learning and the repetition of pledges and platitudes that passes for wisdom in some circles. Our national commitment must be not to conformity of belief but to the thoughtful analysis of verifiable evidence, guided by ethical judgment, and enhanced by group problem-solving skills, with the resulting actions directed toward the advancement of every member of our society.

"Thirdly, the fruits of this education can only be fully enjoyed in a nation that values and embraces intellectual debate. We are starving now for that embrace, bombarded by twenty second shibboleths from media giants gone mad with self-aggrandizement and self-appointed moral authority, frightened by the notion that touching controversy will result in ostracism, excommunication, or punishment that defies what would have been considered cruel and unusual a mere century ago. The unimpeded exchange of ideas in a diverse population weaves a tight fabric, one that will protect this country from the chilling effects of demagoguery and distortion. There is nothing abominable about believing differently, behaving differently, and speaking differently; the abomination is in not respecting the differences. Under my leadership as President, we will restore to its formerly prominent place in our American culture that most critical of clauses in the First Amendment: Congress shall make no law abridging the freedom of speech—not just sanctioned speech; not just reasonable speech; but all speech that seeks to educate, to inform, and to persuade, absent an imminent threat to life and limb."

I began to breathe again. It was working. The entire plan was working!

"Across America today, law has a meaning never intended by the founders. Originally, sovereignty of the people was paramount. Protections against abusive prosecutors and overzealous judges were built into the fourth, fifth, and sixth amendments to the Constitution, codifying hundreds of years of social progress. These protections were repealed by the thirtieth amendment, possibly the most egregious action ever taken by the American political system, in a well intentioned but foolhardy attempt to protect itself from the inevitable criminal minority. Today, three courageous young people lie gravely ill in Springfield, Illinois, starving themselves in an attempt to secure a fair trial. Many people think of them as protestors; I proclaim them patriots. I applaud their courage and their steadfast resolve, at great personal sacrifice. They have earned the country's respect—and its forgiveness. I hereby pardon them, and their fellow students, for all actions taken in the pursuit of truth and justice, and I wish them a speedy recovery. I also commend for consideration by all thoughtful Americans the prompt repeal of the thirtieth amendment.

"Despite our understandable distrust of government at all levels, the affairs of which are conducted by fallible people and the actions of which we frequently perceive as counterproductive to our own personal interests, we must recognize the importance of its role in promoting social order and keeping chaos at bay. We want our property to be secure; we want the freedom to travel comfortably within our fifty-one states without fear of robbery or abduction; we want our borders to provide a safe haven from rogue nations and demented individuals; we want our children to breathe clean air, eat nutritious food, play in safe neighborhoods, and receive quality medical care; in short, we understand, in our better moments, that certain structures and rules, generally imposed, provide the framework within which personal freedoms survive. Government is not an enemy; properly directed, it is a friend, a catalyst for building together what none of us can build by ourselves. We must ensure that governments have the resources and the powers to accomplish what are, in essence, our collective objectives."

The expressions on the faces of Tyler and Chesterfield were priceless. I looked hard enough to remember them, thinking they would sustain me throughout my incarceration, should that come to pass.

"I have taken the Oath of Office of President of the United States for the second time. I am grateful for your vote, although I suspect it may have been intended to support policies I now recognize as wrong-headed, possibly even pernicious. I have returned from the cave, where secrecy and darkness conspire to destroy democracy as intended by the Constitution I have sworn to uphold. Follow me into the light! Dare with me to risk granting the liberties to all citizens that used to make our country the envy of nations around the world."

Bless Jadon's reading ability. He was growing into the speech now, emphasizing just the right words, as if he had rehearsed it a hundred times. He couldn't have delivered it any better had he written it himself and known exactly what he was saying.

"My fellow Americans, freedom will not preserve us; we must preserve freedom. It is our sacred duty to do so, for the sake of the founding fathers, the soldiers who have fallen in battle defending us, and the children born and unborn for whom liberty should be a birthright as natural as loving parents and a nurturing earth. This is not an easy struggle, for its dictates are counter-intuitive in difficult times. Especially in such times, painless and obvious answers are frequently the wrong answers. The intellectually intricate path—remembering that our cherished way of life can be preserved only by adhering to its basic principles every day, without fail, regardless of apparent short-term risks—is the only path that leads to our chosen destination.

"Now I ask that you join me in this perilous journey. Summon the intellect to reject easy answers to complex problems. Summon the courage to confront those who would deprive us of our liberties in the name of preserving them. Summon the personal responsibility to contribute as much to this great country as you take from it. Collectively, it is within our power to restore the mountains to their purple majesty; to bring amber waves of grain to every hungry mouth and every hungry mind; and to work together to ensure life, liberty, and the pursuit of happiness from sea to shining sea!"

The audience erupted into sustained applause. Jadon turned to the side and shook the hand of the Vice President, who had stepped up next to him. I'm not an experienced lip-reader, but I could have sworn that the President asked, "Well, how was that?" Then he was ushered away quickly by Madison and other Secret Service agents.

CHAPTER FOURTEEN

What I observed next could only be described as organized pandemonium. In the crowd around me, a buzz arose—people talking excitedly, gesturing wildly, clearly surprised by the tone of the speech. On the podium, Vice President Tyler was escorted quickly out of sight; his Secret Service guards apparently realized that something was amiss, although they probably didn't know exactly what, and they took no chances. Most of the guests were walking up the stairs or waiting their turn to enter the narrow center aisle that led back into the Capitol, engaging each other in animated conversation. Pete Chesterfield gravitated to the side of the podium, where he was joined almost immediately by Gus LaVelle, who ran in from the left wing. They had whispered back and forth no more than fifteen seconds when LaVelle pointed directly at me and yelled at no one in particular, "That's him! Grab him!"

Chesterfield was slightly more composed. He spoke hurriedly to a man wearing sunglasses, then they both looked at me. The man began barking orders into his watch, and in less than a minute, I was surrounded by men in plain clothes wearing identical glasses and sporting ear pieces resembling hearing aids. I was escorted through the Capitol, hustled into a government vehicle, and whisked away. But my mission had been accomplished, and while I feared the ordeal that would follow, I felt a warm glow inside, a sense of having given my country a unique and valuable gift.

It wasn't clear to me where I was being taken. The windows of the car were darkly tinted. Besides, beefy security agents flanked me on both sides in the narrow back seat and glared at me constantly during a trip that lasted perhaps ten minutes. I heard the clatter of a roll-up door opening, then closing behind us, and we went downhill for another two minutes or so. Then I was pulled from the car roughly by one of the agents, while the other removed my computer from the trunk, handling it with plastic gloves. I was escorted into a small interrogation room, and my left wrist was handcuffed to a chair. I expected to be grilled immediately, but they simply left me alone for about fifteen minutes.

The door opened suddenly, and in walked the Vice President of the United States and the Attorney General! Spying the press pass still hanging around my neck, Tyler pulled it forcefully, breaking the chain, threw it on the floor, then stomped on it like a child frustrated by a toy that won't work properly. He looked at me with disdain. "You won't be needing that any more, traitor," he screamed.

Chesterfield put a hand on the Vice President's shoulder, as if to say "calm down, we need to be careful here." They both took chairs across the table from me.

"Now, Mr. Raines, what the fuck was that all about?" The veins stood out prominently in Tyler's neck. It's a good thing he didn't have a heart condition or he might have had a coronary on the spot.

"I believe it's quite obvious what that was about," I replied, as calmly as I could, but shivering beneath my clothes.

"A neat little trick," Chesterfield said. "How many accomplices did you have? What other assistance did they provide, in addition to unplugging the teleprompter?"

"I'd like to have an attorney present."

"You don't have the right to an attorney, you..." The Vice

President sputtered and gagged, trying to come up with a word that would communicate the intensity of his feelings. "You... evil-doer!"

If that's the best you can do, no wonder the country is in trouble. "No, by your standards, I don't suppose I do. But in the United States of America into which I was born, I would not only have the right to an attorney, but you would have to advise me of that right." I let that sink in—not that it found any fertile ground. "Plus, you'd have to tell me what crime I am being charged with."

"Does being stupid count?" Chesterfield asked, clearly the cleverer of the two. "And how about humiliating the President of the United States?"

"Serious charges indeed. Especially the first."

Tyler stood up and cocked his fist. I escaped a blow only because the Attorney General quickly grabbed his arm.

"There will plenty of time for punishment. Sit down, Shorty."

Tyler complied but needed to vent. "Now you listen to me. You have committed an evil and despicable act." The word "despicable" was accompanied by a shower of spit. "You don't have a snowball's chance in hell of ever seeing the outside world again. You might as well cooperate."

"I am cooperating. I admit I switched the speeches."

"And who are your accomplices?" Chesterfield repeated.

"That I am not at liberty to say."

"We have ways of making you talk," Tyler roared. Whatever was left of his veneer of civility was wearing off quickly.

"Yes, perhaps you do, now that cruel and unusual punishment is permitted. But there will be consequences."

"Are you threatening us, Mr. Raines?" Chesterfield asked incredulously. "Do you have the audacity to threaten the government of the United States?"

"The government of the United States is a sham, gentlemen, and I think you know it. You and your power-hungry cronies have taken advantage of a weak president and a tidal wave of unsophisticated flag-waving war mongers to dismantle the most basic protections written into our constitution." The blow landed on my right cheek, without warning, flinging my head to the left uncontrollably. My right hand went to the point of impact in a vain attempt to reduce the excruciating pain, and I glared at the Vice President. "So that's what this country has come to? A constitutional officer, sworn to uphold the law, beating up a handcuffed prisoner?"

"You're damn right," Tyler raged. "I can't think of anybody who deserves it more than you do."

I had counted on some rationality. My plan presumed that they would want to strike a deal to avoid further humiliation, a public airing of their security lapse, and a congressional investigation. Fortunately, Chesterfield took over. "Shorty, why don't you let me handle this. Go have a cup of coffee or something." When Tyler didn't move, he added, "C'mon, take a break."

Tyler stormed out of the room, muttering incomprehensibly.

"All right, now let's talk, just the two of us. Do you understand the magnitude of the crime you have committed?"

"You haven't told me what crime I committed. Thinking for myself? What is the penalty for that?"

"You are not in an especially strong position to be glib, Mr. Raines. You're the one handcuffed to the chair."

"Then why don't you tell me what I'm being charged with."

"Obstructing the government of the United States in the implementation of its official duties, for one."

"Oh yes, Patriot Act III, if I recall."

"Very good, give the journalist an 'A' for an accurate memory. And do you also recall the penalty?"

"Life in prison without the possibility of parole, unless someone's life is endangered, in which case the penalty is death by public hanging."

Chesterfield smiled broadly. "Right again. Either one will suit you just fine, although personally I prefer the latter."

"Aren't you forgetting something?"

"And what might that be?"

"Do you really want everyone in the world to know what happened? Wouldn't that put a slight damper on your little plot? Wouldn't it, in fact, make the President the laughing stock of every nation on earth, including the United States, limiting his effectiveness to lead the country further into autocracy?"

"With you incommunicado, or dead, how exactly will they find out, smart guy?"

"I've seen to that, Mr. Chief Law Enforcement Officer." I intended irony, but in the midst of serious negotiations, its time had passed. "I took the precaution of ensuring that a handful of reliable, trustworthy people have copies of the speech the President gave, with proof that I had it in my hands before he gave it. Given the secrecy that surrounds inaugural addresses, and this President in particular, there is only one way I could have had a copy of that speech in advance. Together with my explanation of how I did it, and why, I think the story will have considerable credibility." He stared at me silently, apparently trying to absorb the full impact of this new information. I could almost feel the power drain out of his body. "I asked all of my contacts to publish this account in twenty-four hours unless they read my personal account of the Inauguration in the paper tomorrow, signaling that I'm all right. I've given them key words to look for, to ensure that you don't write something and put my name on it.

Furthermore, they will see that the story gets published at any time in the future should anything suspicious happen to me, my family, or anyone associated with the effort to preserve Congress or restore the Bill of Rights. I know you control most of the media in this country, but you don't control all of it, and there are other nations that would love a juicy tidbit like this about our great leader. Once it breaks, you won't be able to prevent it from spreading."

"You son of a bitch."

"I beg to differ. *I* am not the son of a bitch. The sons of bitches are the people who have gradually dismantled the foundations of liberty in this country, spouting meaningless generalizations about freedom at the same time they undermine the principles that secure that freedom."

"Save the lecture, Mr. Raines, you've made your position quite clear."

"That was my intent. To wake up the people who aren't yet fast asleep. Someone needs to warn them about the danger being foisted upon us by people either hungry for power or lacking in wisdom. Or both."

"Okay, you're a modern day Paul Revere. Now what is it exactly you want in exchange for some, shall we say, circumspect judgment being shown about today's little adventure?"

Had I actually won? I felt a spark of optimism in my belly. "I am freed immediately. I write an article for tomorrow's edition of the newspaper praising the President's speech. The one he actually delivered. You see to it that every edition of every newspaper you and your friends secretly control reprints my entire column the following day—and the entire text of the speech. No arrests for the expression of political views as long as you are Attorney General. Public education for everyone aged six to eighteen, with a purposeful and meaningful dialogue about civil liberties, the history of human rights, and the importance of checks and balances in our federal government. And no constitutional convention."

"That's all?" he said, a crooked mouth revealing bitterness and hostility. "You don't want the entire original Bill of Rights restored by next Tuesday?"

"Unlike you, Mr. Attorney General, I have confidence in the people. Given the freedom to debate openly and an educational system that gives students the tools to think, I believe the country will find its way back to the inspirational teachings of our founding fathers."

He had written my points down on a legal pad. "Anything else?"

"Yes. The Jefferson Memorial stays open."

"You shit-head." But he wrote it down. "And in return for this?"

"I promise to keep this matter strictly confidential for twenty-five years. If my confidence is well-placed, I'll be able to publish my account at that time. If not..." The sentence didn't need to be finished; we both understood.

"I'll have to consult with a few people." He stood up.

"I'm not done. Add a few personal things to the list. Be sure the President signs the pardon for those kids in Springfield. Return my neighbor Matthew safely, and restore his house to the way it was before your goons kidnapped him. Have the Vice President send me a hand-written apology for his criminal assault just a few minutes ago, on official stationary. And whoever is tailing my wife, have them cease and desist."

"We're not tailing your wife."

"Don't bullshit me. She says she's being followed."

"Not by us."

The man didn't have the ethical standards of an ant. Somehow I believed him anyway. He wasn't objecting to any of my other demands; why would he lie about the tail? But if it wasn't him, then who the hell was following Alycia? Chesterfield left me alone to ponder that question.

About thirty minutes later one of the agents who arrested me entered the room. "Would you like some water?"

"Yes, thank you. That's the most civilized thing anyone has asked me in the last two hours."

He poured from a pitcher I hadn't previously noticed, on a counter behind me. "You've caused quite a little stir. All the big-wigs are holed up in the White House trying to decide what to do."

"For once, I hope they make the right decision."

"Can't rightly say I understand what they're debating. But there are some pretty good heads in there."

I let the comment slide, and the agent settled into one of the chairs on the other side of the table. Apparently someone had decided I needed babysitting. Having said his piece, he just drummed his fingers on the table incessantly, until the door opened again about fifteen minutes later. "Let him go," the other agent said.

"Let him go?"

"That's right. We're supposed to make sure he gets back to the newspaper office and check to see that he's got fare back to the TDC."

How sweet it is! They were thinking of everything!

CHAPTER FIFTEEN

Once again I was led to a government vehicle, only this time I saw the logo on the side before I got in: "Department of Homeland Security." I was sandwiched between two beefy agents who appeared to have been genetically altered specifically for this line of work. Nevertheless, my mission had been accomplished, and even though my legs hadn't stopped trembling, I was beginning to feel giddy. I was on my way home! I only prayed that Alycia and Devon would be there to meet me. "Do you suppose it would be possible to get a sandwich?" I asked, addressing neither the driver nor the guards specifically. I hadn't had anything to eat since the one-star breakfast at the two-star hotel.

"I guess so," the man on the right replied. "Whaddaya want?"

"A cheeseburger?" I haven't the foggiest notion where that came from. Surrounded by human muscle, not of the friendliest variety, I decided to crack a joke. Nobody carried enough money for a cheeseburger without planning ahead for a week. My remark didn't even elicit a chuckle; whatever genetic modification had been performed had evidently eliminated my guards' sense of humor.

"From what I hear, you're lucky to get a slice of turkey on a soggy bun," the driver replied.

"I'll settle for that. And hold the mayo."

We stopped at a mini-VOX, and the driver returned with two slices of turkey on a Kaiser roll. He even sprang for a large Coke without my asking. Then we headed toward the editorial offices. I ate in silence, keeping my elbows as close to my body as possible. By chance, we passed the Jefferson Memorial on the way. Damned if they weren't already dismantling the fence I had seen the previous night. So far, so good.

Writing is the lifeblood of journalists; it's what we do. Despite my desperate desire to be on the next train home, I knew my first duty was to finish my news report. Back at the office, I headed straight to the bathroom to see how badly I had been injured. The side of my head had stopped throbbing, and I was relieved to discover no blood. However, some evidence of a large black and blue mark was beginning to show. I walked self-consciously into the newsroom, where most of the desks were unoccupied. More than an hour had passed since the end of the speech, and the reporters were out covering the parade or getting ready for the party circuit that night. An intern looked up from the other side of the room and yelled, "Hey, what about that speech?" I waved back and turned away quickly, then settled at my desk. Thirty minutes later the entire article was completed. As had become my habit, most of it had been composed in my head anyway.

> *Washington, D.C.—Jadon P. Hamilton was sworn in for his second term today as President of the United States, promising in an unexpectedly inspiring inaugural address to promote free and universal public education, protect the legislative and judicial branches of government from encroachments on their Constitutional powers, and restore the freedom of speech previously contained in the Bill of Rights.*

I really enjoyed describing my own speech as "inspiring"—how poetic!

> *In a speech lasting just under five minutes, the President asked for the help of all Americans in what he described as a "perilous journey." He defended the role of government in maintaining a stable society, implying that he would ask for a tax increase devoted to that purpose. He asked citizens to reject easy answers to difficult questions and adhere to an "intellectually intricate path."*
>
> *The President emphasized human frailty repeatedly, claiming that the Founding Fathers understood this phenomenon and deliberately created a Constitution that incorporated checks and balances, not only to prevent one branch of government from dominating the others, but to protect us all from "people whose judgment has been clouded by personal ambition." He suggested, without providing details, that some people were already thinking about destroying this important aspect of our Constitution.*
>
> *Combining lyrics from the song "America" and quotes from the preamble to the Declaration of Independence, the President concluded with a burst of optimism and activism, asking Americans to help "bring amber waves of grain to every hungry mouth and every hungry mind, and to work together to ensure life, liberty, and the pursuit of happiness from sea to shining sea."*
>
> *The President's speech was applauded vigorously by an audience consisting largely of invited dignitaries, federal employees, and members of the media. With rumors of terrorism rampant, the general public had been kept two miles away, watching the event on gigantic OmniScreens installed for that purpose.*
>
> *The speech appears to signal a significant deviation from the policies this President pursued during his first term in office. It remains to be seen exactly what that means for the American people.*

I sent the text off to Sid, glanced at my watch, and raced for the door in a single breath. If I hurried, I could make the late afternoon train. I desperately wanted—no, I *needed*—to see Alycia and Devon. Despite the successful operation in Washington, I lived for them. I craved their companionship. Without their love, I was nothing.

Security at the train station had practically disappeared. I guess they were more interested in people trying to sneak into town than out of town. Precisely at 4:47 p.m., I stepped onto the TDC Special and found a seat facing forward. One thing you could say for the first administration of Jadon P. Hamilton: the trains did run on time.

I had been operating on nervous energy for thirty-six consecutive hours, since the previous morning when I'd begun to type the "President's" speech into my laptop. I had almost been killed. I had been assaulted while handcuffed to a chair. And neither of those events compared to the emotional toll taken by more than a day of constant stress, wondering whether more than two months of exhaustive research and meticulous planning would pay off. Finally, it was time to start relaxing. I noticed that my legs had stopped trembling. The enormity of my mission started to settle into my brain. Unless the Vice President and the Attorney General double-crossed me, I had accomplished a nearly unbelievable feat—something neither the northern states nor the vocal minority in Congress had been able to do.

Those bastards wouldn't double-cross me, would they? All the signs so far indicated a complete capitulation. Still, people in search of power typically don't give up easily. They would be angry. They would feel cheated out of what they regarded as their right to rule the country. They would want revenge.

I decided then that it would be too dangerous to tell Alycia about the entire affair. Somehow I had thought, when it was all over, I would be able explain to her the burden I had been carrying the last few months. I had planned to apologize profusely for keeping this enormous secret from her, violating our pledge to be completely open and honest at all times. But now I saw that I couldn't. I had promised to keep the secret for twenty-five years, and knowing that Tyler and Chesterfield would be looking for any opportunity to re-institute their plan, or at least punish me for my role in foiling it, I would keep my word. Just exactly how this would work, given the note she'd left me the day before, I had yet to understand.

My mind wandered during the rest of the trip home. My eyes followed the familiar scenery, shrouded in twilight, without seeing it. I might even have nodded off for a bit, but I knew out of habit to get off at the proper stop. I ran home. The house was still empty.

I had heard of hollow victories—football games won although your star player gets injured; promotions granted with the tacit understanding that retirement would soon follow; opponents vanquished on the battlefield but thousands of brave men and women lost forever. I didn't feel like celebrating what should have been a special moment. Saving the country, or at least attempting to change its course, seemed meaningless without my family. My body ached for emotional release. When my stomach started to heave, trying to rid itself of three months of turmoil and unaccustomed secrecy from the person I loved more than anyone in the world, I went to the bathroom, where a stony face stared back at me in the mirror. I dared not even cry by myself; there would be no end to it.

**

I don't remember going to sleep; obviously I did though, because I woke up in bed in a jumble of sweat-dampened blankets. My first thought was to see if Alycia had come home. Might she have arrived in the middle of the night and gone to sleep on the couch, not wanting to wake me up? I searched the house. Still empty. The pain in my stomach got sharper by the minute.

What about Matthew? I raced to his house and climbed the porch steps three at a time. Peering through the small glass window in the front door, I saw him in a living room chair, leaning forward, his hand on his stomach, coughing convulsively. Not in the mood to engage in conversation, I waited only long enough for the coughing to subside and see him catch his breath. He hadn't seen me, and I hurried home again. At least he was safe.

I pulled the newspaper up on the computer. My article appeared as the lead. The editor had added a note at the end: *Reporter Roland Raines has been on special assignment and will provide an in-depth analysis of the Inauguration viewed from a historical perspective in Sunday's edition.* While I was signed on, a VOXmail arrived: *If you had anything to do with the pardon, please accept our thanks. We appreciate your support more than you can possibly know. Doctors telling us to go slow but predicting a full recovery. Sierra, Ryan, and Tyrone.*

I fixed myself a cup of coffee in the kitchen and sat at the table, heartbroken despite the good news from Springfield. This should have been the day of my greatest triumph. Instead, I was alone. At that moment I would gladly have traded the future of the country for a kiss from my wife and an opportunity to feed my son. Please, just let me bob for Cheerios one more time.

Twenty minutes later, the front door opened. I raced into the living room to find Alycia and Devon, looking worn but happy. Devon gurgled uncontrollably, and I kissed him on the forehead. I looked at Alycia, my eyes full of questions. She gave me an answer I will never forget: "I read the paper, honey." I looked into her eyes. She met my gaze and put her hand gingerly on my wounded cheek. It was clear to me that she knew as much as a person can know without knowing. I put my head on her shoulder and sobbed uncontrollably.

CHAPTER SIXTEEN

Sunday, February 10
Three weeks later we celebrated Devon's thirteenth birthday. Alycia and I had invited the neighbors and our own personal friends, as well as the kids Devon's age. Matthew came over despite not feeling well. His cough had deepened, but he didn't want to miss the historic event. Madison said she would come, if the President's schedule permitted, bringing her dad as well as her kids if that was okay. We had never met her dad and looked forward to it. We had even invited Gordon Richards and his family, with little expectation that they would attend—but they did, causing quite a stir when the black limousine arrived. Everyone ran outside to see it and expressed amazement that we knew such wealthy people. I had never seen Devon so excited. With the arrival of each guest, he squirmed in his chair and gurgled in glee, clearly recognizing that the rapidly growing pile of gifts belonged to him.

We waited for Madison as long as we could, finally concluding that she hadn't been able to break away from the White House. Once the food was put out on the kitchen table—hot dogs, ice cream, and a large rectangular white cake with chocolate frosting—it disappeared quickly. Then we helped Devon open his presents.

He got a lot of clothes, which didn't excite him a great deal, but Alycia and I appreciated it. Matthew bought him a book, *Make Way for Ducklings*, the classic tale of a family of ducks living in Boston. Just looking at Devon's reaction to the front cover, I knew he would treasure it. With a large pile of wrapping paper at his feet, surrounded by family and friends, perhaps a little high on sugar, my little teenager squirmed continuously, glancing eagerly at everyone as if to say "I'm glad you're here!"

Gordon stood up. "We've got a present, too. I need to get it from the car." His children stayed inside, literally bouncing with excitement, and his wife couldn't stop smiling and looking at Devon. Gordon returned with a large object, covered by a white cloth. "All right, family, gather around." They stood directly in front of Devon. Gordon shifted his hands so they supported the bottom of the object, and his children pulled the white cloth up and over the top, revealing a small yellow canary in a bird cage. It started chirping immediately.

Devon looked confused. Then I realized he had never seen a caged bird before. He was having a difficult time figuring out exactly what was going on. "It's for you, sweetheart. Your own personal bird. You'll get to feed it every day. I'll bet we can even take it out of the cage and let it fly around the house." Gordon nodded in agreement. "Here, let's see." I unlatched the little door, and the bird flew out, landing on Devon's shoulder, chirping like it was singing a love song. Then something remarkable happened: Devon looked at Gordon, his wife, and his kids, and just started bawling.

"Doesn't he like it?" the youngest child asked.

"Yes, he does," Gordon answered. "He's crying for joy." And he was.

A few minutes, later Gordon called me aside. We went into the bedroom. "I have a present for you, too."

"It's not my birthday," I chuckled.

"I know that. But our little chat last month triggered a lot of thought. My wife and I have had some intense discussions. When we heard the President's inaugural a couple of weeks ago, we decided to take action. We want to form an endowment fund for your community."

"What exactly does that mean?"

"We'd like to set up a foundation and donate $200,000 every year for five years. If you're willing, you will be Chairman of the Board of Trustees, and the remainder of the Board can be chosen by the other residents. Interest on the investment will be restricted to promoting the general welfare of the members of this community. The trustees can supplement teacher salaries, subsidize medical care, establish a food bank, or whatever they think is necessary."

I might have been a journalism major, but I was no slouch at math. "A million dollars? You want to donate a million dollars to the TDC?"

"Yes." He shrugged his shoulders, as if it made no sense to him either.

"For social services?" I understood what he was doing, but the enormity of the gift tied my tongue.

"Yes."

"The President's speech convinced you to do this?"

"We were thinking about it anyway. But his speech created urgency and supplied the motivation to move the project from dormancy to action. I liked it a lot, actually." He proceeded to quote a few lines. "'Now I ask that you join me in this perilous journey. Summon the intellect to reject easy answers to complex problems. Summon the personal responsibility to contribute as much to this great country as you take from it.' Do you remember our discussion about leadership? I've got to admit I was surprised, but President Hamilton issued a call to arms." I thought I detected a slight smile. "My wife and I decided to answer the call."

What a feeling! The man I so admired for his intellectual brilliance was paying me a high compliment but didn't even know it. I allowed myself to glow on the inside, maintaining a stoic exterior. "But what about the efficacy problem? And the free-rider problem? Did they just disappear?"

"I'm not worried about efficacy. By targeting our philanthropy and putting you in charge, I have no doubt that many good things will result. As for the other, I fully expect that the President's message will generate a change of attitude in this country. But if it doesn't, well, my wife and I will go to sleep every night with a clear conscience."

"I don't know what to say."

"Say 'yes,' and it will be a done deal."

"All right, then, yes. More than that, an emphatic yes!"

"There will be some paperwork to sign, but I anticipated your answer, and all the documents are drawn up already. They will be delivered to you tomorrow, along with a check for the first year's installment."

"You know, Gordon, it's not a day too soon. Matthew needs antibiotics for his bronchitis and has no way to pay for them. I believe that will be the foundation's first expenditure. You've just saved your first life. Thank you."

"And thank you, Roland." His serious face, amplified by a sparkle in his eyes, communicated that he knew more than he was willing to say.

We heard a knock on the front door, followed by excitement in the living room. Alycia called out "Roland, Madison's here."

"I'm coming."

Gordon tugged at my shirt as I walked past. "Will you do me a favor? Don't tell anyone where the money came from. It's not important."

"If that's what you want, by all means."

"That's what we want."

By the time I got to the living room, Madison's two girls

were seated on the floor, playing with Devon, Gordon's kids, and the bird. Madison and an elderly man were seated on the couch, and Alycia stood nearby, looking extremely upset.

Madison stood up. "Hello, Roland. I'd like you to meet my dad."

I walked over and shook his hand. "It's a real pleasure, sir, I've heard a lot about you."

"Likewise, very nice to meet you." He stood up awkwardly, showing his age, but I detected the remnants of physical grace. He noticed me observing him carefully. "I don't get around as well as I used to."

Alycia tugged at me and nodded her head toward the bedroom. I excused myself as casually as possible. "What is it?"

"It's him!"

"It's who?" I asked.

"The guy who was following me. It's Madison's father!"

Ex-FBI. Of course! All the pieces fell into place.

"Madison must have asked him to keep an eye on you," I explained, "for your own protection."

"Was I in danger?" She could only have figured out the broad outlines of all the events of the past few months. I hadn't filled in the details, and wouldn't for another twenty-five years.

"I don't know. It's possible. In any case, it's comforting to know it was him and not...someone else."

"Do we thank her? Do we thank him?"

"I don't think so. What's to be gained by letting him know that you spotted him? He'll just feel badly. Just act like you've never seen him before in your life."

We returned to the living room, where Gordon and his wife had engaged Madison and her father in a discussion about Chinese cooking. Over the course of the next hour, we cursed the weather, concluded that the Cubs had no chance of winning the pennant, and named the bird Shirley, not really knowing if it was male or female. The kids played well together and decided to call the bird Chris, wisely choosing a name that would fit either a male or a female. Their name stuck.

When everyone had left, Alycia and I collapsed on the couch. That's when it really hit me: Operation Capitol Hill had come to an end.

EPILOGUE

January, 2068
My fellow Americans:

I have kept a promise for a very long time. I even delayed publishing this memoir for two additional years, in order to spare my friend Jadon the embarrassment of finding out what really happened at his second inauguration. Now that he has succumbed to cancer, the story can finally be told.

I will summarize in just a moment my view of American history since 2041. First (still first and foremost a writer!), I would like to reflect briefly on my own family's reaction to this account of the events they lived through but saw with different eyes.

As I mentioned, Alycia figured out the broad outlines of the adventure without me saying a word. She also accepted my silence for the last twenty-seven years without asking a single question. When she read the first draft of this book, all she could say was "Oh my God." She has loved me, except for that brief incident with the French translator, during which I didn't deserve to be loved, as no husband has any right to expect. I sure am glad I went to that opera in Bloomington, Indiana, back in 2006!

Devon is an amazing success story. In the third year of Jadon's second term as president, stem cell research—long stymied by conservative forces in this country—was funded again by Congress. Nine years later, a technique was discovered that partially reversed the physical damage inflicted on millions of children by that horrible orange pill. Devon responded to the treatment beautifully, resuming some physical growth, but more importantly, regaining a large measure of cognitive functioning. Now forty years old, he is going to college. He wants to be a doctor. Devon read the first draft, too, and I guess he's pretty proud of his dad. He gives me more credit for turning the country around than I probably deserve, but if he wants to idolize me, who am I to object? After all, idolizing your dad is one of the most profound pleasures of life, and after what he's been through, he deserves every pleasure that comes his way. Of course, he remembers nothing directly about the events of 2040 and 2041—except for the canary he got on his thirteenth birthday. Chris lived to the ripe old age of ten, by the way.

Madison retired in 2050 and moved out of the area. Her dad had passed away by then, and when her daughter was accepted by the University of Western California at Berkeley for graduate work, she decided to move to the West Coast. We still exchange e-mail (that's what they call it these days, since VOX went bankrupt), but I miss her.

I regret to report that Matthew has passed away. He recovered from the bronchitis, thanks to medications purchased with resources from Gordon Richard's foundation, but age finally just caught up with him. He was a wonderful neighbor, and I'm grateful that Devon had such a good friend during his childhood years.

Speaking of Gordon, you might be wondering whether using his name earlier in this book violated my promise to him that he would remain anonymous. I asked Gordon for permission to release his name. He wasn't happy about it at first, but he came to realize that the story would be incomplete without that information. His foundation has helped an enormous number of people in our community. Oh, I should mention, it's not called a

"TDC" anymore. We had a contest to see what we should name it, and the winning entry was "Hope."

I still live in Hope, Virginia. I'm writing from my study, dictating into a computer that recognizes my speech. Arthritis has just about paralyzed my hands, but the stem cell research on that disease has not yet reached the point where treatments are commercially available. At least I have medical care, and the doctors and nurses are doing everything they can to ease the suffering of an old man. Just seeing Alycia's smile every day lessens the pain.

Now, for my personal, historical perspective. Given the direction this country was heading in 2041 and the degree to which our freedoms as citizens had already been restricted, I thought maybe it was already too late. But the reformation and reconstruction we have witnessed in the last twenty-seven years have been nothing short of astounding. Our children are winning awards now for creative thinking and collaborative behavior, not conformity, and the best of them are being elected to public office. Universal medical care has finally been established, and sound judgment has replaced self-interest as the means by which the citizens of the nation tax themselves in order to support vital public services. Our forests are growing again. Our air and water are slowly being reclaimed. The national debt has been reduced to $3 trillion, and we are well on our way toward paying off the burden passed along to us by the leaders of the early twenty-first century. Most importantly, people understand, support, and utilize freedom of expression. Once again, essential public policy issues are resolved based on open debate, relevant facts, and the twin principles of majority rule and respect for minority opinion. The entire original Bill of Rights has been restored to the Constitution.

I have no idea whether my actions saved this country or not.

It occurs to me, if I am correct in my optimism about the resilience and basic good nature of people, that it might have been unnecessary. Indeed, no less a student of human nature than John Milton, speaking in 1644, advanced the idea that truth, given a fair chance, will always prevail over deception. Yet, the slippery slopes of despotism and unbridled power have more than once managed to submerge resilience and natural decency, with devastating results. Lest we forget, Adolph Hitler took the reins of power in early twentieth century Germany by legal means. Twenty years later, Senator Joseph McCarthy engaged in a legal but ill-advised witch hunt for communists in the United States. Now, Jadon Hamilton was no Hitler, and he bore no resemblance to Joseph McCarthy. But those who plotted to betray his trust collectively committed one of the most egregious errors that people with authority can make—believing too strongly in their own infallibility, exacerbated by a willingness to sacrifice basic principles of sound government, developed over four hundred years, for apparent short-term gain.

Tyrants and would-be tyrants do not relinquish their dreams easily, and if I have made it sound like the entire nation turned on a dime following the Inaugural Address of 2041, I apologize for oversimplifying complex historical events. Having lost a battle, Tyler and Chesterfield still attempted to win the war. They both embarked on cross-country speaking tours, contradicting the President's message as boldly as they dared, but their ideas were no longer welcomed. Underground newspapers matured into full-fledged independent publications with large paid circulations. VOX lost its monopoly on OmniScreen channels, and public debate on issues of vital importance to the country flourished. Two years later, the voters threw the majority party out of power in Congress, and Winslow Bell became the leader in the United States Senate. Within a month, rumors began circulating that the Vice President had been involved in some illegal activity during Hamilton's first term. In February of 2043, Andrew Tyler was impeached by the House of Representatives on charges of conspiracy, then removed from office by a vote of the Senate five months later. Chesterfield resigned as Attorney General and struck a plea bargain with his successor to stay out of jail.

Celebrating the election of Thomas Jefferson in 1800 and the consequent overturning of the Alien and Sedition Acts, Samuel Adams wrote, "The storm is over, and we are now in port." Unfortunately, he was wrong. There is no such thing as an ultimate victory for civil liberties, as history has shown on innumerable occasions. Each generation independently affirms those principles, or fails to do so. Parents must pass on to their children the tools to make wise decisions in a complex world where each person's liberty is a restraint on the liberty of others. The human dynamic guarantees a perpetual continuation of the inevitable clash between personal and societal interests, understood only feebly, I fear, by "imperfect man"—quoting the quintessential imperfect man, Thomas Jefferson.

I will die soon. But my life will not have been in vain. I love my family dearly and provided for them to the best of my ability. I cherish the lifelong friendships I have made. But one of my greatest accomplishments was the writing of the Second Inaugural Address of President Jadon P. Hamilton.

I began this story with a description of my visit to the White House in 2040, and the President's birthday party in the East Room. Although I haven't been there in many years, I understand that the portrait of George Washington is hanging in the same place. I hope he is still smiling.

APPENDIX I

Chronology of Amendments to the United States Constitution after the Year 2000

2007	- 28th Amendment, permitting a foreign-born person to become President of the United States, providing that person has been a citizen of the nation for a minimum of twenty years prior to his or her election
2014	- 29th Amendment, repealing the 8th Amendment
2020	- 30th Amendment, repealing the 5th, 6th, and 7th Amendments
2026	- 31st Amendment, rewording of the 2nd Amendment
2027	- 32nd Amendment, repealing the 9th Amendment, rewording the 10th Amendment
2035	- 33rd Amendment, rewording of the 1st Amendment

APPENDIX II

Text of the Proposed 34th Amendment to the United States Constitution

Section 1. Article I of the Constitution of the United States of America is hereby repealed.

Section 2. All powers heretofore vested in the Congress of the United States are hereby vested in the President of the United States.

Section 3. The President of the United States shall have the power to enforce this article by any appropriate means.

APPENDIX III

Preface to *Historical Foundations of a Just Society,*
by Gordon Richards

The history of modern civilization is essentially the story of the never-ending attempt to conceive a form of government that approaches perfection despite the imperfections of the people who create it. There is no certain road to success in this endeavor; but the failure to travel any road in the desired direction inevitably results in human tragedy.

The popular adage, "That government is best which governs least," provides no assistance. It suggests that the primary function of government is to stay out of the way. Then why have one at all?

A more thoughtful solution rests on a simple premise: that government is best which furthers the natural purposes of mankind and complements the instinctive functions of the species. Indeed, any other form of government would be doomed to failure, challenged by the inherently unachievable task of countermanding the most fundamental behavioral patterns of its creators—known colloquially as "swimming upstream."

The task then becomes a matter of ascertaining what the natural purposes of mankind are and how they can be furthered by a self-imposed social order.

Many philosophers and psychologists have suggested that the most fundamental purpose of the species is self-perpetuation. The concept is easily traced as far back as the 17th century, in which Thomas Hobbes wrote convincingly about the principle of self-preservation and its ramifications for individual members of the species. Also in the 17th century, John Locke referred to it as "the fundamental law of nature." The eminent 18th century philosopher Jean-Jacques Rousseau put it eloquently: "It is a contradiction in terms to say that any human being should wish to consent to something that is the reverse of his own good" (*The Social Contract*, p. 70). Similarly, the psychologist Abraham Maslow, in his famous hierarchy of needs, puts at the base of his pyramid the desire for food, water, and shelter, thus satisfying the most fundamental physiological requirements of the organism for staying alive.

While it may not be a "purpose" of mankind per se, it could hardly be denied that its members are by nature social creatures. The propagation of the species through sexual reproduction guarantees at least nominal contact with other members of the group. The complexity of raising a child with a long maturational process also ensures the formation of a social order of at least minimal scope—an order known as a family, normally characterized by extremely strong internal bonds of affection commonly known as love. It hardly seems necessary to document the existence of this phenomenon. Nevertheless, it may be noted for academic purposes that the process of bonding was well established by psychologists in the late twentieth century, notably through the seminal book *Attachment and Loss* (Bowlby, 1973).

Finally, common observations as well as studies in genetics reveal that members of the human species come into the world as diverse individuals, possessing strengths and skills—including those required for survival—in widely varying degrees.

It follows from these principles that, absent any form of government as commonly defined, the human world would best be described as a disorganized collection of family units, each competing for the resources required for self-preservation, deriving such resources exclusively from the exercise of power. In such a world, while day-to-day survival might be achieved by those blessed with strength, speed, or cunning, it would be a constant struggle. There would no such thing as ownership of resources. Indeed, great effort would probably need to be expended merely to keep them long enough to use them, with the closest competing family unit under no obligation to pass up any viable opportunity to seize them for its own gratification.

The question then arises, is such a world the best that can be envisioned? Does it contribute better than any other to the preservation of the species and its individual representatives?

The answer is a resounding "No." This can be seen, first, through a logical extension of the concept of family. If it makes sense for a few individuals to enhance their chances of survival by forming a small cohesive unit, might it not also make sense for such units to extend their reach, collaborating rather than competing, for the benefit of all? Secondly, in a society that inevitably expands geographically to parts of the natural habitat that are less inviting, and advances technologically in a manner that requires an increasing need for specialization, is it not counterproductive for the small units to maintain insular and essentially antagonistic boundaries?

Therefore, the fundamental principle of self-preservation in a complex world requires positive social interaction on a scale that extends beyond the immediate family. This interaction, intended to maximize the availability of resources essential for the preservation of the community as a whole, is commonly known as collaboration. As Rousseau put it, "Since men cannot create new forces, but merely combine and control those which already exist, the only way in which they can preserve themselves is by uniting their separate powers in a combination strong enough to overcome any resistance" (pp. 59-60). Using slightly different language to arrive at essentially the same idea, Sommerville (1992) describes Hobbes as believing that, "Since peace is unattainable as long as people exercise the right of nature—the right to do absolutely anything that they think conduces to their preservation—it is necessary that they lay down or transfer this right. But no one has any reason to part with rights unless others do so too. What is needed to escape from the state of nature, therefore, is a mutual transference of rights by which each person agrees to hand over his rights…on condition that the rest do so too" (p. 31).

Collaboration within families is natural, due to the intense bonds of love referred to previously. However, such bonds do not frequently extend beyond the family, at least to the same degree. Friendships may form among people who come into frequent contact. But friendship with an unknown and abstract individual living hundreds or thousands of miles away is at best an ideal and at worst a figment of imagination. Indeed, it is more common for people to distrust or even despise those they have never met—perhaps a genetic holdover from simpler yet more dangerous times. It follows that collaboration is not a natural phenomenon in complex societies and must be enforced by rules established for the common good—rules that have come to be known as laws.

With the advent of laws, many complex processes spring into motion. Laws that govern the ownership of property give rise to a less transitory world, one in which successful families can build the means to ensure their survival in the long term. The ownership of a great deal of property, in excess of that required solely for survival, is called wealth. As we will shortly discover, the aggregation of wealth, while a natural consequence of laws among men and women with diverse skills and abilities, comes with its own set of benefits and problems.

Another consequence of the existence of laws is the necessity for some person or some group to establish and enforce the law. This requirement also results in a predicament that has plagued every government and will continue to do so until mankind becomes perfect—in other words, into eternity.

Let us deal first with the aggregation of wealth and its ramifications. First, it is important to recognize the significant returns that accrue to society as a result of this phenomenon, for they can scarcely be overstated. As Andrew Carnegie noted in his famous commentary on the subject in 1889, "upon the sacredness of property civilization itself depends" ("Wealth," North American Review, CXLVIII (June 1889), p. 656). In the absence of the ability to keep what one produces, there is no incentive to earn more than one needs for daily subsistence. Furthermore, as Carnegie also noted, the production of wealth has the capacity to banish "universal squalor" (p. 653).

But the coin has another side, equally important in understanding the complex dynamics of government. In a world populated by diverse people with inherently varying abilities, wealth is always distributed unevenly. Despite the benefits that wealth may bring even to the poorest of families, disparities between the poor and the rich can result in social unrest. Indeed, in the most aggravated cases, unrest becomes upheaval, also known as revolution. Revolution occurs in two circumstances: one, when the disparity between rich and poor is perceived to be unfair; two, when the poor have so little that there is nothing to be gained through peaceful compliance with rules designed to protect the status quo.

It seems logical enough, then, that it is in the best interests of the wealthy to ensure that distribution of property, though inherently unequal, is sufficiently egalitarian to prevent revolution, the outcome of which is inevitable and universal human suffering. History demonstrates that revolutions are, in the long run, invariably successful, resulting in the loss of wealth among those who fought to preserve it. Once again, Rousseau foresaw this development: "The strongest man is never strong enough to be master all the time" (p. 52). Furthermore, the reader need not be reminded that our United States began with a revolution against a powerful British Empire, catalyzed by no more than a tax on tea, viewed as symbolic of an unfair, tyrannical, and uncaring monarch.

By a strange and complex twist of logic, then, it behooves those who accumulate wealth through natural and lawful means to distribute a part of that wealth to those in need. This seemingly unnecessary, counterproductive, and illogical act conforms to the rationale established at the beginning of this essay for the very existence of government, namely, to help protect the species from self-destruction. Although it is far from obvious, the judicious redistribution of wealth is a form of behavior whose outcome actually enhances the preservation of wealth—thereby benefiting the entire community. Ironically, giving away a significant portion of his accumulated property to the community protects the wealthy man's children far more effectively than the seemingly more efficacious act of leaving the entire estate to them directly.

It is easy for the rich person to wonder why he should support his poorer counterpart who, due to laziness or lack of ability, has not developed the capacity to care for himself. The answer—by virtue of the fact that it is counter-intuitive and does not emerge from a cursory analysis—is not one that the average person can be expected to ascertain for himself.

People are easily distracted from long-range necessity by

perceived short-range desirability. As Rousseau pointed out, "Perspectives which are general and goals remote are alike beyond the range of the common herd; it is difficult for the individual, who has no taste for any scheme of government but that which serves his private interest, to appreciate the advantages to be derived from the lasting austerities which good laws impose" (p. 86). Alexander Hamilton noted the same characteristic in Federalist Paper #6: "Has it not...invariably been found, that momentary passions and immediate interests have a more active and imperious control over human conduct than general or remote considerations of policy, utility, or justice?" Even if people understand, in general, that philanthropy is a worthy enterprise—which many will not agree with under any circumstances—the proper moment for handing off something that belongs to them may forever be procrastinated in response to emotions dominated by momentary considerations. In short, in the absence of public sanction, individuals will typically not make decisions that support the public good; therefore, society, for its own welfare and preservation, must regulate the distribution of wealth through law. Various public policies for accomplishing this objective can be established—through the minimum wage, for example—but by far the most common is through taxation.

It would be a gross understatement to suggest that laws of this nature are easy to devise. Even Carnegie's suggestion regarding "the test of extravagance" is not especially useful. There is no objective standard for the amount of wealth that "should" be accumulated; indeed, in common parlance, the label "rich" is usually applied simply to those who make more money than the person applying the label. This brings us back to the predicament identified but not dealt with earlier: who shall make the law?

Society long ago dispensed with the notion that any one

person should be empowered with such enormous responsibility. This type of government is known as benevolent monarchy in its best incarnation and malevolent dictatorship in its worst. An informed, well-intentioned group almost always makes better decisions than an informed, well-intentioned individual.

Furthermore, individuals may or may not be well intentioned. Indeed, the power to make important decisions tends to detract from this desirable characteristic. As Alexander Hamilton noted in Federalist Paper #1, "So numerous indeed and so powerful are the causes, which serve to give a false bias to the judgment, that we upon many occasions, see wise and good men on the wrong as well as on the right side of questions, of the first magnitude to society." President Andrew Jackson made much the same observation more than a hundred years later when he said, "It is to be regretted that the rich and powerful too often bend the acts of government to their selfish purposes."

We may therefore conclude that some group of people must be chosen by an organized society to create laws that may be counter-intuitive to some individuals—especially those individuals with the most to lose through a sharing of resources—and that these laws, in order to protect public order and preserve the species, must provide for some measure of involuntary distribution of wealth. We may further conclude that the best government will be devised in a manner that prevents any group of people, especially those with a tendency to protect self-interest, from putting such interest above the good of the community they are supposed to serve.

The most common method of ensuring the latter is to divide the government into separate and equal institutions, each of which has some power to curb excesses of the others. The United States Constitution embodied this principle in an exquisite balancing act, putting people into positions of power in a manner that used their fallible human characteristics to guarantee a clash of interests unless the common good became so obvious that agreement was assured. As James Madison pointed out in Federalist Paper #51, "Ambition must be made to counteract ambition."

Establishing a body of law regulating the members of society, including the levying of taxes to pay for community-wide services, is one thing; ensuring compliance is another. Widespread noncompliance eventually disenfranchises an unpopular law, or requires so many resources to be spent in its enforcement that it becomes counterproductive. Therefore, the great majority of people must believe that the law is fair and worthy of being complied with, despite its occasional inconvenience. This consideration brings us to the final elements required to establish a successful government: leadership, education, and freedom of expression. Without education, no one will understand what society is, much less feel any loyalty to the common good. Or as Thomas Jefferson put it, "Enlighten the people generally, and tyranny and oppressions of body and mind will vanish like evil spirits at the dawn of day." Without freedom of expression, information of the kind necessary to provide education and to elect capable lawgivers cannot be transmitted. Without leadership, the people will drown in the torrent of cross currents that modern society has become—pulled downstream by short-term, self-indulgent thinking, unable to see the shore that provides a safe haven from human frailty.

So we return to the original question: "What is the best form of government?" The founders of our country and the philosophers of the intellectually golden age in which they lived understood it fairly well. Self-preservation, the ultimate goal, requires that individuals participate in the formation and maintenance of a lawful society in which resources are shared even though they are produced in unequal amounts by individuals with varying degrees of wealth-producing skills. Neither strict egalitarianism nor pure selfishness produces stability. Some measure of compromise between these extremes must be codified into law by intelligent representatives of the people, working through institutions configured to lessen the probability that human frailties will result in the aggrandizement of personal power at the expense of the community-at-large. When societies are so established, they form symbiotic bonds with their individual members, protecting them even from themselves.

Does the current government measure up to these fundamental principles? That subject is beyond the scope of Volume I and will be addressed in Volume II.

APPENDIX IV

Some of the Materials Provided to Roland Raines at the Library of Congress

Amar, A. (1998). *The bill of rights.* New Haven: Yale University Press.

Bowlby, J. (1973). *Attachment and loss.* New York: Basic Books.

Carnegie, A. (1889). *Wealth.* North American Review, CXLVIII (June 1889), 653-64.

Freedman, R. (2003). *In defense of liberty—the story of America's Bill of Rights.* New York: Holiday House.

Hamilton, A., Madison, J. & Jay, J. (1787-1788). *The federalist papers.* New York: Bantam Books.

Kovach, B., and Rosenstiel, T. (2001). *The elements of journalism—what newspeople should know and the public should expect.* New York: Three Rivers Press.

Locke, J. (2003) *Two treatises of government and a Letter concerning toleration.* (Ian Shapiro, Ed.) New Haven: Yale University Press.

McClosky, H. and Brill, A. (1983). *Dimensions of tolerance—what Americans believe about civil liberties.* New York: Russell Sage Foundation.

Merritt, D., and McCombs, M. (2004). *The two W's of journalism—The why and what of public affairs reporting.* Mahwah, New Jersey: Lawrence Erlbaum Associates, Publishers.

Powell, J. (2000). *The triumph of liberty—a 2,000 year history told through the lives of freedom's greatest champions.* New York: The Free Press.

Ramonet, Ignacio, "The Social Wars," <u>Le Monde Diplomatique</u>, November, 2002.

Richards, Gordon (2036). *Historical foundations of a just society.* Berkeley: University of Western California Press.

Rousseau, J. (1968). *The social contract* (M. Cranston, Trans.). London: Penguin Books. (Original work published 1762)

Schweitzer, A. (1987). *The philosophy of civilization* (C.T. Campion, Trans.). Amherst, N.Y.: Prometheus Books. (Original work published 1923)

Sommerville, J.P. (1992). *Thomas Hobbes: Political ideas in historical context.* New York: St. Martin's Press.

Stone, G. R. (2004). *Perilous times—free speech in wartime.* New York: W. W. Norton & Company, Inc.

Sunstein, C. (2003). *Why societies need dissent.* Cambridge: Harvard University Press.

Waldman, M. (2003). *My fellow Americans—the most important speeches of America's Presidents, from George Washington to George W. Bush.* Naperville, Illinois: Sourcebooks Inc.

White, R.C. Jr. (2002). *Lincoln's greatest speech—the second Inaugural.* New York: Simon & Schuster.